Johann Wolfgang von Goethe, Robert Slater

Letters to Leipzig friends

Johann Wolfgang von Goethe, Robert Slater

Letters to Leipzig friends

ISBN/EAN: 9783741115578

Manufactured in Europe, USA, Canada, Australia, Japa

Cover: Foto ©Andreas Hilbeck / pixelio.de

Manufactured and distributed by brebook publishing software (www.brebook.com)

Johann Wolfgang von Goethe, Robert Slater

Letters to Leipzig friends

GOETHE'S LETTERS

TO

LEIPZIG FRIENDS.

EDITED BY

PROFESSOR OTTO JAHN.

TRANSLATED BY

ROBERT SLATER, Jun.

WITH THREE LITHOGRAPHED PORTRAITS.

LONDON:
LONGMANS, GREEN, READER & DYER.
1866.

TRANSLATOR'S PREFACE.

"As the twig is bent the tree's inclined," is an aphorism no less trite than true in its usual application to the human subject; hence we study with the deepest interest all those circumstances in the early youth of a man distinguished later as a genius, which may possibly have directed the current of his thoughts and actions into a channel destined to swell into a mighty torrent, bearing all before it by its innate strength of character.

Amongst the great minds which have arisen in modern times few have been productive of more powerful effect on their age than the prince of German writers, Goethe, who, by the force of his intellect and the breadth of his views, initiated a new era in the literature of his own land, and at the same time operated with considerable effect upon reflecting minds in other countries. It is beyond my province to refer more particularly to the mode in which the influence he thus exercised made itself felt; the fact is sufficiently attested by the crowd of authors who have striven to follow where he so nobly led.

The original of the present translation had its

origin in a desire on the part of Professor Otto Jahn to perpetuate, in a tangible shape, the memorials of the early youth of Goethe given to the world on the occasion of the festival in honour of the poet held at Leipzig in 1849, with the addition of some early correspondence which, from its character, can be more relied on for accuracy than Goethe's own account as furnished in his autobiography, written at a later period of his life, when time had blended somewhat indistinctly in his memory the incidents referred to. And the translator conceives that in its present form the work may prove not unacceptable to the English public.

The endeavour of the translator has been to render as closely as possible the ideas conveyed by the originals; and, in the case of the few odes, he has sought to retain in most instances the rhythm of the poems, whilst giving a translation of them as nearly literal as in his power. For this portion of the work he must ask, therefore, the kind indulgence of his readers.

In conclusion, the translator refers with pleasure to the assistance he has received from Messrs. Breitkopf and Härtel (the publishers of the German work) in his efforts to place the work before the public in a shape which may be considered as adding to its interest.

BLACKHEATH, *September, 1866.*

DEDICATION

TO

HERR SALOMON HIRZEL.

You, my dear friend, have not only given occasion for the production of this book, but have exercised so decided an influence upon its character and contents, that you cannot but consent to your name appearing in connection with it. I know assuredly that no one will take more delight in the relics which the Goethe Festival here has brought to light, and will more sincerely join me than yourself in the expression of our thanks to those whose kindness has authorized their publication. On this account, therefore, I trust you will, with your accustomed consideration, excuse the somewhat motley collection of the contents, for which not even an appropriate title could be found.

With this explanation, I dedicate the book to you as a memento of days passed agreeably in joyful occupation, as well as of a sincere and true friend.

OTTO JAHN.

LEIPZIG, *18th October, 1849.*

CONTENTS.

GOETHE'S YOUTH IN LEIPZIG.

At the sight of the Olympian Zeus the Greek in solemn awe forgot his trials and sorrows,—enchanted by the godlike presence, found peace and strength, and quitted the sacred fane proud that he was a Greek. This day the German experiences a similar feeling. This day he is permitted to lay aside even his most anxious care,—the care for his country,—his deep regret at blasted hopes and struggles,—in the remembrance of the great genius, the common property of all Fatherland, to express that in which all agree—wonder and reverence for Goethe. To give utterance to his thankfulness and devotion requires no particular stimulus; for all who take part in German progress are called to celebrate the memory of Goethe, whilst for us it is an admonishing duty to ornament with a commemorative chaplet the brow of the poet so intimately connected with us.

Goethe commenced his studies in Leipzig, and for three years was a member of our University. It is here that his impressions were formed and ripened by his association

with artists and friends of art; friendships and affections
chained him in many ways to the spot; here it was he
passed the restless period when he was first thrown on
his own resources—truly a not unimportant part of his
life may be claimed by us. We may cite himself as a
witness of his attachment to Leipzig, the remembrance of
which was ever so dear to him :—" He who has never
seen Leipzig," he writes to his friend Breitkopf, on
his return home to Frankfort, " might pass his existence
here in a town so much the antithesis of Leipzig as to
possess little to satisfy me." " You are right, my
friend," he observes in another letter, " in supposing
that I am now punished for my sins against Leipzig ;
my residence here is as unpleasant as my residence
in Leipzig would have proved delightful had certain parties
not felt interested in making it disagreeable to me."
Such were the impressions of the youth, saddened by
his departure from agreeable and pleasing associations,
who greatly missed " in the dearth of good taste in
Frankfort " the higher, and more particularly the literary,
accomplishments for which Leipzig was so noted in consequence of the free and unrestrained intercourse which
obtained there, especially with the fair sex. Goethe, at
a later period, renewed his connection with Leipzig by
repeated visits from Weimar; he wrote, in December,
1782, to Mad. Von Stein :—" Since '69, when I left this,
I had never been here for more than a day or two at a
time, and then I only visited my old acquaintances ; so
that I was under as much restraint as in former years.
On this occasion, however, I am making myself acquainted
with the city in another manner, and I have found it a

new little world. I should be glad to have it in my power
to remain for a month or two, for it is inconceivable how
much is to be met with. The inhabitants may be looked
upon as a small moral republic. Each stands for himself,
has but few friends, and pursues his course alone; no
superior gives a tone, but every one produces his small
original, be it sensible, learned, stupid, or in bad taste,
bustling, benevolent, insipid, egotistical, or what else you
will. Wealth, science, talents, properties of every kind
combine to create a whole which a stranger, if he can
comprehend it, may very well enjoy and turn to advantage.
It is only requisite that he should preserve a strict
neutrality, and take no part in their passions, actions,
prepossessions, or antipathies. There are some living
here quite retired, and if I may use the term, lodged here
by fate, from whom I should derive great advantage did
time permit. I have every reason to be satisfied with the
reception I meet with. They show me much good will
and the greatest respect, whilst on my part I am friendly,
attentive, frank, and courteous to all." It will be seen
from this that Goethe not only cherished the acquaintance-
ships formed during his academic career, but also those of
a more recent period. I need only name Gottfried Hermann, Friedrich Rochlitz, and Blümner, who were closely
connected with him. It is true that the condemnation of
the " Xenien " was general in Leipzig as elsewhere; so
that when the good folks of the city had acted rather
absurdly on the occasion of a visit by Catalani, he could
not forego the opportunity of bitterly observing that "it
was to be regretted that the various opinions of such a set
of people could not be bottled up for future analysis

and classification ;"* but it should, at the same time, be borne in mind that not long before he was zealously engaged in making known throughout a wider circle the old German paintings discovered here by Quandt, which now ornament our city museum.† Many other little traits show the interest and delight Goethe took in recalling to memory anything relating to his former residence in Leipzig.

On an occasion like the present, when we are assembled to celebrate the hundredth anniversary of his birth, we wish above all things to realize the presence of Goethe in Leipzig. His image, it is true, does not thus represent the man in the possession of his full powers, nor the prince among poets in the full radiance of his fame, but the struggling youth, entering a grand path of victory, in whom is already visible the whole Goethe. The wondrous unity of purpose and force of nature which admitted of his experiencing, and placing clearly and fully before us, every step of human development, fill us more than anything else, with astonishment at his character. Goethe, from youth to old age, presents the type of the natural ripening and advancement of a great and expansive mind, to those who do not look for the fire of youth in old age, nor the tardy experience of grey hairs in the morning of life ; and who do not demand of the man rash pride, nor of the youth calm reflection, making allowance for the bounds within which human nature in its development is confined. Were creative poetical feeling extant in our

---

* Letters to Felter, II., p. 306 (28 August, 1816).
† Morgenblatt, 1815, No. 69 (March).

people, Goethe would undoubtedly have been transfigured by tradition into the representation of the spirit of Germany in its noblest aspects ; as it is, the poet, with rare facility and distinctness, has pourtrayed himself. Were it the task of an orator to undertake the refutation of Goethe's masterpiece, who would assume the office? But let us not forget that the matured man depicts his own youth, looking back with a complacency on his efforts and foibles, which casts over them a sense of repose he in vain strove for in his earlier years. We will, therefore, attempt, from the unfortunately spare means at our command, which have been handed down to us either orally or by documents, to present a tangible representation of the persons and circumstances amongst which Goethe lived when here, and the influence these connections exercised over him. Even comparatively unimportant facts, which at a later period may have lost their interest for him, may thus command a certain degree of attention.

In the autumn of 1765, Goethe, who had just completed his sixteenth year, travelled to Leipzig with a bookseller named Fleischer, and his wife, who were on their way to attend the fair. In those days merchants visiting the fairs were prayed for in the churches—Goethe was not destined to reach Leipzig without accident—near Anerstaedt the coach was upset, and Goethe, in his efforts to get the vehicle righted, exerted himself so much that he felt the evil effects for some time afterwards. On his arrival here he hired two neat chambers at the "Fireball," in the Newmarket, which looked upon the yard ; and on the 19th of October was received by the

then Rector, Councillor Ludwig, as a student in the
Bavarian nation.* We see him then in the happy yet
restless condition of the young student, freed for the first
time from paternal restraint, with the determination to
enjoy his liberty although at times irksome to him; full
of confidence in the world which lay open before him;
lavish of his time and money, which in his eyes appeared
inexhaustible; and with the firm determination to prepare
himself for life, of which he as yet knew so little.
Trials and disappointments follow each other, enjoyment
and denial succeed each other in rapid succession, and
passion gives place to passion,—experience thus ploughs
deep and saddening furrows in the youthful mind, which
easily* receives its impressions, invigorating manly
powers, and bearing timely fruit. During the whole
period of his stay in this city, Goethe presents this image
of restlessness, with no fixity of purpose, and no clear
conception of his latent power, pursuing eagerly now this
object, and now the opposite, only to fall back speedily,
deceived and wearied. He was vacillating in his occupations, yielding first to one impulse, then to another, never
satisfied with his exertions; so decided, however, was the
call of his nature, and so powerful the effect of the inner-
most wants of his mind, that his thoughts invariably
reverted to the consideration of art. Not less variable
was his temperament, at one time gay and joyous, at

---

* Until very lately, all members of the University, whether tutors
or students, were attached to one of the four nations fixed at the
foundation—namely, Meissen, Saxony, Bavaria, or Poland. As a
native of Frankfort, Goethe was included in the Bavarian nation.

another moody and self-tormenting, by turns haughty and satirical, or kind and full of feeling, but so superior in the power of his grand and deeply seated nature, as always to reconcile and command those about him whose sensibilities he had offended or touched.

When entering the University, Goethe was placed in a peculiar position. His father, although he viewed with pleasure his poetic and artistic ideas, and even forwarded them as a desirable occupation for his leisure hours, decided upon Jurisprudence as his principal study, in which he personally aided and prepared him. The son, however, felt no particular attraction for the law; but, whilst it certainly did not enter his mind to devote himself entirely to the Muses, his wishes led him to the thorough investigation of antiquity, and he desired to go to Göttingen and place himself under Heyne and Michaelis. His father, however, insisted on Leipzig. Goethe did not venture to give utterance to his views to the strict, pedantic and severe man, but resolved that the first use made of his academic freedom should be formally and decidedly to absolve himself from Jurisprudence, and to devote himself to the study of the Ancients and of Science. He frankly and honourably informed Councillor Böhme, to whom he carried introductions, of his intentions; but soon gave way to the earnest representations of this gentleman, and the kindly expressions of his wife. The newly formed decision to remain true to Jurisprudence does not, however, appear to have proved lasting. It is true he at first attended juridical and philosophical lectures, and wrote them up with much self-devotion, except when, as a recreation, he preferred to illustrate the margin of his paper with caricatures; however, towards Lent, the classes had to endure a severe struggle with the attractive pancakes baked in St. Thomas's church-yard, and the number of scholars became considerably thinned. The grammatically critical tendency of Saxon philology does not seem to have proved attractive to him; nor did Ernesti's lectures on Cicero come up to his expectations, or give a tone to his studies, the aim of which remained, as ever, his preparation for a poet. Whatever his occupation or pursuit, his taste for poesy constantly cropped up, and unconsciously led his thoughts back thither again. During the period of the development of German literature, Leipzig occupied a singular and important place. True it is that it could not continue to hold this position when Goethe first entered on the scene; but the men whose names were in every one's mouth were for the greater part still alive, and their fame diffused around them an autumnal radiance, giving promise of the fulfilment of services which it was not seen they were incapable of. It is not a little remarkable that the youth Goethe should personally have been impressed with a style similar to that which he was ultimately destined to uproot.

Gottsched, who had formerly possessed much influence by his services to literature, and by the controversies he had originated through the rigid character of his style, was still alive, but had little weight, and had ceased to be more than a mere celebrity. "I have not yet seen Gottsched," we find in his earliest communication to his friend Riese, but a few days subsequently he wrote, "All Leipzig despises him. No one

associates with him," appending this to a poetic sketch
of the man :

> Gottsched, a man of bulk, as were he of ancient extraction,
> Like him, who in Gath,—you terrible Philistine warrior,—
> Was born to be Israel's terror down deep in the valley.
> Yea, such is his aspect and bearing,—his stature,—
> Himself the authority,—six Parisian feet, or e'en more.

He pursues this strain for a time, and towards the conclusion continues :—

> I saw him take his stand upon the bench on high,
> I heard the words he spake, and will not now deny
> His subject matter's good, and that his speech is pliant
> As tender saplings are ; but still he stands a giant
> Upon his lofty chair ; and, were he not well known,
> His words him soon betray,—richly with boasts they're sown.

Such was the first impression ; the laughable position
in which he found him on a later visit, when he was putting
on his wig with one hand, and dealing out a fearful box
on the ear to his servant with the other, is well known.
There can, of course, be no talk of influence, as Gottsched
died in the year 1766.

Amongst the writers of a younger generation, who in
their services were not excelled even by Gottsched, and
might be looked upon as landmarks in the advance of
German literature, Gellert and C. F. Weisse were sur-
passed by none. Goethe enjoyed personal intercourse
with, and was bound by a lasting attachment to the kindly
disposed and amiable Weisse, who at that period was
fully occupied as theatrical poet, and as editor of the
Library of *Belles Lettres* ; and as late even as 1801, he
sends his respects to the honoured old man through

Rochlitz. Gellert, equally as man and author, was the
object of a general and almost enthusiastic adoration; the
simplicity and straightforwardness of his manners, the
genuineness of his interest in others, and even his physical
infirmities, combined to produce a deep impression on youth;
and neither the tearful tenderness with which he brought
forward his subject, nor his moralising habits excited
their dislike or sarcasm.   Gellert found an attentive
listener, desirous of profiting both by his lectures and by the
style of his exercises, in Goethe, who took pleasure in communicating his so recently acquired information, in his
letters to his sister.   But, as might have been expected,
no lasting impression was produced upon the mind of
Goethe—the teacher and his scholar were too widely at
variance in their natural inclinations.   Gellert commanded
but little confidence, and that simply personal and
immediate, and failed altogether of influence.   His chief
topic of private conversation consisted of admonition
to attend divine service regularly, which was both distasteful and irksome to Goethe, who would not curtail his
academic freedom by ecclesiastical restraint, and had altogether discarded theological studies, although in opposition
both to his previous and subsequent pursuits.   Goethe
by his style did not excite Gellert's particular attention,
for we find that he corrected his exercises, as well as those
of others, without considering them worthy of distinction.
They had no charm for him, as we may readily believe
from the few fragments which have been preserved, chiefly
in the form of letters,* since they evince a freedom and

---

* Scholl.   Letters and Essays by Goethe, p. 20.

passion, both in their conception and form, that doubtless could not give satisfaction to Gellert, although they serve to show us that Goethe strove to mould into an artistic shape his actual experiences.

Besides those by Gellert, whose bodily infirmities so much restricted his usefulness, lectures and classes were held by Clodius, which Goethe also attended. The estimation in which Clodius was held as a diligent poet, was not based on his genuine piety, as in the case of Gellert; such students as devoted themselves to poetry felt by no means disposed to subject themselves unreservedly to his criticism, and soon discovered his weakness, and the technical ideas he had formed of the art; in addition to which his remarkable appearance excited their derision, and made him a mark for their sarcasm. Thus Goethe on one occasion, for a freak, composed in the Kuchen garden, the poem on the confectioner Handel, in which all the pompous and inflated words Clodius was in the habit of using, were introduced:

Oh! Handel, thy widely spread fame, from the *North* to the *South* it doth ring,
While thy glories I try to proclaim, oh! list to the *Pæan* I sing,
A mind, so *creative* as thine as a type of thy *genius* supplies
An *original* cake most sublime, which the *Gauls* and the *Britons* both prize;
And an *Ocean* of coffee so clear, and so luscious that *Hymettus'* land
Its honey may scarcely compare, thou pour'st with a liberal hand;
Thy house is no *monument* mean, of the ardour of students for art,
Rich *trophies* of *Nations* are seen embellishing every part.

No *diadem* charms has for thee such as those which great
    gains do convey,
And many's the shilling we see diverted from *Cothurn's* café.
But when that thy *urn* shall adorn in *pomp* all majestic thy
    tomb,
Ah! then shall the *Patriot* mourn with grief o'er thy drear
    catacomb.
Yet live! Be thy *Torus* the *nest* of an offspring ennobled by thee!
Stand high as *Olympus* the blest, and firm as *Parnassus* the free!
Every *phalanx* of Greece we defy, we scorn ev'ry Roman *Ballist*.
Let their efforts united but try *Germania* and Handel to waste.
O'er our spirit thy *weal joy* suffuses—thy *woe* causes *pain* to our
    mind
In their heart have the sons of the Muses thy temple, oh! Handel,
    enshrined.

As these lines had a malevolent intention attributed to
them by Horn in his play of Medon, they became known, and
were subsequently printed, exciting general attention and
much animadversion, so that even Goethe himself was
much annoyed thereby. Clodius, however, shortly after
expressed his satisfaction with Goethe's conduct in this
matter; and in his letters our poet did not fail constantly
to transmit his friendly respects to Clodius.

It is clear that the University, in the persons of its professors, could have no positive influence over the mind of
Goethe. Those once shining lights were fading from day
to day; Klopstock had had a mighty effect upon Goethe
as a boy; Wieland was read by the youth with astonishment; and, above all, Lessing (himself educated in
Leipzig), had already trodden the path which Goethe was
to follow. His Minna von Barnhelm (1730) " rose as the
Island of Delos from the flood of the Gottsched-Gellert-
Weiss school, graciously to receive the travailing god-

dess." No other work had exercised similar power over Goethe. We gather from occasional remarks, how deeply rooted a feeling, of almost veneration, this work had acquired in the circles in which Goethe mixed. Thus in one of his letters to a lady, for whom he entertained the warmest regard, he observes :—" Could the countrywoman of Minna write otherwise?" And again, " You know what made me discontented, wilful, and sullen. The roof was good, but the beds might have been better, says Francisca." A few of his friends had ventured on a private representation of the piece, and subsequently addressed one another by the names of the characters each had assumed. " What is Francisca doing?" he asks, and inquires whether she can get on with Just, now that her captain is away. Minna von Barnhelm engrossed his mind as a work, and drew his attention to the fact, " that a something higher existed, of which the weak literature of that period had no conception," and encouraged him to strive after this higher ideal, whilst it taught him how to reach it. This work was, however, the only one of its kind.*

Speaking generally, the productions of that era, as well as the intercourse Goethe had in Leipzig, did not tend so much to incite his emulation, as to confuse him, and render his course unsteady. He had been recommended to several respectable intelligent families, where he had always the *entrée*. The numerous literary productions radiating from Leipzig as a centre, had aroused in widening circles a growing interest in *Belles Lettres*, which,

---

* Eckermann's Conversations, II., p. 328 ; compare I., p. 340 and Riemer's Communications II., p. 663.

being supported by an increasing acquaintance with the
subject, and a more general degree of mental culture,
diffused a certain facility of criticism. . This, however,
being chiefly exercised for amusement, had no better
result than the pronouncing moderate productions to be of
but humble merit, and blunted rather than encouraged any
desire for improvement, taking from the youth all his
belief and veneration ; and whilst causing him to feel deeply
his need of support in his exertions by example and productive emulation, gave him only stones for bread. The
natural result was discouragement, uncertainty, dissatis-
faction with others, and with himself; at last he burnt all
that he had up to that time attempted or projected.

He was destined to experience this fate, not in one way
only. Shortly after his arrival in Leipzig, he lived, as he
tells us himself :—

> Like to a bird who on a lofty bough,
> The freshest in the wood, sweet freedom breathes,
> And without hindrance, on light pinions borne,
> From tree to tree, from bush to bush hops on,
> And cheers the grove with loud and gladsome warblings.

After his introduction, however, into the *beau monde*,
he speedily found that the " little Paris which gave the
ton " made demands on him which he felt to be rather
irksome. Neither his dress nor manners had the proper
cut, his Frankfort accent, and the pithy expressions he
made use of, were not of the first water of the genuine
Meissen German, and but few encouraged him in so mild
and friendly a manner as the worthy wife of Councillor
Böhme, from whom, by the way, he learned to play cards.
Besides this his views and feelings were on all hands

regarded as strange, his enthusiasm for Frederick the Great met naturally with no return, although his surprise at this speedily vanished. But he did not long suffer himself to be annoyed by this perpetual schooling and consequent restraint; for, as he gradually dropped his attendance at these readings, he withdrew himself, more particularly after the death of Madame Böhme, from this kind of society, which, happy as he might otherwise be, only made him feel the more keenly the want of intercourse congenial to his youthful tastes. "I sigh for my friends and my sweethearts," he writes to Riese, 28th April, 1766, "and when I feel that I sigh in vain,

> My heart is filled with grief's fell load,
> Mine eyes gleam sadly.

However, in his second term, this was all changed, and Goethe joined quite a different circle. John Adam Horn, with whom he had been intimate in Frankfort, came to Leipzig, and by his unceasing flow of spirits and former acquaintance, had a beneficial effect on our hero, who was in a fair way of becoming untrue to himself and to his poetical calling. In the above-mentioned letter to Riese, he states, "Horn's arrival has in a measure dissipated my melancholy, he is surprised to find me so altered—

> He seeks the hidden cause—but vainly—
> Smiles 'midst his thoughts, and looks me in the face,
> Yet how can he the cause see plainly,
> I fail myself to trace?

John George Schlosser, subsequently his brother-in-law, also resided for a time in Leipzig, and introduced him to a joyous company, formed of students and of others

who had not long completed their studies. Amongst
these we may name the brother of the Poet Zacharias,
Pfeil, and Hermann (who afterwards became burgomaster),
the latter of whom attended with true devotion on Goethe
during his subsequent illness, and was much distinguished
by his hearty equanimity of character. Behrisch, the
majordomo of Count Lindenau, was altogether of a different stamp. He was descended from a noble family, and
although careless in money matters, was upright, honest,
and well informed, passionately fond of music, but at the
same time quite an original—he wore, for instance, clothes
always of fashionable shape, but all of grey material, the
various shades of which he was quite an adept in employ-
ing. He was one of that race of beings always to be
found in universities, who possess the peculiar gift of
wasting their time in satirizing themselves and others,
and are as dangerous to spirits of a middling or inferior
order, as they are attractive and even exciting to bolder
minds. The humour with which he could carry out his
follies in a most serious manner, whilst he gave a
ridiculous character to everything grave, was boundless
and irresistible, and fascinated Goethe, notwithstanding
the domineering manner in which he always lorded it over
him. A man of cultivated taste, he took a lively interest
in Goethe's poetical labours, encouraging him continually to
improve himself; but always dissuaded him from trusting
himself to print, personally transcribing in an elegant
book, with a neatness and art peculiar to him, such pieces
as had stood the test of his criticism. On Behrisch
leaving Leipzig for Dessau, where, at the recommendation
of Gellert, whose favorite he was, he became tutor to the

crown prince, and afterwards master of the pages, he carried with him farewell odes of Goethe's of a heavy calibre. At a later period Goethe renewed this acquaintance from Weimar, and found his old friend quite the courtier, highly esteemed by all around him; but full of fun as of old, "clothing sapient remarks in ridiculous language, and *vice versâ*."* The reception he met with, he informs us, was, " Did I not tell you so? Was it not good counsel that you should wait until you had written something altogether good, before rushing into print? It is true that what you then wrote was not bad, or I should not have transcribed it; but had we remained together, you should not have printed the others. I should have written them into the book, and it would have been just as well for you."† Langer, afterwards majordomo to Count Lindenau, in place of Behrisch, and subsequently librarian in Wolfenbuttel, who, as a soldier, had gathered a varied and extensive experience,‡ and although never at college, had acquired a vast amount of learning, became a great consolation to Goethe in his sickness, and by his mild earnestness obtained much influence over his feelings, whilst his knowledge and experience advanced the cultivation of his mind.

Amongst the younger companions we find Bergmann, afterwards pastor in Livonia,§ a skilful fighter who scarred Goethe's arm; Wagner, to whom Goethe, when up in years, addressed these lines :—

---

* Riemer, II., p. 60. He died at Dessau in 1809, unmarried, in his 60th year.

† Eckermann's Conversations, II., p. 175.

‡ Blum. A Picture of the Baltic Provinces, p. 29.

§ Original Papers, 1832, No. 83.

> Though we eighty years have sped
>   Along life's weary way,
> And (altho' with silvered head)
>   Dare not from duty stray,
> Many paths to Death's dark portal,
>   Smooth and decked with flowers we find.
> But once clad in form immortal
>   Our griefs we leave behind.

In the company were found also the two brothers Breit-kopf, and Horn. The latter, whose small figure and deformed limbs* always attracted notice, was the most jovial in the party, which he always delighted with his talent for mimicry, ready at all times to mystify or to be mystified; in other respects a worthy and true-hearted companion, as he also proved in Goethe's illness.

Goethe now no longer attended the dinners given by Councillor Ludwig to his students, according to the customs of that period, but gave himself up entirely to this new circle, in which life, and intellect, and the unrestrained joyousness and mirth of youth reigned supreme. Meetings were appointed for mid-day and for the evening at the various places of amusement—Apel's (now Reichel's) Garden, the Cake Gardens, Gohlis, Raschwitz and Kon-newitz—all of which were regularly frequented. The wild vagaries permitted on these occasions we can surmise from the scene in Auerbach's cellar, depicted in " Faust."

---

* Horn writes to Kate Schoenkopf—"We should have made a good impression, for I had put on a small hump;" and on another occasion, "During the journey I nearly came to grief, for my crooked legs, as Miss calls them, had got so entangled with those of Andrae, that in order to separate us they had some thoughts of breaking them."

It is true that no thorough investigation has as yet shown us the Leipzig originals from which his characters were drawn, but they all bear an unmistakeably local colouring : this the joke about Hans von Rippach proves, which it is the privilege of any inhabitant of Leipzig to comprehend without elucidation. Little as was their restraint in the matter of present enjoyment, we find they placed even fewer bounds on the most unmeasured impertinence and un-sparing exercise of their wit, which proved frequently a stumbling-block, and afforded occasion for evil reports. Amours were then the order of the day, and several of the circle were paying their devotions to damsels, with whom (although they were, it is true, better than they were reported to be) it was, to say the least, not desirable, for their reputations' sake, to be mixed up. There can be no question that the contemplation of the fickleness and lightness of behaviour of these females engendered the wanton and sensual expressions found in Goethe's poems and letters of that date. At the same time we must not forget that our opinions of propriety of conduct are liable to undergo great changes ; and we need only glance at the paintings of that period to understand much which now astonishes us. If Goethe, in the fire of youthful power, gave himself up rashly to an irregular course of life, the punishment for this and other follies before long overtook him, seriously undermining his health. The bursting of a blood-vessel brought him to the verge of the grave ; and although saved by the careful treatment of his physician, Reichel, and the affectionate nursing of his friends, he continued weakly and suffering during the remainder of his stay in Leipzig, and afterwards in

Frankfort. This illness had no unimportant effect upon his
spirits, which ever after his recovery were much subdued
—the gaiety and pride of his youth was broken.   He did
not conceal from himself the fact of his having thought-
lessly made inroads on his health.   Not content with
exercising for himself a certain degree of caution, he
ventured to admonish his friends to greater moderation,
and, in consequence, did not escape their ridicule—as we
learn from one of his own verses.

> You laugh and jeer, and cry : the fool !
> The fox who lost his bushy tail
> Would cut all ours most gladly.
> Heed not the fable of the school ;
> The trusty fox's loss can't fail
> To point a moral sadly.

And this joke of the fox must have grown into a proverb
amongst his friends, for it is frequently adverted to in
their letters.

But do not let us forget that this lively company was
composed of young men of considerable talent, and really
sound ideas, who, in the whirl of enjoyment, did not lose
sight of the goal they were striving for. The invaluable
advantage of an academical life consists in the freedom of
intercourse, grounded on similarity of tastes, in common
struggles after scientific attainments, and in the continued
tension of the powers in the exciting contest with others,
so healthful in its effects, because originating in motives
based on the actual experience of life. Here Goethe found
for his productions an encouragement as warm as the
criticisms they met with were sharp, communicating a
positive impulse to his artistic efforts, which, if confined

by the bounds of youth, were yet as fresh as they were free in their conceptions. Here it was that the individuality of his poetical nature was first developed,—that nature which made him great above all others, and has constituted him the emancipator of German poesy, the sole fountain of which flowed from his own mind, impelling him, as a necessity, to give artistic utterance to what he so deeply conceived and felt, and relieving him, as it were, from a load. Nothing, however, operated with so great an effect on his mind, or so continually gave it employment, as his passionate attachment, during his residence here, to the girl whom he depicts to us as Annie—an attachment embodied in a more lively form in his letters still in existence, than in his later representation.

Christian Gottlob Schoenkopf, a wine merchant, was the occupant of the house* in which the company Goethe frequented used to meet at midday. His wife, a talented and lively woman, whose maiden name was Hauk, was descended from a Frankfort patrician family. Goethe early became intimate with his townswoman, made himself quite at home there, and was regarded soon almost as one of the family ; and we find he introduces them to us in his first letter from Frankfort, dated 1st October, 1768 :—" Your servant, Mr. Schoenkopf. How are you, Madame ? Good evening, Miss. Good evening, Peter. You must imagine I enter at the side door. You, Mr. Schoenkopf, are on the sofa by the warm stove ; Madame

---

* This house, No. 79, Brühl, next the sign of the Golden Apple, remained until a few years ago in the occupation of the family ; since changing hands it has been almost entirely rebuilt.

in her corner at the writing table ; Peter beyond the stove ;
and if Kitty is sitting in my place by the window, she may
just get up, and make way for the stranger. Now we
begin the discourse." He then narrates the incidents of
his journey ; tells them how little he likes Frankfort, and
how indifferent his health is ; excuses himself for not
having taken leave of them ; says he went there, saw the
lamp burning, and stood at the foot of the stairs,—"but
how could I have come down again, knowing it would be
for the last time?" In all his letters he mentions many
little circumstances attesting the intimacy of his acquaintance with this family and their friends. A circle of intelligent men occasionally met together there, and over a
glass of punch* enjoyed this life in unrestrained hilarity.
Concerts were frequently arranged, in which parts were
taken by Obermann, a merchant, who lived opposite, with
his two daughters, the eldest of whom was distinguished
as a singer ; and by Häser, father of the celebrated vocalist,
who both frequented the house ; Goethe played the flute
until illness forbade this ; and Peter, the youngest son,
born in 1756, already, as a boy, remarkable for his performances on the piano, joined in. A drawing, representing
Peter seated at the piano with his sister, Häser, and
Lelei, also an excellent musician, beside him—said to
have been the production of Goethe, was in existence
until the war, when it was burnt. Comedies were also
occasionally acted : " Minna von Barnhelm " had even been

---

* " I should like to have a glass of punch with you this evening,"
Horn writes ; and again, " What would I not give to be able to
drink punch with you once again ?"

attempted; and much delight had been given by the representation of J. C. Krüger's comedy of "Duke Michael." Goethe had taken the part of *Michael*, Kitty, of *Hannah*—and in one of the rooms of Schoenkopf's house, the principal scene had been depicted on the wall, and was preserved for a considerable time. Goethe inquired from Frankfort after the welfare of Manager Schoenkopf and his actors, and sent Miss Schoenkopf a humorous letter, signed "Michael, formerly entitled Duke, but, after the loss of his duchy, a trusty tenant on the ducal estate "— accompanying a pair of scissors and a knife with leather for a couple of pairs of slippers. In the same circle we find also Reich, the prince of Leipzig booksellers, with whom Goethe, from his interest in Lavater's work on physiognomy, was subsequently connected; the book- seller, Junius; Miss Weidmann; the Breitkopf family; Stock, "the comic copperplate engraver, who had the habit of telling such wonderful and horrible tales," as Horn says; the Receiver-General Richter; the younger Kapp, afterwards celebrated as a physician; and Horn, who resided in the house. He closes his first letter, referred to above, with the request that Kitty will let him hear from her at least once a month.

Kitty, as she was called by intimate friends, or Anna Katharine (her name in full), no doubt, attracted him to the house. Born on the 22nd August, 1746, she was three years older than Goethe—a pretty girl, of middling stature and elegant figure, with a full, fresh-coloured face, brown eyes full of arch brightness, of a lively and pleasing disposition, warm and unconstrained in her feelings. She soon gained the passionate affection of the youth who, on

23rd January, 1770, wrote :—" You know that ever since
I have been acquainted with you I have existed only as
one with you ;" which feelings she reciprocated. Neckties,
kerchiefs, and shoes, painted by his own hand, served here,
as later in Sesenheim and Weimar, as tributes of his
affection. She partook of his interest for poetry, which
he often read to her, assisting him also in his productions ;
and after his departure, he called her attention to the
songs he had written, telling her to let Peter play one of
them, when she would think of him. Goethe frequently
disturbed the happiness of their common attachment by
the violent fits of unfounded jealousy with which he tormented both himself and the poor girl, and which, often
as he repented of them, only led to new scenes of passion,
that eventually estranged the heart of his mistress. " A
year ago to-day," he writes, on 26th August, 1769, " I
saw you for the last time. Three years ago I could have
sworn it would have been far different. Oh, that I could
recall the last two years and a-half! By my faith, my
dearest Kitty, I would act more wisely." Besides many
poems afterwards destroyed, he wrote in 1768, as a
penance, the play, " A Lover's Whims," in which the
pointed and pithy expressions general at that period, as
well as the shepherd's costume, threw a strong light which
we can even now discern, upon the condition under which
the piece was written, proving the severe struggles he had
to contend with in consequence of this affection. Be this
as it may, the production of the artist might excuse the
poet, but could not give him back the heart of his mistress, and he saw her turn her affections over to another.

It is evident from his letters that he departed full of love for Kitty, and in the hope and conviction that he would at some future time possess her. His request above alluded to was fulfilled. Kitty wrote to him, and he at once replied to her (1st November, 1768) as his dearest friend, who has all his love and friendship, and in an enclosed sheet, he corrected, at her request, the errors of orthography in her letter to him. She was in fears about his health; he immediately (30th December, 1768) allays her anxiety, telling her that he was improving, and hopeful of being able to travel; but that if he should die before Easter, he would order a gravestone to be erected in Leipzig churchyard, so that she might visit his monument on St. John's (his saint's) day. A month later (31st January, 1769) he complains bitterly of being ill and miserable, and without news from her. This is conceivable; for towards the end of May, Horn, who left Leipzig in April, received information of Kitty's betrothal to Dr. C. K. Kanne, who had been introduced to the family by Goethe himself, and as whose wife she died on the 20th May, 1810. Whilst Horn, as schoolmaster and *ludimagister*, wrote an amusing letter of congratulation, we find that Goethe on 1st June, 1769, also wrote, commencing with a calm command of temper; but as he progressed, showing an excited bitterness of feeling, which was eventually turned against the loved one, whose certain loss weighed so heavily on him. We perceive distinctly the lover's feelings in this letter in the sentiment that "the heart most deserving of love, is that which loves the most readily, but that which loves the most readily, forgets also the most readily." But the exclamation "It is a heartrending sight to see one's love expire!" shows us how deeply

his feelings were affected. There would be no occasion for
him now to go to Leipzig, as the discarded lover would
play but a poor figure as a friend; it must certainly
strike her as amusing to reflect on all the lovers she had
had, and whom she had salted, as it were, like fishes, for
fear they should spoil; but yet she should not altogether
break off the correspondence as he was still bearable,
although in pickle. In his subsequent letters, the painful
sense of his loss was also expressed, at one time with the
impetuosity of passion, and at another with a quiet saddened tone, in which, under the impression that she was
already married, he takes leave of her, and begs her not to
answer him. " This is a sad request, my best one, the
only one of your sex whom I may not call friend, for my
feeling towards you is deserving of a much more important
name. I desire as little to see your handwriting as to
hear your voice; it is sufficient suffering for me that my
dreams are so intense. I can send you no nuptial ode;
some I have indeed composed, but they gave either too
much, or too little expression to my feelings." However,
she *did* reply, and advised him she was not yet married—
the ceremony took place on the 7th March, 1770—and
that she expected he would continue to write to her, and
in fact brought him back to his senses. He replied by
writing (23rd January, 1770), since she requested it.
This, written in a more cheerful tone than former letters,
reflects clearly the esteem she commanded, but no less
his painful sense of her loss. He tells her that he is living
quietly, and is hearty, healthy, and busy, having no
maiden in his head; that he purposes going to Strasburg,
where his title would be equally changed with hers, both
receiving something of the doctor, and really after all

"the difference between Madame Dr. C. and Madame
Dr. G. is miserably small."* He did not again correspond with her; in Strasburg the attractions of Frederica
banished the last painful thoughts of Kitty, and held him
bound in fresh chains; when he, however, came thoroughly
to know Frederica, he could bear to remember cheerfully
all who esteemed him, "and even Kitty, of whom I am
assured that she will be true to herself, and that my
letters would meet the reception she had formerly accorded
to me." And on his next visit to Leipzig, in 1776, we
find he sought out his first love. "All remains as it was,
I only am altered," he writes to Madame von Stein, "and
there is no change in my former intimate relations—*Mais
ce n'est plus Julie.*"

His intercourse with the Breitkopf family, the centre of
a wide circle, introduced him to another sphere, in which a
thorough grounding in science and art, more particularly
in music, could be acquired. Bernhard, known as the
Magister, born 1749, the eldest of two sons (who were
both Goethe's fellow-students), was even then noted for
his talent as a musician. He died later in St. Petersburg.
In 1770 the first collection of Goethe's songs was printed,
with Bernhard's melodies, which even at the present day
command favour, if we disregard certain sacrifices he made
to the then ruling fashion. Gottlob, the younger, born 1750,
who died as warden of the guild in 1800, also greatly skilled
in music, was, as Goethe writes from Frankfort in 1769, a

---

* Custom grants to wives in Germany the honours of their hus-
bands. We have, for example, Professoresses, Privy Councilloresses,
&c.

good fellow, and a man of sound sense, possessing a facility of conception rarely met with. In a circle such as this, the prevailing taste was for music, as may be imagined; and in this Goethe joined, for although he had no conspicuous talent, he was fond of music, and had acquired the power of playing on several instruments. He made the acquaintance of Hiller, and was received by him in a friendly manner. Hiller's comic operas were then in everybody's mouth; Goethe found, however, that like many others, he did not know how to gain friends, in consequence of his obtrusiveness, although he was well meaning and evinced an anxiety for information which no mere teaching could satisfy. Goethe was also an enthusiastic admirer of the two vocalists, Mesdames Schmeling and Schröter, with whom every one was then in raptures. The former, subsequently known all over Europe as Madame Mara, celebrated her jubilee in 1831, when Goethe, with pleasure, remembered having heard her in Hasse's Oratorios, "and having violently applauded her, as an excitable student only can," at the same time he addressed a poem to her, refreshing the memory of his youth. As a student he admired Corona Schröter at a distance only, writing poems to her for others—afterwards, however, he became more intimate with her, and was the means of bringing her to Weimar.

The theatre was, however, of more importance to Goethe than the musical enjoyments Leipzig could offer him. The development of art on the German stage commenced in Leipzig, where the drama was in the zenith of its power. Koch, having obtained a fresh theatrical concession and a standing troop, came to Leipzig, and built a new house,

which was opened on the 6th October, 1766, with
Schlegel's "Hermann." Shortly after Goethe's departure,
this brilliant epoch terminated; for on the 18th October,
1668, Koch closed the house, and left Leipzig. At that
period the interest in theatricals became general, and was
uppermost in all circles formed for literary improvement.
The influence this had on Goethe is undeniable, and his
preference for clothing everything in a dramatic form
showed itself early, and is even visible in his exercises in
style, causing him to give the form of romance to his
letters. As he had the precious gift of grasping and
expressing in "well filed words" the thoughts which
thronged his mind, every circumstance that excited him
called forth a lyric poem—his study was chiefly directed
to the drama, and the translation, as well as imitation of
French pieces continually and busily occupied his time,
although we have but a faint trace of this left us in a fragment of Corneille's "Liar." For at a later period he
destroyed most of his attempts of this date, and the only
evidence of the earnestness with which he pursued the
study of this branch is the "Mitschuldigen" (The
"Equally guilty ones," or, as it is generally, but incorrectly,
translated, the "Accomplices"). This piece evinces, for
the period, a remarkable dexterity of expression and knowledge of his subject, both on the point of composition and
of adaptation for the stage, which certainly could only
have been acquired after diligent and careful study.* In

* Goethe offered this piece in vain to the publisher Fleischer, in
Frankfort; and it was not printed until 1787. It had, however,
repeatedly been represented on the amateurs' stage in Weimar,
where Goethe took the part of *Alcest*, Bertuch that of *Soller*

other respects, too, this play affords a remarkable evidence of how Goethe, even at that early period, was enabled, by the spirit of poetry with which he was imbued, to throw off life's troubles and annoyances. From early youth a witness and partaker of an unhappy state of family circumstances, it was not from choice that he selected such a subject for a comedy; but, having made his selection, he discharged his mind of all prejudice such circumstances might have excited, by giving them, as a poet, a form which, whilst depriving them of their individuality, made them seem as if they were strange to him, and to exist beyond him.

Goethe subsequently had the opportunity of expressing his obligations and thanks to the Leipzig stage, on the Weimar players giving several representations there during the summer of 1807. In the beautiful prologue composed at Rochlitz's desire, he says :—

> Reward ! in truth it cannot here be wanting,
> Here, where so soon, before most German towns,
> Taste and high talent well combined have budded,
> Giving the Drama order, and high place.
> Who cannot but reflect on noble spirits
> Whose words and verses on our Fatherland
> Have worked much good, by precept and by practice?
> Those also are not yet forgotten, who,
> Taught long since on these boards, have learnt
> Nature with art entwined to represent.
> Which bears the palm off? Those, or these more recent?

Musæus, of the *Host*, and Corona Schröter that of *Sophia*. It may also be observed, as an interesting fact, that a prose version, by Albrecht, was produced in Leipzig.—Blumner's History of the Leipzig Theatre, p. 302.

He also expressed to Rochlitz his expectation that this
visit to Leipzig would prove beneficial to the company,
and later his satisfaction at their engagement having been
so fortunately concluded, and rewarded with such honour
and success. He was also much gratified by the production of a little pastoral he had written in Leipzig in
1768, which was very well received, and at the representation of which (on 29th August, 1807) Kitty herself was
in all probability present.

Adam Frederick Oeser, an individual we have not yet
had occasion to notice, also exercised an important influence over Goethe in the matter of the fine arts. He had
been appointed in 1763 to the office of Director of the
Academy of Arts in Leipzig, and was highly esteemed
both as a painter and sculptor, as well as a man.
Goethe, whose natural talent for art had already been
cultivated under his father's eye, exerted himself in
Leipzig to improve his style, and took lessons in drawing
from Oeser, together with Hardenberg (afterwards Chancellor), Prince Lieven, and Gröning of Bremen. At a
later period he did not content himself with drawing
simply, but turned his attention to etching, (as is proved
by the existence of some small plates prepared for
Schönkopf and Kitty, as well as two larger subjects)
induced to this most probably by his connection with the
copperplate engraver Stock—the same whose daughter
Minna became the wife of Körner, whilst Dora, another
daughter, was intimately connected with Schiller. Oeser's
merit as an artist, though valued too highly by his contemporaries, has had justice rendered to it by Goethe;
his influence over whom extended, however, far beyond

mere instruction in his art, for our hero felt clearly " that the studio of the great artist unfolds more to the mind of the budding poet and philosopher than the lecture-room of the worldly wise, or of the critic." Oeser was a talented, reflective man, of powerful originality and no small share of information, suggesting by hints rather than by clear explanations, quick and abrupt in manner, although good-humoured and indeed jovial; in short, a man who could not fail to make a deep impression on youth. By encouraging acknowledgment of Goethe's capacity he won his confidence and esteem, and grounded in him a sure starting point from which to regard the beautiful in art, so attractive to him because it rendered other fields so fruitful. Oeser had been the confidential friend of Winckelmann, upon whose views of art he exercised great influence. The enthusiasm with which Winckelmann was received on all sides threw a greater halo on Oeser, the weight of whose opinion contributed, in a certain degree, a more personal character to the honour paid to Winckelmann. The sudden news of the death of Winckelmann came, therefore, like a thunder-clap *sub Jove* upon all in Leipzig, a visit from this artist being looked forward to at the time. In this same field also Lessing, by the production of his " Laocoon," threw an unlooked for light upon youthful minds, purifying and invigorating them as no other work had done, showing them not alone the truth, but also the way by which it might be attained, and with modest earnestness demanded of them not to fear the labour or pain of exertion in the struggle for truth. To this day we can recognise traces of the enthusiasm with which Lessing inspired Goethe, who had fixed his glance on him, as on his leading star.

It proved of the greatest importance to Goethe's subquent development that, through Oeser, he formed that just conception of art, more particularly of ancient art, which he cherished till his latest years. He halted long between poetry and figurative art, and only perceived late, and even then with pain, that he could be no more than a *dilettante* in the latter;* yet the plastic nature of his poetry was so intimately connected with his taste for figurative art, that the conceptions and views he thus became imbued with in early life, continued to the last full of influence, and acted as a corrective upon him. He gives expression in his letters to the most devoted thankfulness towards, and a truly respectful affection for, Oeser; and to Reich he writes, "Oeser's discoveries have given me a fresh opportunity of blessing myself that I had him for my instructor. He entered into our very souls, and we must indeed have been without souls not to have derived benefit from him. His lessons will produce their effects during all the rest of my existence. He taught me

---

* Riemer's Communications, Vol. II. p. 301—"I shall derive one advantage from my sojourn in Rome, and that is, that my notions of following figurative art are silenced." Eckermann's Conversations, Vol. I., p. 132—"What I was about to observe is, that in my fortieth year, when in Rome, I was wise enough to know myself so far as to perceive that I have no talent for figurative art, and that my inclination that way was a mistaken one." Page 139—"I mention this, remembering how many years it took before I perceived that my taste for figurative art was a mistaken one, and how many more, after I perceived it, before I could shake off the old notion."

that the ideal of beauty is simplicity and repose."* He renewed this acquaintance from Weimar. On the 25th December, 1782, he wrote to Madame Von Stein :—" How delightful is the intercourse with an upright, sensible and discerning man who knows the world, and the part he has to play in it; and who, to enjoy this life, has no need of superlunary excitement, but lives in the pure sphere of attractions afforded by correct tastes and passions. Grant, in addition, that such a man be an artist, capable of production as well as of imitation, and of enjoying with a double or even threefold zest the works of others, and you cannot picture to yourself any one more fortunate than he. Such is Oeser; and what must I not add if I would tell you all that he is." Similar remarks are repeated as often as he sees Oeser, and testify how deeply he felt indebted even in manhood to Oeser's worth. Presented by Goethe at the court at Weimar, Oeser's extensive acquaintance with art commended him to the notice of the Duke Charles Augustus, and of the Duchess Amalia; the latter, particularly, held him in high esteem, and induced him to repeat his visits to Weimar, where his vivacity, his witty joviality, and his worldly experience always made him a welcome guest.

His acquaintance with Oeser was a ready introduction

---

* Schöll's Letters and Maxims of Goethe, p. 107—" The speech by Reynolds on the occasion of the opening of the Academy at London contains excellent thoughts of an artist regarding the education of young painters. He dwells particularly on the importance of correction, and on the effect of ideal quiet grandeur. He is right. Great minds are thereby wonderfully raised, whilst more modest genius gains at least somewhat."

for Goethe to all the collections of art in Leipzig, amongst which Winkler's justly held a high position. By this means, Goethe gathered round him a circle of connoisseurs and friends of art, amongst whom, besides Huber, we may particularly mention Kreuchauff, formerly devoted to mercantile pursuits, but who now lived solely for art, his interest in which is evinced by his writings. This circle was in the habit of assembling with unrestrained hilarity at Oeser's hospitable dwelling in the Pleissenburg, or in summer at his villa in Dölitz. A sermon, written by Goethe in the dialect of the Frankfort Jews, which he delighted in producing there, is a proof of the innocent and youthful gaiety which prevailed. The soul of this company, at least for the youthful portion of it, was Oeser's eldest daughter, Frederica Elizabeth, born in 1748, who died in this city, unmarried, in the year 1829. From her childhood she had been the darling of her father, and was always in his company, even whilst engaged upon his labours. As a girl she delighted him by her sauciness, which she exercised particularly upon her phlegmatic brother ; and later, her capacity and the development of her talent made her yet dearer to him; he frequently employed her pen, until at last his correspondence was conducted wholly by her. Her full face, with a small nose somewhat *retroussé*, and sparkling brown eyes, contrasted well with her small but neat shape, and, although disfigured with marks of smallpox, betrayed an active mind and understanding, as well as the lively temperament which caused her to attack Goethe in an ironical and overbearing mood—or in a too severe and merciless one, as he thought—whenever he felt sad and depressed. Yet

he always sought consolation from her when tormented by
love or jealousy ; and she had so much the greater influence
over him, since no passionate attachment existed between
them.   For several years after his departure from Leipzig
he cultivated a regular correspondence with her ; and on
one occasion, as a mark of his continued devotedness to
her, sent her the portrait of his much loved sister, Cornelia,
hastily sketched on a proof-sheet of his Götz.   In the
woods and meadows of Dölitz he gave himself up to
poetical day-dreams ; and if Kitty—or Annette, as the
poet named her—was generally at once the cause and
object of his effusions, these were generally laid before the
highly-cultivated and keenly-criticising Frederica for her
approval.   A collection of " Songs with melodies, dedicated to Mdle. Frederica Oeser, by Goethe," the oldest
and most peculiar memento of his poetry, is still preserved
in manuscript in a library in Leipzig.   As these pieces,
" of which some were so unfortunate as to meet with her
disapprobation " (we can readily suppose why), were
afterwards printed with additions, " he might, perhaps,
have taken the freedom of dedicating a copy bearing
his autograph to her, did he not know how easily she was
moved to abuse by trivialities."   These new songs, set to
melodies by Bernhard Theodore Breitkopf, appeared,
without Goethe's name, in 1770.   Hiller, when criticising
them, was of opinion, that on reading them, it was evident that the poet possessed a happy talent for humorous
poems of this description.   For us they are an interesting
and genuine monument of his residence in Leipzig.   The
dedication with which he closes expresses his feeling as
truly and sincerely, and at the same time as simply and

beautifully, as was in the power of any other poet of the period :—

> Behold them then !   You have them there !
> Such verses free from art or care
> As bubbling brooks inspire.
> In love and joy with throbbing heart,
> I've played a youthful, joyous part,
> And thus have tuned my lyre.
>
> So sing them then, who sing them may !
> Upon a brilliant vernal day
> Some youth may use a number.
> The poet from afar approves
> Whilst dietetic quiet moves
> His heavy lids to slumber.
>
> With look, askance half, and half sage,
> As nascent tears o'ercloud his page,
> Your joy in bursts he praises.
> List, then, to these, his parting strains :
> Like you, of joy he drank the drains
> And learned its fleeting phases.

At last he took his departure from Leipzig, on the 28th August, 1768.   Neither he himself nor his friends anticipated that future greatness to which he attained, and to which we still gaze upward with wonder and admiration. Leipzig placed no laurels on Goethe's brow, but the flowers the youth plucked here possess a fresh, undying fragrance.

GOETHE'S LETTERS

TO

JOHN JACOB RIESE.

I.*

LEIPZIG, *20th October, 1765.*

SIX A.M.

RIESE,

    Good morning !

21st—Five P.M.

RIESE,

    Good evening !

I had hardly seated myself yesterday to devote an hour to you, when suddenly a letter reached me from Horn, and tore me away from the sheet I had already commenced. To-day I expect I will not remain with you much longer. I am going to the play. We have an excellent theatre here. But yet ! I am quite undecided ! Shall I stay ?

---

* John Jacob Riese, a young friend of Goethe, studied in Marburg whilst the latter was in Leipzig. On his subsequent return to Frankfort he continued in intimate relations with Riese, whose portrait, taken in chalk by the hand of Goethe, of life-size, is now in the possession of his nephew, Herr J. Riese, of Frankfort. All of Goethe's letters to him are unfortunately destroyed, with the exception of these college letters, made known by H. König in "Lewald's Europa" (1837, Vol. I., p. 145), from his facsimiles. It is from these we have taken the following letters. The character of the two first letters is blunt and rough, without many distinguishing signs, whilst in the third it is much more ornamental, a fresh pen appearing to have been employed.

Shall I go to the play? What is it to be? Quick! Let the dice decide. But I have no dice! I am going! Good-bye!

Halt! No! I'll stop. To-morrow I can't, for there's college to attend, visits to pay, and an evening engagement. Then let me write now. Let me know what sort of life you are leading. Whether you sometimes think of me. Who your professors are, *et cetera*, and I mean a *long et cetera*. I live like—like—I don't know what like; something

> Like to a bird who on a lofty bough,
> The freshest in the wood, sweet freedom breathes,
> And without hindrance, on light pinions borne,
> From tree to tree, from bush to bush, hops on
> And cheers the grove with loud and gladsome warblings.

In fact, picture to yourself a bird on a green bough, revelling in joy, and you have me. To-day I have commenced my classes.

What are they? Is it worth the trouble to ask? *Institutiones Imperiales, Historium Juris, Pandectas,* and a *privatissimum* on the seven first and seven last paragraphs of the *Codex.* That's enough; the rest is soon forgotten. No, your most obedient, that we'll drop by the way. But, jesting apart: I have to-day attended two lectures, one by Professor Böhmer, on the History of States, the other by Ernesti, on Cicero's *De Oratore.* That was doing pretty well, was it not? Next week we commence *Collegium philosophicum et mathematicum.*

I have not yet seen Gottsched. He is lately married again, to a Lieutenant-Major's daughter; but you know of it. She is nineteen and he sixty-five years old. She, four feet high, and he, seven. She is as thin as a lath, and he as fat as a porpoise. I am making quite a figure here. Yet I am no boaster, and will not become one. I use all my art to be busy, and succeed pretty well—what with societies, concerts, the theatre, dinners, suppers, and drives, so far as the weather at present permits. Ha! it is capital! It *is* capital, and costs capital too. The deuce take it, my purse tells me that! What ho! Save us! Stop! Don't you see them fly? There went two louis d'ors. Help! there's another. Heavens! two more off! Groschens here are of no more account than kreuzers in the Empire. And still one may live cheaply here. The fair has come round again. I shall live in a right managing style. I hope with 300 dollars—what am I saying?—*with 200 dollars*, to make both ends meet. N.B.—Not including that already gone to the devil. My meals are rather expensive. Look at our bill of fare,—fowls, geese, turkeys, ducks, partridge, snipe, woodcock, trout, hares, venison, pike, pheasants, oysters, &c. All this daily; nothing of other vulgar meats, *ut sunt*, beef, veal, mutton, and so forth; I have forgotten how they taste. And all these delicacies not dear—by no means dear. I see, however, that my sheet is almost full, and no verses on it, although I had intended giving you some. This another time. Tell Kehren that I shall write to him. I learn from Horn that you are complaining *ob absentiam puellarum forma elegantium.* Ask him for the opinion I gave him of you.

GOETHE.

II.

Leipzig, *30th October, 1765.*

Dear Riese,

I have just received your letter of the 27th, which has given me much pleasure. The assurance of your affection towards me, and your regret at my being situated at such a distance from you, would have caused more satisfaction had they not been expressed in so formal a tone. Sir! Sir!* sounds so insupportably strange in my ears, more especially from my dearest friends, that I can scarcely restrain my feelings. Horn was equally stiff in his communication, and I have taken him right well to task about it. I have more than half a mind to take you also to task. Yet! *Transeat!* Only don't venture to repeat it.

I am living here quite contented. Indeed, you may guess as much from the enclosed letter, which has been some time written, and which you would have had long ago had Horn not forgotten to send me your address. The description of Marpurg is really comic.

---

* Translator's Note.—This is not a faithful translation of the expression employed by Goethe, but perhaps explains sufficiently his meaning, which turns on the personal pronoun in which Riese addressed him—the third person plural. This mode of address (for the information of readers not acquainted with the idiom of the German language) is commonly used amongst equals, or to superiors or strangers. Intimate friends, on the other hand, use the second person singular. Inferiors may be addressed in the second person plural, or even in the third person singular, when it is desirable in the speaker to impress the party he is addressing with the sense of his condescension.

I did not again see the best of tragedy maidens.
Should you not ascertain before your departure what she
thinks of Belshazzar my fate remains undecided.   Little
is wanting to complete the fifth act.   In five-footed
iambics,—

The rhythm which yon maiden most did please,
Whom to please most, oh, friend ! I did desire,
The rhythm which the learned Schlegel used,
And which most critics use, for tragedy,
Esteeming it most fit and apt t' employ,
The rhythm which to most men sounds not well,
As most on Alexandrines love to dwell,
The long six-footed verse.   'Tis this, my friend,
That I have chosen in my tragedy
To close with.   But, why write more thereof ?
Your ears are dinned therewith full oft, my friend ;
I pray you, therefore, let me now narrate
Somewhat more pleasing both to you and me.
I have seen Gellert with Gottsched, and haste
Truly to picture them to your mind's eye.

Gottsched, a man of bulk, as were he of ancient extraction
Like him, who in Gath—yon terrible Philistine warrior—
Was born to be Israel's terror down deep in the valley.
Yea, such is his aspect and bearing ; his stature,—
Himself the authority,—six Parisian feet, or e'en more.
Did I aright depict him, I had need use a proper design
To give of his form but a notion.   But this, I fear me, were vain.
In short, my friend, did'st thou now wander from country to
      country,
From the far distant east down to the sun's western setting,
Thou would'st, believe me, no being, our Gottsched resembling,
      discover.
Often—often I thought, and at last conceived the means
How clearly to show him ; but laugh not, my loved one, I
      pray you.

Humano capiti, cervicem jungens equinam
Derisus a Flacco non sine jure fuit.
Hinc ego Kolbeliis imponens pedibus magnis,
*Immane corpus crassasque Sculpulas Augusti,**
Et magna, magni, brachiaque manusque Rolandi,
Addensque tumidum morosi Rostii † *caput.*
Ridebor forsan? Ne rideatis amici.

Such is a faithful sketch of this most learned man
As well as by mere words his likeness sketch I can.
Read, then, beloved friend, this brief but clear description
And Gottsched, I may hope, will rise before my diction.
I saw him take his stand upon the bench on high,
I heard the words he spake, and will not now deny
His subject matter's good, and that his speech is pliant
As tender saplings are ; but still he stands a giant
Upon his lofty chair : and, were he not well known,
His words him soon betray,—richly with boasts they're sown.
In fine, he told us much of his collections, varied,
How much he paid for this,—the value that one carried.

Besides many other matters,—suffice it, my friend, I must close. You know he has a wife. He has again married, the old goat that he is ! All Leipzig despises him. Nobody associates with him.

Apropos. Have you not heard that the Councillor complains of the want of lasses in Göttingen?

What will he with a maiden?

That figures rhetorical he oft may exercise,
Whilst in the style ‡ Hübneric his love he well applies,

---

* You must know him—the fat sweep !

† You cannot have forgotten the fox's father.

‡ Johannes Hübner, the well-known geographer and historian, wrote also "Oratorical Enquiries" (Leipzig, 1726—30, 5 vols., Fragen aus der Oratorie).

To see if the protasm may melt a stony heart,
If love is bound by axioms which fix'd rules may impart,
Or else if Mimesis, or Ploce, or sarcasms
Possess attractions rich as Neukirch's pleonasms ;
Or whether by the ardour with which he Ulfo sings
Corvinus' potent verses may move a maid's heart-strings ;
Or whether—But my sheet is filled to overflowing.
Here's love to all your girls, for whom my heart is glowing !

6th Nov., 1765.   GOETHE.

III.

DEAR RIESE,

It is long since I have written to you. Pray
excuse me, and do not ask for a reason. I cannot certainly
plead full engagements. You live contented in M., and I
also here. But lonely—lonely—altogether lonely. My
dearest Riese, this loneliness has impressed my soul with
a certain sadness.

> It is my sole, my constant pleasure,
>   Wrapt up in self, from cares apart,
> By shaded brooks to lounge in leisure,
>   Thinking of loved ones near my heart.

Still, although well pleased, I feel all the want of
society. I sigh for my friends and my sweethearts, and
when I feel that I sigh in vain,

> My heart is filled with grief's fell load,
>   Mine eyes gleam sadly.
>   Yon brook tears by, foaming and madly,
> Which but e'en now with music flowed.

No more the warbler's notes so cheering
  Refresh the groves bereft
Of leaves and zephyr's sweets endearing.
  By storms the trees are cleft,
And blossoms scatter'd o'er the plain.
Filled then with anguish and with pain
I flee and seek some lonely place
For solitude's solace.

Yet I am happy, quite happy. Horn's arrival has, in a measure, dissipated my melancholy. He is surprised to find me so much altered.

He seeks the hidden cause—but vainly—
  Smiles 'midst his thoughts, and looks me in the face,
Yet how can he the cause see plainly,
  I fail myself to trace?

You speak in your letter of Geyer. Does the good man really think that the auditors sit here by hundreds? It may have been so formerly in Leipzig; but were the benches at his lectures not nearly empty?

But I must tell you a little of self.

Changed altogether are the wishes now,
Beloved friend, that occupy my breast.
Thou dost remember how my taste inclin'd
To Poesy,—with what contempt I viewed
Those, whose sole bent was study of the law
And all its mysteries, who refused to listen
Unto the Muse's soft persuasive voice,
Nor lent a willing ear, nor stretched their arms forth
To court her presence. Thou can'st tell, my friend,
How oft I (though in error) have conceived
The Muse affected me, and oft inspired
My verse. True, not a few resonant notes
Sprung from my lyre, though tuned by neither Muses'

Nor great Apollo's hand.   And yet my pride
Permitted vagrant thoughts my mind to fill,
Of gods whose condescension had so willed
That masterpieces not more beauties covered,
Than did those pieces my poor hand wrote down.
I failed to feel that pinions were denied
To me, vain groveller on this earth, to soar with,
And that perchance the godlike hands would never
Aid me, when upwards mounting feebly.   Still
Methought I had possessed them, fledged long time since.
Howe'er, scarce here arrived, the thick cloud faded
And 'fore mine eyes sank down, when the fair fame
Of many great ones shone, full in my sight,
Clearly revealing what 'tis fame to merit.
Then did I find that my presumpt'ous flight,
As it had seemed, was nought but the attempt,
Amidst most vile dust, of the worm which sees
The eagle rising, and like him would soar
On high.   He twists and winds, stretching aloft,
With straining nerves he puts forth all his power—
Nor leaves the dust.   But sudden comes the wind
Raising the dust in eddies up.   The worm
Is carried with these eddies forth, and deems
Himself the eagle's match, and revels then
In gladness.   But the breathing of the wind
At once is stopt.   The dust sinks to the ground,
With it the worm.   He now crawls as before.

Do not lose your temper over my " Galimathias."
Farewell!   Horn will enclose my letter.   My regards
to Kehr.   Look more to your *collegia* in future.   Horn is
to attend five, I six.   Farewell!   Do not acquire academical manners.   Remember me.   Farewell—farewell!

GOETHE.

Leipzig, 28th April, 1766.

D

GOETHE'S LETTERS

TO

CH. G. SCHOENKOPF AND HIS DAUGHTER KITTY.

I.*

Your servant, Mr. Schoenkopf,—how are you, madame,
—good evening miss,—how d'ye do, Peter?

N.B.—You must imagine that I enter at the side door.
You, Mr. Schoenkopf, are on the sofa by the warm stove,
Madame in her corner at the desk, Peter beyond the stove;
and if Kitty is sitting in my place, by the window, she
may just get up, and make way for the stranger. Now
we begin the discourse.

What a long time it is since I last saw you. 'Tis now
fully five weeks, or more, since I was here, and enjoyed
your conversation. Such a thing has not happened for
two or three years before, but unfortunately will now
occur more frequently. You would like to know how I
have been getting on all this time? Well, that I can tell
you,—middling—only middling.

Apropos, I am sure you will forgive me for not having
come to take leave of you. I was in the neighbourhood,

* These letters are in the possession of Mad. Sickel (widow of the
President), *née* Kanne, of Leipzig, granddaughter of Schoenkopf,
daughter of Kitty; and with her kind permission I am allowed to
publish them. I am also indebted to the same lady for many letters
of Horn addressed to Schoenkopf's family, from which I have extracted not a few items to elucidate my subject. I beg at the same
time to express my thanks to Mad. Sickel for many interesting communications having reference to the youth of her mother.

indeed at the door, saw your lamp burning, and went to the foot of the stairs, but had not the heart to mount them. Knowing it was for the last time, how should I ever have been able to come down again.

I must, therefore, now do what I should have done then, thank you for all the affection and friendship you have shown me, which I can never forget. I need not beg of you not to forget me, a thousand circumstances must occur recalling to your memory him, who for two years and a half made one of your family, who, although at heart a good fellow, gave you cause frequently to feel pain, and whom I hope you will sometimes miss. At any rate I miss you frequently. But let us think no more of this, which for me at least is always a sad subject. I reached the end of my journey without anything worth recording, and found all friends here well, except my grandfather, who, although almost recovered from the attack of paralysis which had deprived him of the use of one side, still suffers in his speech. I found myself as well as any one can be who is in doubt as to whether he has pulmonary disease or not, and think I am somewhat improved; my cheeks are filling up again, and as I have neither girls nor worldly cares to plague me here, I hope to progress satisfactorily from day to day.

A word to you, miss! Did my messenger hand you the nic-nacks I sent? and if so, how did you receive them? The other commissions I have not forgotten, although as yet they remain unexecuted. The neckerchief I have completed with great gusto, and will send it you by the first opportunity. If you would like one of the enclosed colour, you have only to command it, telling

me at the same time the tint you would like on it. The fan
is in hand ; the ground will be flesh-coloured, with natural
flowers. Have you still got the shoes? See that your
shoemaker takes care in making them up, when the
colours are well fixed, not to spoil them, and then send
me your pattern, and I will paint as many as you please,
in any colours you may choose, for they are soon got up.
Time will settle other matters. Let me hear from you
when you like, but under any circumstances before the
1st November, when I intend writing you again ; and now
my dear Mr. Schoenkopf, I know you will not write yourself, but urge Kitty on a little that I may soon receive
news of you. What think you, miss ? It would be unreasonable did I not receive, at least once a month, a
letter from the house in which, up to this time, I was to
be found every day. And if you should not write me, it is
all one. On the 1st November you will certainly hear
again from me.

Respects to Madame Obermann, Mr. O. and Miss
Obermann particularly, to Mr. Reich, Mr. Junius, besides
Miss Weidemann to whom you must apologize for my
neglecting to take leave. Adieu, all of you. Kitty, if
you do not write me, you shall see !

Sent off 3rd October.

IA.

MADEMOISELLE,

  Mr. Goethe, to whom it is well known that
scissors, knives, and slippers are articles particularly in
demand with you, sends you herewith a pair of pretty

good scissors, an excellent knife, and sufficient leather for
two pairs of slippers.   All are of sound material, and most
substantial, and my good master has instructed me to
commend to you at the same time the utmost patience.   I
may, however, observe, that in my opinion neither blade
nor leather will be able to hold out in your hands so long
as he.   Do not take it ill of me.   I speak as I think;
but two and a half years you cannot demand of either
slipper, knife, or—I need not say what—for most cruelly
do you treat all that subjects itself, or must be subjected
to your authority.   Tear and break them all up as you
please until Easter, when a new supply will be at your
service, and may these trifles occasionally remind you that
my master ever as before remains your most devoted.   He
has not thought fit himself to write you, that his vow never
to send you a letter before the first of the month may not
be broken.

In the mean time, that is from to-day until the 1st
October, he commends himself to you through me, and I
myself take this opportunity of offering you my respects.

MICHAEL,

Formerly entitled Duke, but after the loss of his
Duchy, a trusty tenant on the ducal estate.*

---

* Goethe here refers to the representation of Kruger's comedy,
mentioned at page 23, in which a servant named *Michael*, who had
captured a nightingale which he hoped to dispose of for a considerable sum, dreams that he will so profitably employ the produce as to
be able at last to purchase a duchy; and in anticipation plays the
part of the overbearing noble towards his master and his daughter
Hannah.   As he is announcing his plans to the wondering maiden,
he suffers his nightingale to escape, descends to reason, and comforts
himself with her affection.

II.

FRANKFORT, *1st November, 1768.*

MY DEAREST FRIEND,

Still so lively, but still so malicious.   So happy
in showing up good in a false light, so unmerciful as to
deride the sufferings of the unfortunate, and jeer at his
complaints,—all these wicked pleasantries are exhibited
in your letter : could, indeed, the countrywoman of Minna
write otherwise ?

Sincerely do I thank you for so unexpectedly early a
reply ; and I beg of you in future in happy hours to think
of me, and, when you can, to write to me.   It affords me
the greatest delight to witness your liveliness, your
vivacity, your wit, salient and bitter though it be.

No one knows better than I the figure I have cut, and
the figures my letters cut I can well suppose.   When we
remember what has happened with others, it needs no
prophetic soul to divine what will happen with us.   With
that, however, I am well content ; it is the usual lot
of the departed, that those left behind and those coming
after should dance on their graves.

How does our manager, our director, our majordomo,
our friend Schoenkopf get on ?

Does he ever think of his leading actor, who all this
time has played to the best of his poor powers, in comedy
and tragedy, the onerous and difficult parts of lover and
deserted friend ?   Has anyone yet offered to take up my
parts ?—I fear not all of them.   You may sooner find ten

actors to play *Duke Michael* than one to play *Don Sassa-fras*.*   Do you understand my meaning?

Our good Mamma has reminded me of Stark's Manual† ; I will not forget it.   You remind me of Gleim ; be assured I will forget nothing.   Absent, as well as present, I seek to satisfy the wishes of those I love.   I very frequently think of your library ; you may calculate on its being increased very soon.   If I do not immediately perform what I have promised, I generally do more than I had undertaken.

You are right, my friend, in supposing that I am now punished for my sins against Leipzig.   My present residence is as unpleasant as my residence in Leipzig would have proved delightful, had certain parties not felt interested in making it disagreeable to me. ·If you *will* blame me you must act fairly.   You know what made me discontented, wilful, and sullen.   The roof was good, but the beds might have been better, says Francisca.

Apropos, what news of *our* Francisca?   Will she soon have made it up with Just?   I fancy so.   As long as the Captain was there she thought of her promise ; but now that he is off to Persia, why, out of sight out of mind. She will sooner take up with a lover she would rather not have had, than not have any.   My regards to the good girl.   You complain with stiffness of the particular compliment I paid your fair neighbour.   What remains for you?   Why, what a question !   You have my whole

---

* We have not been enabled to discover who this hero is.

† Probably H. F. Stark's "Daily Manual for Good and Evil Days."   Frankfort, 1739.

heart, all my affection; and the most pointed compliment does not amount to the thousandth part of that, and that you well know, although you act, for the torment or amusement of your friend (either is the same to you), as if you did not think so; and you take care in your letter to tell me this—for instance, where you speak of my departure;—but let us pass this over.

Show this letter, and all my letters, to your parents, and, if you like, to all your *best friends*, but to no one besides. I write, as I have spoken, in all honesty; but at the same time, I wish no one who might distort my meaning, to put eyes on it.

Constant as ever,
Faithfully yours,
J. W. GOETHE.

III.

FRANKFORT, *30th December, 1768.*

MY BEST, MY MOST ANXIOUS FRIEND,

Horn will doubtless have brightened your prospects for the new year with the intelligence of my recovery, and I hasten to confirm his statement. Yes, my dearest one, the cloud has rolled by, and it will serve to comfort you in future when you hear—he is again laid up! You know my constitution occasionally makes a false step, but in a week I am generally well again. This time it went hard with me, and looked worse than it really proved, for I was tormented with dreadful pains. But in much evil there is some good. I have learnt during my sickness

many things I should otherwise have been ignorant of.
Now that all is over, I am quite lively again ; although I
have not left my room for fully three weeks ; and scarcely
anyone visits me but my doctor, who, thank God, is an
estimable man.   What a foolish creature is man !   In
lively company I was always retired ; now that I am forsaken of all the world I am full of vivacity : indeed,
during my illness this was a source of relief to my family,
who were hardly in the position to console themselves, let
alone me.   In a fit of folly I composed the lines on the
new year,* which you will of course have received, and, to
kill time, I have had them printed.   Besides, I draw a
good deal, write tales, and am altogether contented.   God
grant me in the new year everything good for me.   May
he grant this to all of us ; and if we ask for nothing more
we may certainly hope to receive it.   If I can only rub on
till April, I shall be able to resign myself to my fate.
Then I hope to get on better, more particularly as my
health may be expected to improve daily, now that my
complaint seems to be known.   My lungs are as healthy
as can be, but my chest seems oppressed with something.
I have been given to understand, in confidence, that I may
look forward to an agreeable and pleasant mode of life :
my mind, therefore, is contented and at ease.   As soon
as I recover, I am to visit foreign countries ; and it will
only rest with you, and somebody else, to decide how soon
I shall again see Leipzig.   In the meanwhile, I contemplate starting for France, to study life there, and to
learn the language.   You can therefore form a notion of

* This piece appears to have escaped every search made for it.

what a polite man I shall doubtless have become by the time I return. Sometimes the idea strikes me—what a stupid fate mine would be were I to die before Easter, notwithstanding all my fine projects. In that case, I would order a gravestone for the Leipzig churchyard, so that on St. John's, my saint's day, you might visit the mannikin and my grave at the same time.* What say you?

Commend me to the continued regard of your parents. Kiss for me your dear fair friend, and thank her on my part for the kind interest she takes in me. I will soon write to her.

Your neighbour I really am sorry for. Will not the circumstance that has happened prove a disagreeable episode in the affairs of the loving couple? The poor creatures! They are in great straits; and if Heaven help them or not, they will not be thankful—you will live to see, and say,—Has not Goethe told us so? Certes, marriage, now-a-days, has become a grand affair; none of them, or at least one of them, has not consideration enough to lay out a penny. Oh! holy Andrew! descend, and work a miracle, or we shall have a piggery. N.B.— Take care that nobody sees this but those that can profitably employ it. Farewell, my darling; in sickness or health,

Altogether yours,

GOETHE.

---

* It is still customary in Leipzig on St. John's Day to visit the churchyard, and ornament the graves with flowers. On the same occasion, the small figure of St. John, carved in wood, is placed on the fountain and decked with garlands.

IV.

FRANKFORT, *31st January, 1769.*

To-day or to-morrow, it is all one when I write, so that you learn how I am getting on. I would rather be in Leipzig than here. Neither you, nor Horn, nor anyone else writes to me. Possibly you are enjoying balls and twelfth-night revelries, whilst I am moping here. Miserable carnival. For a fortnight have I again been kept within doors. At the commencement of the new year I was released on parole; the little license accorded me is now expired, and, in all likelihood, I shall be caged for a good part of February. Heaven knows when this is to end. However, I make myself as comfortable as I can, and trust you do likewise. I shall have been here half-a-year, come the 3rd of March, and ill for the six months. Truly, I have learned much in this half-year. Horn, I fancy, must have improved all this time; we shall not know one another again when we meet. Horn cannot have half the desire to see me that I have to see him. The good fellow is to leave Leipzig, and, as yet, has not spit blood. Sad fate! "Can you be so merry who have only this day left Leipzig?" said a Saxon officer to me, when I supped in Naumburg with him on the 28th August. I replied, "Our hearts frequently know nothing of the hilarity of our blood." After a time, he commenced,— "You appear unwell?" I added, "I really am so. I have spit blood." "Spit blood!" he cried; "Ah! then I see it all. You have already made a great march on the road out of the world, and Leipzig became indifferent to you because you could no longer enjoy it." "You have hit it," I answered; "the fear of death has dispelled all other regret." "Naturally enough," he said, taking me up; "for life is always the grand point: without life is no enjoyment. But," he continued, "has not your departure been made easy?" "Easy?" I inquired; "How so?" "Why, plainly on the side of the ladies," said he; "you have the aspect of being not altogether unwelcome amongst the sex." I expressed my sense of the compliment by a deep bow. "I carry my meaning on my tongue," he added; "You seem to me a deserving young man, but you are ill; and I wager, therefore, ten to one that no maiden has held you back by the arm." I held my tongue, and he laughed. Stretching his hand to me across the table, he said, "Now I have lost ten dollars if you say in your conscience, one has held me back." "Done, Captain!" I cried, seizing his hand; "you keep your ten dollars. You are well versed in the affairs of this world, and do not throw your money away." "Bravo!" said he; "I see that you, too, know its ways well. God preserve you! And when you have recovered your health, you will derive advantage from your experience. I"—— and then he plunged into his history, which I will pass over in silence. I sat listening, and when he had ended, assured him I was confounded; and my history, as well as the history of my friend, Don Sassafras, has since confirmed in my mind the philosophy of the captain.

Unfortunate Horn! He has always prided himself on the symmetry of his calves; they will certainly bring him now to destruction. Pray let him off alive.* You may still look at him to your heart's content, for he is the last Frankforter of any note left in Leipzig; and when he has gone, you may wait awhile before you set eyes on another. But console yourselves, I will soon be with you again.

Good heavens! here am I joking again in the midst of my affliction. How should I get on were I not in such good spirits? Chained up now for almost two months.

Adieu my best of friends. Present my regards to your parents, and your fair friend, and when you next write let me know how the several members of the former Sunday company are agreeing. Continue in your affections for your friend,

Ill or in health, till death,

GOETHE.

---

* Horn returned to Frankfort in the beginning of April. In his first letter he says :—" Goethe desires to be remembered to you, Miss. He still looks far from well, and has grown very stupid. The air of the Empire must have affected him. I must see that I pack off, or I shall be in the same predicament; and I am yet too young to become stupid. The time hangs heavy on my hands, although I am seldom alone. Goethe tells me to hang myself; but here at any rate I shall not do so: had I been wise I would have hanged myself in Leipzig."

V.

FRANKFORT, *1st June, 1769.*

MY DEAR FRIEND,

 From your letter to Horn,* I have learnt your

---

* In May she had advised Horn of her betrothal to Dr. Kanne, and received a reply, which we subjoin, for comparison with Goethe's letter :—

FRANKFORT, *26th May, 1769.*

MOST WORTHY BRIDE,

 Without water we should die of thirst; without bread starve; and without matrimony our existence would lose half its pleasure. How happy are you, excellent bride, in having resolved to change your condition for one esteemed the most happy by even savage nations. As regularly installed *magister* and publisher of the banns here in Frankfort and in Sachsenhausen, I feel the most sincere delight, and esteem myself particularly fortunate in having the honour at this time to offer my congratulations to the bridegroom, as well as to yourself. Human beings seek their greatest pleasure in social intercourse one with the other. This in the case of men gives rise to friendship; when ladies are in the case, to love; love to matrimony; matrimony to children; children to grandchildren, and so on. As all this, my dear lady, is likely to be your portion, it naturally causes unbounded delight to my pedagogueish heart. Would to heaven that I could assist at the wedding, and take the lead of my community in singing the hymn! How beautiful it is! Unfortunately, however, the distance of a matter of two hundred miles will render this impracticable, and nothing therefore remains for me but to metamorphose my official assistance into a poetic effusion, and send you for the occasion the glad result of my appeal to the Muses. Pray, therefore, let me know the happy day fixed on, that I may make my arrangements accordingly.

Your friend,

HORN,
Schoolmaster and Ludimagister in
Frankfort and Sachsenhausen.

P.S.—King Horn begs to enquire after the state of health of his

happiness and seen your joy; what my feelings were, and what my joy was, you can picture to yourself, if you can still picture to yourself the great love I bear you. Present my regards to your dear doctor, and commend me to his friendship. I might well have considered myself guilty of

---

ministers in the Schoenkopfic house. By these presents he also accords his most gracious permission to such members as are desirous of entering into the holy state of wedlock to carry their designs into effect when it shall seem unto them fitting, with the proviso that they do so in the legal form and with all due ceremonies. Given at our residence in Frankfort-on-the-Maine, this 22nd May, 1769.

HORNIUS REX.

But, joking apart, I experience the most heartfelt pleasure when I reflect on your family. Papa and Mamma contented, Mademoiselle a bride, and Peter regarding the whole affair with apparent indifference; truly it contributes much to my happiness that you know that I have always taken so great an interest in your welfare. Would to heaven that I could be present at the wedding!—it would certainly come off as merrily again. You know me. Without boasting, I may say that I always play the part of the jolly friend. But now I have lost all taste for enjoyment; the life I lead here is altogether miserable. I study as if I were mad, so as to pass away my time. Sometimes a letter from Leipzig brightens me up a little; but hardly have I read it than I fall again into settled melancholy. Who knows whether I shall ever see Leipzig again; whether I shall ever be made as happy as you have made our friend Kanne. I must not yet give up all hope, but my happiness is still very uncertain. My dear friend, do not altogether forget me. Do not let your joy altogether drive me, unhappy one, from your memory. Remember me and my Constantia on your wedding day. May you enjoy as much happiness as we now suffer pain. Farewell! and console with an early communication.

Your sincere friend,

HORN.

My regards to the Receiver-General.
Goethe intends writing you soon.

neglect for not writing long since, had you looked forward with impatience to a letter from me. This I knew, however, —and therefore for a time have not communicated with you,—that a letter from me was as little worthy of your attention as the " Erlangen Journal;" indeed, taking all in all, I am like a fish out of the watery element, and could swear that,—but swear I will not, since you might imagine I am not in earnest. Horn is beginning to improve ; on his arrival I could make nothing of him. He has grown so tender and susceptible for his absent Ariadne as to provoke my mirth. He unhesitatingly believes what you have written to him, that his Constantia has actually grown pale through her grief for his absence. Talking of becoming pale-faced, one would suppose that his affection could not be very strong ; his cheeks have acquired a ruddier hue than ever.* When I assure him that Sophy will take a leaf out of her friend's book, and by degrees learn, &c., &c., he curses me to his heart's content, wishes me and the book at the devil, and swears that the characters of tenderness have been indelibly engraven on her heart by the might of his love. The poor soul does not reflect that maidens' hearts may not be of marble. The

---

* Horn had an attachment for Sophia Constantia Breitkopf (unknown to the lady's father), to which he frequently gave utterance in his correspondence. She subsequently married Dr. Oehme, and died 1819. Horn, writing to Kitty on 30th June, 1769, says :— " My dear friend, you do me injustice when you believe what Goethe in jest wrote you regarding me. Are, then, ruddy cheeks always the sure sign of the state of our minds ? I pray you, my friend, not to blame me for what I do not deserve.

susceptible heart is one which loves the most readily, but that which the most readily loves, forgets the most readily. But of that he does not think, and very properly; oh! it is a heart-rending sight to see one's love expire. A lover who cannot command attention is not nearly so unfortunate as a forsaken one: the first still cherishes hope, and at least dreads not hate; the other, yes the other—he that has once felt what it is to be cast out of a heart that was altogether devoted to him, shuns even reflecting upon, much less speaking of such a subject.

Constantia is a good girl, and I sincerely trust she may find a consoler; not a tiresome one, who says, " Well! so it is, you must take things as you find them," but such an one as in consoling, is in himself consolation, inasmuch as he replaces all that we have lost. She will soon find one of this nature. Mark my words, my dear friend, and when you see her thus led away to solitary walks and— but you know how all this occurs, and what it is that is not altogether as it should be, then advise me of it,—you will readily conceive how it will interest me.

My songs are still unpublished; were they ready I would willingly send you a copy, but I know no one in Leipzig to whom I could intrust them. Give the few groschens they will cost you for my sake, and sometimes when you would think of me, let Peter play one to you. When I wrote these songs, I was altogether a different fellow to what I am now. The poor fox; were you to see how I employ myself the livelong day, you would be amused.

Writing, particularly to you, has grown distasteful to me. If you do not expressly command it, you need look for no letter from me before October. For my dear friend, even though you address me as your *dear* friend, and sometimes your *best* friend, such a friend is at best but *ennuyant*. No one asks for preserved beans, whilst fresh ones are to be had. Fresh jacks are always most esteemed; but when one fears they may grow stale, he pickles them, particularly if he wishes them to travel. You must at times smile when you reflect on all the admirers you have salted with friendship, big ones, and little ones, crooked or straight ones; I laugh myself when I think of them. Yet you must not altogether break off your correspondence with me, since for a fish in pickle I am still polite enough.

Apropos, lest I forget it, I send you herewith a trifle you can dispose of as you see fit, either in making something for your own headdress, or for another person's wrists.

The neckerchief and fans have not yet advanced a finger's breadth. You see I am candid; when I would set to painting, a something produces a choking in my throat. It is only in spring tide that the shepherd carves on the trees, only when flowers abound, that he weaves garlands. Pardon me; but the remembrance grows too saddening for me, when I would do that for you which I have formerly done, without being more to you than I am.

I have always told you that my fate depended on yours. Probably you may soon see how truly I have spoken, perhaps you may soon learn what you little expected.

Present my regards to your parents, and all your family.
My respects to the Receiver-General.*

I remain as much as possible,

Your devoted friend,

GOETHE.

VI.

FRANKFORT, August 26th, 1769.

MY DEAR FRIEND,

I thank you for the interest you take in my
health, and must tell you for your consolation, that the
last report of my illness was not altogether well founded.
I found myself pretty well, although at times undoubtedly
less so than I could wish to be. You may readily suppose
that nothing but indisposition prevented my writing you
long since, possibly other circumstances may shortly
hinder you from communicating with me. It is a curious
coincidence that a year ago to-day I saw you for the last
time; it is somewhat ridiculous that the face of things
may be so changed in one short year; I wager that were
I to see you again, I should no longer remember you.
Three years ago I had sworn it would have become otherwise than it is. We should swear to nothing I maintain.
Time was when I could not cease talking to you, now my
imagination fails to provide matter sufficient to fill one
side of a letter to you. For I can think of nothing that
would be agreeable to you. When I once hear from you

---

* The Receiver-General Richter, also referred to in Oeser's letters.

that you are happy, altogether happy, I shall be please d. Do you not believe so? Horn desires his regards to you, he is more unfortunate than I. As all things are, however, wonderfully ruled, his folly aids in curing him of his passion. Farewell my dear friend, give my regards to your mother and Peter. I am to-day in a sulky mood. Were I in Leipzig I would take my seat at your side, and show it in my looks. You may remember some such scenes of old. But no; were I beside you, how happy I should feel my existence. Oh! that I could recal the last two years and a half. Kitty, I swear to you my dearest Kitty, that I would act more wisely.

G.

VII.

FRANKFORT, 12th December, 1769.

MY VERY DEAR FRIEND,

A dream reminded me last night that I owe you a reply to your last. Not as if I had altogether forgotten it; no: not as if I never thought of you; no, my friend, every day brings with it remembrance of you and all I owe you. Yet it is a strange sensation, which you may not be altogether unacquainted with, to feel the memory of absent friends dimmed, although not effaced by time. The distractions of our engagements, acquaintance with fresh objects, in short every change in our condition works upon our hearts as dust and smoke on a painting, preventing our recognising the finely-drawn lines, whilst we fail to perceive how this all takes place. A thousand circum-

stances bring you before my mind, a thousand times do I
see your image before me, but as faintly, and with as little
of excitement as if I thought of some stranger.   It frequently occurs to me that I owe you a reply, without my
experiencing the slightest desire to write to you.   If I now
take up your kind letter, already some months old, and
see your friendship and care for so unworthy an individual,
I am shocked at myself; and then only feel what a sad
change must have come over my heart, when I suffer that
to pass by without gladness, which formerly would have
raised me to the very heavens.   Pray pardon me !   May
not a miserable being be excused for his inability to
appreciate joy.   My wretchedness has made me proof
against the good that still remains in me.   My body is
restored to health, but my mind is not yet healed.   I enjoy
a quiet inactivity, which brings no pleasure.   In this state
of rest my power of conception is so tame, that I can no
longer conjure up that which of old was so dear to me.
It is only in my dreams that my heart sometimes appears
to me in its real state; a dream only can recal those
sweet impressions, touching my very heart-strings;   as
I have already mentioned, you are indebted to a dream
for the present letter.   I have seen you; I was beside
you as of old, and yet so strangely that I must tell you
of it.   In a word you were married.   Can this be so ?   I
took up your dear letter, and found the time corresponded ;
should it prove so, oh ! may this be the beginning of
your happiness.

When I cast off all selfish feelings, and reflect on this,
how does it gladden me to know that you, my best friend,
you the envied of all who thought more of themselves

than of you, are in the arms of an estimable husband, to know that you are happy, and that you are freed from all the unpleasantness to which a single existence, and more especially your single existence exposed you. I am thankful to my dream for having so vividly pictured to me your happiness, and the happiness of your husband, and his reward for having rendered you so happy. Preserve for me his friendship by remaining my friend, for now in friends even you must have community. If I may believe my dream, we shall see each other again, but for my part I shall strive to defer its fulfilment, if a man may seek to resist fate. I formerly wrote you somewhat ambiguously regarding my future intentions. I can now tell you more plainly, that I shall change my present residence, and remove farther from you. Nought more shall remind me of Leipzig, save perhaps some fitful dream. I shall see neither friend nor letter from that quarter. And yet I feel that all this will not help me. Patience, time, and distance may effect what all else fails to do, may blot out all unpleasant reminiscences, and at last restore to glad life that friendship, which after a lapse of years, we shall regard with other eyes, but with unchanged heart. Till then, farewell! Yet not quite till then. In two or three months I will acquaint you with my destination, and the period of my departure, and once again tell you, if need be, that which I have already told you a thousand times. I pray you not to reply, but to let me know, through my friend, if you would say more to me. This is a sad request, my dearest one, the only one of your sex I may not call friend, for that is too trivial an appellation by which to express my feelings. I desire as little to see your handwriting as to hear your voice; sad enough it is to be so haunted by my dreams. You may count on yet one letter from me; this I will hold sacred; a part of my debt shall be expunged, the remainder you must overlook. Fancy that our connection has ceased when I have completed this point.

The large book you ask for shall be sent you. I am glad that you have demanded this of me; it is the most glorious gift I could make you; a gift which will preserve me in your memory longer and more worthily than any other.

I can send you no nuptial ode. I had composed several for you, but they gave either too much or too little expression to my feelings. Besides, how is it you ask of *me* a worthy song for a joyous festival? For a long time past my verses have been peevish, and as misplaced as my head, as you will observe from most of those already published, and from the remainder should they appear.

I will soon send you " Hagedorn " and some other works. May you take as much pleasure in the verses of this delightful poet as he deserves. In conclusion, present my regards to your dear mother, and to your no longer little brother, who will doubtless by this time have become a good musician. Remember me to all kind friends, and, in some measure, recall me to the memory of your circle.

Farewell, my dearest friend; receive this letter with love and kindness. My heart could not but give utterance to my feelings at a time that a dream only could give me information on a matter which would otherwise have forbidden it.   A thousand times, farewell, and think occasionally of the tender devotedness of

Yours,

GOETHE.

VIII.

FRANKFORT, 23rd January, 1770.

MY DEAR FRIEND,

Indeed it was fully my intention when I last wrote, never again to take pen in hand to indite a letter to you.   However, in times gone by, it was frequently my fixed intention not to do something or another, and as frequently could Kitty compel me to do it when she pleased ; and if the Doctor's wife possesses the same gift to rule as she may think fit, I suppose I must write to Madame Canne, although I had sworn even a thousand times not to do so.   If my memory serves me well, my last letter was written in a doleful strain ; the present, on the other hand, is in a more lively tone, as you have given me grace until Easter.   Would that you were already married, and Heaven knows what more.   But, truly, at heart I am vexed, as you can readily imagine.

I know not whether you have received the books from me.   I had no time to get them bound.   Let me recommend the small French one to your notice.   You already have a translation of it, and I know that you have studied French a little.

I cannot tell you more of myself than that I am living very quietly, and am hearty, healthy, and busy, for I have no maiden in my head.   Horn and I still remain good friends; but, as is the case with the rest of the world, he is absorbed with his thoughts and ways, and I with mine; so that a week passes by without our seeing each other more than once.

All things considered, I am now fairly tired of Frankfort, and purpose leaving it towards the end of March. I see that I must not go to you; for if I arrived at Easter you would perhaps not be married, and I have no desire to see Kitty Schoenkopf again unless I can see her under some other name. If then it is of interest to you, I leave at the above time for Strasburg. Will you also write to me at Strasburg? You will not play me any prank. For, Kitty Schoenkopf—well, I know better than anyone that a letter from you is dearer to me than from any other hand.

You are still the same estimable girl, and will always be the estimable wife. And I—I shall remain Goethe. You can comprehend that. When I mention my name, I mention my all; and you know well, that ever since I have been acquainted with you I have existed only as one with you.

Before I leave this you shall have the book not yet sent. I shall be a fan and a neckerchief in your debt until my return from France.

I purpose remaining some time in Strasburg, where my title will be changed as well as your own; both will acquire something of the *Doctor*.

From Strasburg I go to Paris, where I hope to enjoy myself, and may perhaps stay some time. And afterwards?—God only knows what is to come. Well now, if it is not at Easter, it will be at Michaelmas; and if it does *not* happen at Michaelmas; why I shall certainly not hang myself.

What if, on bringing you the fan and the neckerchief, I could still say Mdlle. S., or Kitty S. I should then be also a doctor, and, what is more, a *French* doctor. And after all, there is a miserably small difference between Madame Doctor C. and Madame Doctor G.

In the meantime, farewell; and present my respects to Father Schoenkopf, the dear mother, and Friend Peter.

My connection with the Breitkopfs, as well as with all the world, has almost ceased. It is true I received letters not long ago, but I have not the heart to reply to them.

Stenzel still loves the* Peguan to distraction, which strikes me as ridiculous, and makes me angry; you can suppose why. "The grapes are sour," says the fox. We may actually have a wedding yet, and that would be an affair. But I know another wedding that would be a still stranger affair; and it is not impossible, only improbable.

Our arrangements here are excellent. We have a whole house; and if my sister marries she must quit. I will suffer no brother-in-law. If I marry, my parents and I will divide the house between us—I getting ten rooms, all handsomely furnished after the Frankfort taste.

Well, Kitty, it really looks as if you would not have me. Court for me one of your acquaintances, whoever is most like *you*. What of my journey? In two years I am back again. Then! I have a house; I have money. Heart, what dost thou still desire?—A wife.

---

* Constantia and Horn are here referred to.

My dear friend, adieu. To-day I am disposed to be joyous, and have written badly. Adieu, my best one.*

GOETHE.

In "Merck's Letters" (Vol. III., page 13) the subjoined poem in French is quoted. It is described by Dr. Wolff, of Darmstadt, the possessor, as being written by Goethe, and as having been composed by him.

. . . . Que l'amour soit mon Maître,
J'écouterai lui seul, lui seul doit me guider
Au sommet du bonheur, par lui je veux monter,
Au sommet de la science monté par l'industrie.
Je reviens, cher ami, pour revoir ma patrie
Et viens voir, en dépit de tout altier censeur,
Si elle est en état d'achever mon bonheur.
Mais il faut jusques-là, que votre main m'assiste.
Laissés parler toujours ce docte Moraliste.
Ecrivés moi. Que fait l'enfant autant aimé ?
Se souvient-il de moi ? Ou m'a-t-il oublié ?
Ah ! ne me cachés rien qu'il m'élève ou m'accable,
Un poignard de sa main me seroit agréable ;
Ecrivés. C'est alors que, de mon coeur chéri
Comme elle est mon amante, vous sérés mon ami.

Cher . . . .

le votre,
GOETHE.

Leipzig, le 2 Juin, 1769.

That the date must be incorrect is plain. For on the

---

* On 5th March, 1770, Horn wrote :—"Goethe desires to be remembered to you. He goes to Strasburg." Again, on 9th April, " Goethe left a week ago for Strasburg. I accompanied him to Mayence. He will soon write to you." This he did not do, although he had not forgotten her.

2nd June, 1769, Goethe was not in Leipzig, but in Frankfort; and the above letter, dated 1st June, 1769, renders
it hardly probable that he would have written these lines
the next day.   If written in Leipzig—and the year incorrectly given—it is difficult to conceive under what circumstances they were composed.

ETCHING BY GOETHE,

taken by the electro process from the original plate.
See page 31.

GOETHE'S LETTERS

TO

ADAM FRED. OESER AND HIS DAUGHTER FREDERIKA.

Adam Friedrich Oeser was born in Pressburg on the 17th February, 1717, and evinced in early youth taste and talent for painting. In 1730 he proceeded to Vienna, where he attended the Academy, and, under Donner, studied modelling and sculpture. By his composition— "The Offering of Abraham," he gained the gold medal in his eighteenth year. About the end of 1739 he left for Dresden. Here he made the acquaintance of Winckelmann, who, after leaving Nœthenitz, in 1754, took up his residence with him in Dresden, and for whom he was the medium of procuring several commissions whilst the latter was in Italy; so that Winckelmann speaks of him as his only and constant friend. Oeser, as Winckelmann himself gratefully acknowledges, exercised much influence in the cultivation of this artist's talent (whose style he sought to improve by lessons in sketching), as may be observed in his treatise on the imitation of ancient art;—indeed, at the close of his preface, he mentions that, "the conversations with my friend, Mr. Friedrich Oeser, a true follower of Aristides, who gave expression to the soul, and painted for the understanding, afforded me, in a measure, an inducement to write this treatise." It is said that he took part particularly in the chapter on Allegory (commenced in Dresden), which is the more probable, as

Oeser's passion for allegory gained so much the upper hand, that frequently matters, introduced by him as accessories, acquired a too prominent position, to the damage of art in his compositions, from their overshadowing his main idea, and rendering it undecided in character. His friend, Kreuchauff, wrote, in 1783, regarding Oeser's latest allegorical painting, as he had written in 1774 respecting Gellert's monument.

During the seven years' war, Oeser, who was married in 1745, resided several years with his family in Dahlen, and after the termination of hostilities, removed to Leipzig, where Hagedorn, at the instance of Weiss, procured his nomination, in 1763, to the post of director of the newly-erected Academy of Arts. At the same time he was professor in the Dresden Academy, and painter to the court.

How powerfully, and with what lasting effect, his teaching and intercourse worked on Goethe, whilst the latter was in Leipzig, we gather from Goethe's own accounts, and more distinctly from the letters he addressed to Oeser from Frankfort, whilst from Strasburg the intercourse was still maintained. And when Goethe, on seeing in Mannheim, for the first time, a cast of the Laocoon (in Leipzig the only antique was a cast of the faun with cymbals), expressed to him the new lights which had dawned upon him on beholding it, Oeser, who, it is true, did not lay much stress on his views, acknowledged them with a general incitement to improvement. However, when Goethe was fixed in Weimar, he renewed his personal intercourse with Oeser.

This opportunity was afforded by the journeys the Duke

took to Leipzig almost every year during fair time, in which he was accompanied by Goethe, when Oeser was invariably visited. As early as March, 1776, Goethe came to Leipzig, where he remained for several days, and saw again his old friends, Kitty and Oeser, and formed a more intimate acquaintance with Corona Schröter. Towards the end of the same year he made another flying visit. In May, 1778, they returned to Leipzig, going thence to Dessau, Berlin, and Potsdam. Wieland, writing of this journey, states,—"All the country where they have been is full of their fame." Goethe, in company with the Duke, visited Leipzig again in April, 1780, in May, 1781, and in September of the last year with the youthful Frederick von Stein. Goethe, accompanying the Duke again in December of the next year, remained after the latter left on Christmas, until the commencement of 1782, making himself acquainted in a new manner with the town, which seemed a new little world to him, as, besides enjoying himself amongst his old friends, he formed many fresh acquaintances. At a ball he visited, he found about 180 persons present,—many pretty faces and pleasant men; and he thought,—"How was it that fifteen years ago you did not see mankind as you see them now? and yet there is nothing more natural than that they really are what they seem to be." There can be no doubt but that his affection and respect for Oeser remained the same as ever, as the beautiful sketch he gives of him in a letter to Madame von Stein testifies, as well as the kind communication he subsequently made to him. For some years we hear of no further journey to Leipzig, until December, 1796, when Goethe again visited

the city with the Duke, and met many men, amongst them
some interesting ones, as well as old friends and acquaintances, and at a crowded ball was regarded with some
apprehension as the embodiment of the evil principle by
Messrs. Dyk and company, and such as imagined themselves injured and terrified by the Xenien. The last
journey on record was made in 1800, after Oeser's death.
It was on this occasion that Goethe visited G. Hermann,
and after a lengthy conversation on the subject of rhythm,
called on him to write an epic poem in German, on which
the latter replied, that Goethe must first create a German
style.

Goethe introduced Oeser to the notice of the court of
Weimar. The Duke made his acquaintance in Leipzig,
and much enjoyed his society. It was in Oeser's company
that he first met with the aged Forster, and he was delighted to observe the friendship existing between the two.
" Oeser and he draw well together; he is delighted with
the boisterous manner of the rolicking sailor. As Oeser's
good nature permits him to turn his attention to many
subjects, particularly such as may afford him a little amusement, he appears, when in Forster's company, to give
himself up altogether to enjoyment."

Invitations to Weimar soon followed, and these Oeser
accepted as early as 1776. His visit was renewed in the
following year; and Oeser subsequently came to Weimar
once or twice annually. We find him there in January,
June, and (after accompanying the Duchess Amalia to
Mannheim) in the autumn of 1780; in the spring and fall
of 1782; in July, 1783; and during the same month in
1785. In Weimar he was not only welcome as a guest

and experienced connoisseur, whose advice and mediation
was gladly sought in the acquisition of objects of art, but
occupied a prominent position in all artistic undertakings.
" Oeser is here," writes Goethe; " and I have already
taken the benefit of his kind advice in many matters.   He
can tell at once *how* a thing is to be done, whilst I am
perhaps more fortunate in discovering what the thing is."
After he had left, Goethe thought,—" If I had him only
half a day each month, I would mount other colours."
Oeser painted decorations and a curtain for the amateur
theatre, in particular for the representation of " The
Birds," given at Ettersburg, on the 18th August, 1780.
He also took art and part in the plans for the park and
Tiefurt, and completed the monument which the Duchess
Louisa erected to the Duke Leopold of Brunswick.   In a
letter to Knebel, dated 25th January, 1780, he communicated to him a sketch of this monument, illustrating it
with some remarks, and concluding characteristically with
these words,—" I do not think I have anything to be
ashamed of in this idea of a monument; to my knowledge
the thought is a new one, which, I trust, will meet with
the approval of connoisseurs.   The thought started by the
General Superintendent is one I cannot possibly fall in
with.   It seems to me that it would look as if he and I
did not know how to answer the expectations of the public
better than by his reading a passage from some hackneyed
author, whilst I held the book; instead of both of us
saying something new, and not laying ourselves open to
the charge of presenting that to the public which they
could have turned to themselves without having the
trouble of coming to read it.   To study the ancients, and

to copy them, are two very different things, according to my notion."

The man full of taste and talent, the quiet artist rich in worldly wisdom, as he is styled by Goethe, could not fail, by his genial manners and attractive conversation, to win general admiration. He gained in a particular degree the esteem of the Duchess Amelia, on whose recurring birthday (24th October), her old Oeser, as she called him, generally made his appearance with sundry elegant presents. "The Duchess," Goethe writes, "was highly delighted so long as Oeser was here; now things move on more quietly. The old man was engaged the whole day long, either in objecting to, showing, altering, drawing, hinting, debating, or teaching something; so that every moment was occupied." And she herself writes:—" During the time that you, and almost everyone else here, were gadding about this summer, I lived retired at Tiefurt, my sole companion, the old professor Oeser, of Leipzig, who was with me for five weeks; and in wet weather or fine—the former predominated this season—no hour appeared long to me." With her accustomed liberality, she aided him in the education of his son, a circumstance confirmed by the following note of hers to Commissioner Ludecus, preserved in the album of the Schiller house in Weimar:—

" Do you still remember what amount I promised last year to young Oeser for his advancement in the world. His old father has again made application to me, through a third party. I am in a measure indebted to the old man, although the son deserves nothing. If I do not

mistake it was some fifty or a hundred florins. If you
have them by you hand the amount over to Goethe, who
will deliver it to the old man.   Adieu.

" AMELIA."

In later years we learn nothing of Oeser's visits to
Weimar, which possibly may be accounted for by his
advanced age ; still, after Goethe's journey to Italy, his
connection with him would appear to have fallen off.

Oeser died of catarrh on the 18th March, 1799. Goethe
honoured his memory in a manner worthy of his services,
in his Propylae of the year 1800.

It has caused great, and not unfounded surprise, that
Goethe, in his treatise, " Winckelmann and his Age,"
has even not mentioned Oeser, who had so great
an influence on both.   This silence, as well as the
somewhat sceptical manner in which Goethe alludes to
Oeser's influence on Winckelmann, in his " Truth and
Poesy," may perhaps be attributed to the Italian journey.
That Oeser worked powerfully on Goethe's conceptions,
and was afterwards highly esteemed by him as a lover and
master of art, cannot be doubted.   His residence in Italy,
however, considerably modified his views on this subject.
" I fully expected," he observes, " to learn something of
consequence here, but that I should have to go so far back
in the school, and again learn, or rather unlearn, what
I already knew, was more than I had anticipated." Yet
here he proceeded thankfully from Winckelmann's position
and returned to it, admitting at same time that his general
ideas were in the end correct, and wonderfully represented,
but that individual points were involved in uncertain

darkness. He found in Heinrich Meyer a guide who quietly pursued the sure path pointed out by Winckelmann and Mengs. Writing of him, he says,—" He has a heavenly clear conception. Never do I converse with him but I wish I could note down all that falls from his lips, so decidedly yet so correctly do his words describe the only true course. His instruction affords me what no other man can give. All that I learned, heard, or imagined in Germany, compared with his guidance, is as the bark of the tree to the kernel of the fruit." Meyer was distinguished for a comprehensive knowledge of art, founded on careful observation. His system was ordered after Winckelmann's, which he fully comprehended, and had the feeling to enlarge. By his modest, clear understanding, and his quiet manner, he offered a wonderful contrast to Oeser, thus laying before Goethe that which he at that period so much required. On the other hand, his intercourse with Moritz excited and advanced his acquaintance with the beautiful in art, supplementing in so peculiar a degree Goethe's studies in the natural sciences. Without being ungrateful to Oeser, whose former influence on himself he had so truly and so warmly depicted, he learned to recognise his value as an artist and critic, and probably came to the conclusion that Winckelmann's obligations to Oeser in former years had been too highly estimated in comparison with what he became through his own application in Rome, and through the advice of Mengs. He, therefore, preferred not to speak of Oeser, rather than express himself more harshly of him than he could wish.

Such of Goethe's letters to Oeser and his daughter Frederika as are still preserved, are in the library at

Weimar, whence we have obtained permission to publish them. A part of them were already issued in the *Morning Journal*, in 1846, No. 112, page 117.

For several papers and some information referring to Oeser and his family, we are indebted to the kind communications of his grandson, Mr. Geyser, who possesses the portrait of Frederica Oeser, painted by Tischbein, of Cassel, here represented.

TO ADAM FREDERICK OESER.

My dear Professor,

I have now been twelve days in my native town, surrounded by relatives, friends and acquaintances, part of whom rejoice, and some of whom are surprised at my return, whilst all of them unite in kind professions to the newly arrived half stranger, and by friendly intercourse, strive to render bearable to him a city too greatly the antithesis of Leipzig to possess much attraction for him. We shall see how they succeed; at present I can form no opinion.   I am too much distracted, and too busily engaged with my new arrangements, to permit of my heart having much feeling for what I have lost, and what I here regain.   At the present time I only write to advise you that my arrival, after a pleasant journey, has allayed the long-continued anxiety of my family, and that my illness, according to the report of the physicians here, does not so much affect my lungs, as the passages to them, and appears daily to diminish, so that your cabinet-maker,* after staying some days with us, left for his

---

* John Christian Jung (who is afterwards referred to), attendant at the Academy of Art in the Pleissenberg, and who, from his occupation as a cabinet-maker, was named the model cabinet-maker.

destination with good introductions, in the full hope of succeeding in his object, and with respects to yourself and your whole house. For the present that is all. Let me defer until a more quiet and seasonable period—and I trust this will soon arrive—all my grateful acknowledgments for your past kindness, to which I purpose giving expression in a longer and better letter; in the meantime preserve for me all your attachment, your friendship which is so flattering to me, and has so elated me; also the remembrance of your honoured lady, and of your estimable children, as well as of all my friends. In particular I desire my regards to Messrs. Kreuchauf, Cravinus, von Hardenberg, von Lieven, and Huber, and I wish my successor Mr. Groening rapid progress in art.

Ever respectfully,
My dear Professor,
Yours most obediently,
GOETHE.

Frankfort-on-the-Maine, 13th Sept., 1768.

II.

FRANKFORT-ON-THE-MAINE,
9th Nov., 1768.

MY DEAR PROFESSOR,

The protracted absence of your man Jung has delayed the present letter, which I had promised to write you earlier. I had hoped to have forwarded by him to Leipzig a packet of letters, and sundry small matters, which must now wait for some other opportunity.

Should you not have received more tidings of him than I have, you will be more anxious than I; for I console myself with the reflection that he will either have written to you, or have returned by some other route. I hope soon to ascertain what has occurred, as a kind friend has undertaken to inquire for me in Grehweiler as to how he has got on.

My health begins to improve, although I am yet but little removed from a precarious condition. The enclosed letter, which I have taken the liberty of addressing to your daughter, gives more information on this point, and on my mode of life.

Art, now as before, forms my chief occupation, although I read and think on the subject more than I exercise it by the pencil, for now that I am to run alone, I begin to feel all my weakness; I can hardly get on at all, my dear Professor, and as a last resource have nothing left me but to take ruler in hand, and see how far I can progress with this support in Architecture and Perspective.

What am I not indebted to you, most worthy Professor, for having pointed out to me the path to the true and the beautiful, and for having made my heart susceptible of their charms. I owe you more than I can hope to thank you for. My taste for the beautiful, my acquirements, my ideas, have they not all been derived from you? How certainly, and with what bright truth, can I now appreciate the strange and almost incomprehensible phrase that the studio of the great artist developes sooner the budding thoughts of the philosopher and poet, than the lecture rooms of the worldly wise and of critics. Instruction does much, but encouragement everything. Who amongst all my teachers has considered me worthy of encouragement, except yourself. They either unconditionally condemned, or inconsiderately lauded, than which nothing can be more injurious to progress. Encouragement following on the steps of blame, like sunshine after rain, is pregnant with fruitful results. Indeed, Professor, had you not given my love for the muses a helping hand, I should have for ever despaired. What I was when I came to you you well know, as well as what I was on leaving; the difference is your work. I am aware that it happened to me as it did to Prince Biribincker,* after his bath in flames, I saw altogether differently, I saw more than before; and, what was of most consequence, I saw what I still have before me to do, if I hope to be great.

You have taught me to be modest without losing confidence,—proud without being presumptuous. I should find no end, were I to tell all I have learned from you; excuse these apostrophes, these sentences, flowing from a thankful heart; I have this in common with most tragic heroes, that my passion seeks vent in tirades, and woe be he who would dam the current of my lava stream.

The company of the muses, and a correspondence maintained with my friends, will this winter render pleasant my sickly, solitary life, which for a young man of twenty years of age would otherwise be a source of torment to him if absent from you.

My friend Seekatz died a few weeks before my arrival. From my love for art, and my gratitude to artists, you can form some idea of the measure of my grief. If Mr.

---

* In Wieland's "Don Sylvio de Rosalva."

Collector Weise would oblige me by inserting a notice of his life and works in the "Library," I should be happy to furnish you with information.* Pray take the opportunity at your leisure of speaking to him on this subject. I have just read "Idris,"—of my thoughts on this, more another time. My parents desire their regards to you and your family, with all the affection and gratitude they owe to a man to whom their son is so much indebted. Farewell.

I remain, my dear Professor,

Yours devotedly,
GOETHE.

III.

FRANKFORT, 24th November, 1768.

HONOURED PROFESSOR,

Jung leaves to-morrow; can I neglect this opportunity of writing to you? I envy every one and every thing going to Saxony, my letters included; and yet my correspondence with Saxony is now almost the only thing in which I take real delight.

You will be astonished at seeing all the treasures your cabinet-maker takes with him; we were all rejoiced to find that his journey has proved so successful—his sickness excepted—and hope that his return journey at this bad time of the year will be as pleasant as can be expected.

* In the "New Library of the Fine Arts" appears a short notice of Seekatz, which did not emanate from Goethe.

Were it not that the road to Leipzig is so bad, and so long, I should some day or other take you by surprise; for I have much to say to you. You will remember that I had always an abundant stock of reflections, which I generally produced for the benefit of your opinion; some it is true were very far fetched, but then you taught me better; there are, however, a thousand things one can talk of without hesitation, but which one would hesitate to write about.

My thoughts on "Idris," and the letter to Riedel,* on Ugolino, on Weisse's Magnanimity, on the Essay upon Prints, from the English,† are all of them fitting subjects for conversation, but poor topics for correspondence.

The galleries here, are, it is true, small, but all the more numerous and choice; my greatest delight is to make myself thoroughly acquainted with them. It is well that you have taught me how to look around.

Generally speaking, however, I suffer much for art; it is my usual fortune to suffer for my friends. Apostles, prophets, and poets are seldom much honoured in their own country, and still less so when they are to be seen every day; but, notwithstanding this, I cannot forbear preaching in favour of good taste; if my exertions are not attended with any great result, I always gather fresh information therefrom, were it only the conviction experience carries with it,—that widely spread learning, reflective,

---

* Wieland's letter to Riedel was published before the first edition of Idris and Zenide, 1767.

† An essay upon prints. London, 1768. 8vo.

F

pointed wisdom, errant wit, and well based acquirements,
compared with good taste, are very heterogeneous in their
nature.

The ladies here lay great store by the wonderful, and
think less of the beautiful, *naïve*, or comic. Consequently,
all such tales as "Grandison," "Eugenic,"* the "Galley
Slave,"† and like fantastic stuff are in great demand here.
Of "Wilhelmina,"‡ which, thank Heaven, has gone
through three editions, I have failed, after the most diligent inquiries, to find a single copy in any of the ladies'
libraries here. In my next I shall tell you more of this
sad state of affairs.

If you find the red stone and the black chalk good, I
have more at your service. Have the kindness to present
my respects to your good lady, and all the family, as well
as to my patrons and friends, among whom I particularly
mention Messieurs Creuchauf, Weisse, Clodius Hubert,
von Hartenberg, Cravinus, and Gröning. My parents
desire their regards to you.

With the most sincere respect, I remain,

Your obedient scholar and servant,

GOETHE.

---

* A translation of Beaumarchais' Eugenie (Paris, 1767), appeared
at Leipzig in 1768.

† The "Galley Slave" (Leipzig, 1768) was a translation of
L'honnête Criminel of Fenouillot de Falbaire (Paris, 1766). Lessing
at one time entertained thoughts of writing another version of the
same incidents; "for he was not at all satisfied with the French
original, great as was the applause bestowed on the German translation."—Lessing's Theatrical Remains, Vol. XLVII.

‡ Thümmel's "Wilhelmina" appeared in Leipzig in 1764, 1766,
and 1768.

IV.*

As I had appeared, so I disappeared. My dearest friend, a thousand thanks for all your kindness, and unchangeable love *in sæcla sæclorum.* Regards to all your family and to Becker.† Do not forget the casts, and let me have them soon. My description of the Snayers has caused the Duke to long to possess them, and we must see how he likes them on beholding them. I beg you, therefore, to send them to me well *cleaned,* and carefully packed, by the mail. I left Leipzig with regret. M. Becker might write me occasionally.

GOETHE.

WEIMAR, *6th April, 1776.*

V.

We are thinking of producing a new piece on our boards in honour of the Duchess Louisa's birthday,‡ and require a new back drop scene for a wood. We should like to have the prospect of a beautiful neighbourhood abounding in trim hedges, and lakes, with but few architectural points; it should represent a park.

---

* Several letters are wanting here.

† W. G. Becker, Editor of " Recreations and the Pocket-Book for Social Amusement," afterwards Superintendent of the Collection of Antiquities in Dresden, and a frequent visitor at Oeser's house.

‡ " Proserpina " was given on the 30th January, 1777.—Riemer, II., page 38.

If you have anything of this description on hand, pray send it by first post, at any rate a plate of Poussin's, or some such idea. If I remember right, you have something of this description on a curtain in Leipzig. The bust shall be sent you without delay. Your memory is cherished by us all. The Duchess Louisa has reproached me for not introducing you to her, you must therefore soon visit us again, that I may repair my fault—Addio. Has nothing further respecting my divinity been revealed to you?

GOETHE.

7th Jany., 1777.

VI.

Having returned home by another route,* we were prevented bringing you with us. The Dowager Duchess is at present in Ilmenau, but she would have been glad could we have followed her there.

Pray do me the kindness to send me the bas-reliefs, as I should much wish to complete the frames during her absence.

I would gladly amuse you with an account of the table I asked for, and other matters, but I well know the inclination of your tastes.

---

* In the beginning of May Goethe accompanied the Duke to Leipzig, and afterwards went with him to Berlin, whence they returned to Weimar in the beginning of June.—See Letters to Madame Von Stein and Riemer.

Send me one or two drawings for stone garden seats, elegant in shape, but at the same time simple in design.

On my return from Ilmenau, you shall hear from me again.

I shall give you my ideas of the table. I see clearly in my mind's eye what sort of appearance it should have,— something Gothic in style again. I know we shall be at sixes and sevens about it. I am as difficult to please in this as any Philistine. Write and send to me again.

GOETHE.

5th June, 1778.

VII.*

WEIMAR, *the 10th March, 1780.*

I return you my best thanks, my dear Professor, for what you have kindly sent me. The sketch for the prison shall be returned to you immediately, completed.

You write: "Schuman is to carry out in the above style the sketch I have made on the subjoined paper," but I find nothing to which these remarks will apply.

The drawing for the table leg has been again laid aside. I have fixed the terms, and beg that, in accordance with your promise, you will attend as well to the purity of the details, as to the position, construction, and unity of the whole.

I must also request you to send me as soon as possible a chandelier for our theatre, for we have arrived at that point that we now want light.

---

* From this point onwards, the letters are no longer written by Goethe himself.

I have your name down on my tablets for many other matters, and I beg of you again and again, so to make your arrangements as to join us at the commencement of spring.

I will attend to the letter, and await the box.

GOETHE.

VIII.

I have delivered your letters, and attended to your commissions. You will in all probability receive by this day's mail your bust, and I hope you will in some measure be pleased with the workmanship.* I have mentioned to Klauer your desire to see him with you for a short time. He seems undecided, and I myself should wish to ascertain, before mentioning the subject to his Highness the Duke, and asking for leave of absence for him, in what way, and for how long and for what object you wish to have him with you, for these are all questions his Highness is sure to ask. Klauer himself appears to consider some more decided understanding desirable, and I would myself counsel you to treat fully and distinctly with him on this point. Unless a clear arrangement be come to at the commencement, it is difficult to attach a value to the productions of an artist, and discontent is generally the result. Besides, he has several matters in hand here,

---

* This bust was modelled by the sculptor Klauer when Oeser was in Weimar during the summer of 1780. Goethe more than once expresses his satisfaction with the manner in which it had been executed.—Letters to Madame Von Stein and to Merck.

which he can scarcely hope to complete in less than three months.

As promised, I herewith send you a copy of the celebrated correspondence, which, when read, please return to me. I do not know whether your opinion will agree with mine, but in the form of a narrative it appeared to me more delightful and pleasant than it now does in type.

If you would kindly send me a few architectural designs for his Highness the Prince,* I will take care that they are copied.

At the time I write this you will doubtless be engaged in an important transaction, to which I wish you every success.† It may be that the statue is already fixed, and I am curious to see it.

Farewell—remember at your convenience the commissions with which we have troubled you.

Wiemar, *3rd August, 1780.*

Goethe.

IX.

My time being fully occupied with a multiplicity of affairs on my arrival here, I cannot do more than merely express to you, my dear Professor, my thanks for the large measure of love and friendship you evinced towards me during my stay in Leipzig. My every hour there

---

* Prince Constantine, brother of the Duke.

† Oeser's monument of Fred. Augustus III., erected on the Königsplatz, in Leipzig, was inaugurated with every ceremony on the 3rd August, 1780.

being devoted to some special object, how much I feel indebted to you for having enabled me to pass the greater part of my time pleasantly, as well as usefully.

Having to leave this again on the day after to-morrow, (the 3rd,)* do me the favour to correspond with Councillor Bertuch (with whom I leave full instructions) about the statue to be sent.

I must close with kindest regards to you and yours, in which I am joined by my little fellow-traveller.† Excuse me for troubling you with so many matters, and rest assured of my sincere devotion.

WEIMAR, *1st October, 1781.*

The bas-relief referred to before may be shortly expected to arrive.

GOETHE.

X.

My thanks reach you rather late, my dear Professor, but are not less warm than when I parted from you, for I certainly left Leipzig with regret.‡ You rendered my stay there as agreeable and useful as it possibly could be, and, as usual, I left all the richer.

It is true I have acted like the people of Israel in their flight out of Egypt. You will miss sundry articles,

---

* For Gotha.—Letters to Madame Von Stein.

† Frederick Von Stein.—Letters to Madame Von Stein.

‡ Frederika Oeser, writing on 6th January, 1783, to her brother, said—"Privy Councillor Goethe was in Leipzig during the holidays, when a good deal was talked over."

amongst which I may particularly mention a large pencil that I appropriated without any compunctions of conscience. If we are so fortunate as to see you here in the spring,* I will lay before you the result of my labours with it. The colour is boiled, works of art attempted, but unfortunately the border is the part of such works that I succeed best with.

The bust you requested for Mr. Breitkopf, has been packed up, and will be sent by Schauri's coach. The elevation of the observatory I have enclosed in a box to Rost, and trust it will reach you in time.

But I must now pressingly beg of you to send me the celebrated fountain. We have made an experiment, and find that the water rises sufficiently high; it is true it flows in rather a strong jet, but at the same time does not fall quite satisfactorily. Be good enough to send me the drawing as soon as possible, for until I receive it, we cannot lay out either the paths or the plantations; and, notwithstanding the severity of the season, their Highnesses urge on the work.

Large stones have been procured for the rockwork, and only await your creative commands to form a beautiful whole. Do not therefore dash down our hopes, but come as soon as the weather will permit.†

---

* Oeser came to Weimar in July, and "was very merry, Herder good, Wieland talkative, Musæus good-humoured and unpolished as ever."—Letters to Madame Von Stein.

† A leaf upon which Goethe wrote his Epigram on Amor feeding the nightingale, in a similar form to that in which it is chiselled on the stone at Tiefurt, testifies to Oeser's participation in the arrangements in the park.—See Letters to Madame Von Stein. Is the small statue likely to have been executed by Oeser?

Commend me to your family, and thank all a thousand times for the liberal aid and friendly entertainment so freely rendered to me during my stay.

Many compliments to Herr Creuchauf.

How is Burscher engaged? May I count on seeing soon a new work of art of the modern Hogarth?

Immediately on my arrival here, I caused the fine card board to be imitated; the result, however, of the first attempt has not been altogether successful, as the size does not take well, which the papermaker attributes to the weather.

When you join us, you will be delighted with the excellent iron stairs I have obtained from Treves. I have also procured others from Hungary; but by no means so beautiful as yours.

Afford me an early opportunity of at least partially repaying the many obligations I am under to you.

Again, farewell.

WEIMAR, *30th January, 1783.*

GOETHE.

TO FREDERIKA OESER.

I.

FRANKFORT, 6th Nov., 1768.

MAM'SELL,

      As fractious as a teething child ;
Now downcast, like a man by writs made wild,
Or meek, like any one who's hipped,
And moral, with love's wings close clipped,
Obedient as a very lamb ;
Then as a bridegroom brisk, I am
Half ill, and then anon half well once more,
My body stout and sound, my throat with quinsey sore ;
.Disgusted much that my defective
Lungs scarce inhale enough, with strains effective
To tell the world around in proudly measured staves,
What I enjoyed with you, what here my spirit craves.

They strive to clothe me with fresh animation,
Fresh spirits and fresh strength ; hence for probation
I'm handed by my Doctor *Medicinæ*
An extract made from *Cortex Chinæ*
To brace my nerves, relaxed and stricken,
And foot, and hand, and eye
Anew to strengthen, memory
And faculties to quicken.

Especial care he next devotes,
By regimen those ills to banish
Which rash excess so much promotes,
And bids my fierce desires to vanish.

" By day, and above all, by night,
Give not your fancy too great flight !"
What a command this for an active mind,
Which e'en the slightest charm in chains can bind.
The maiden limned by Boucher's art
Must from my chamber's wall depart,
And be replaced by an old frow
With deeply wrinkled face, and jaws half void and toothless,
By careful, frigid, Gerhard Dow.
Instead of wine, with cruel hand and ruthless,
He proffers wretched tisanne tea.

Oh ! tell thou me,
Can worse befal me than at present ?
My body old, though adolescent—
Infirm, whilst yet in partial health—
What melancholy fits this raises,
And even wealth
Untold would fail to banish such dark phases.
What profit should I find in heaps of gold ?
An invalid to joy is cold.

Yet at my fate I would not murmur,
For in the school of woe too well I'm versed,
Had I but that which makes us firmer
To bear with sickness' load accurs'd,

Which makes our hearts yet quicker beat
Than inuate virtue, consolation
'Midst hours o'ercast by desperation ;
E'en kindred spirits' converse sweet.

'Tis true that round me are collected
Friends sympathizing with my sadness,
Who when I grieve are much dejected,
When I rejoice join in my gladness,
I fail myself alone to make my heart o'erflow,
But yet I know of none who such a glow
Of peace, content, and happiness diffuse
As you, whose glance my soul with life endues.

I came to thee a very apparition
Whom death's hand soon again a second blow had dealt ;
And he who round his heart that icy grasp has felt,
Does melt
With fear when he recals yon hour he abject knelt.
I know how sad was my condition,
Yet mad'st thou with thine own sweet disposition
A bed of flowers replace the vision
Of the dark tomb.   Thou didst narrate to me
How fair, and sweet, and holy, life might be,
And this with flatt'ring tone so blythe and free,
Methought the bliss which misery had ravish'd
I yet enjoyed, since upon thee 'twas lavished.
Content I journeyed forth,—indeed, yet more, with joy,
Which on the road knew no alloy.

I reached my home, and found the girls as ever,
So dull—since truth must out—that all endeavour

To touch my heart has proved but labour vain.*
Though faint praise, such as Hamburg's beauties
From Schübler met with,† I refrain
To give them,—yet a critic's duties
Will not permit me to compare
Their gifts with the seductive graces,—
So constant in my thoughts,—of Leipzig's maidens fair,
Before whom they must veil their faces.
For sprightliness, intelligence so choice,
Good heavens! or for wit, none may with thee compare.
Yet how would thy harmonious voice
Within the Empire's limits fare?

Such converse as we often held 'midst flowers,
Or on some summer seat, strange though its wonted bent,—
So lively, yet so sapient,—
Cheers not my dreary hours.

----

* Horn after his return to Frankfort also writes :—" Here in the
Empire existence is intolerable, the people are as stupid as you can
well conceive.   At times I cannot but laugh at this, but more
frequently I am annoyed at it.   The girls! they are quite unbearable
here, very proud, and devoid of all common sense.   I could at times
go mad when I remember Leipzig.   Not one amongst them is
capable of conducting a conversation, unless it be about the weather,
or the last new cap."

† Daniel Schübler, of Hamburg, resided in Leipzig from 1765 to
1768, and occupied his time with music and poetry.   His select
works were published by Eschenburg (Hamburg, 1773).   He would
appear to have been intimate with the Oesers.   In his poem " Pyg-
malion," when addressing the God of Love, he compares the ladies
of his native city to exquisite. statues, and calls on the Deity to
breathe upon them, and inspire them with life.

When 'midst our damsels joy I show,
By frowns my levity's demolished—
'Tis then, " Good sir, come you from Bergamo ?"
Nor is this asked with tone so polished.
If wise I look, they still are not content,
For if my thoughts I do not measure
By Grandison, or should dissent
One jot or tittle from the man they treasure
As all in all, I wot
I'm laughed to scorn,—they hear me not.

Ye maidens are so good, for self-improvement caring,
Your own faults strict to mark, of others' most forbearing ;
Joy to diffuse no pains you spare,
Your gentle sway all hearts entrances.
Ah ! all your virtues own, though seen only by glances,
And love you e'er they are aware ;
A Frankfort girl with pride expanding
Leads one in truth a weary game,
She lacks, for friendship, understanding,
For love, a heart to feed the flame.

My course had soon been run, but that my innate gladness,
Though thus hedged in, breaks through all sense of sadness ;
My laugh is heard, where not a smile I see,
Cheered by the thought,—you often think of me.

For think of me you oft must in connexion
With rural scenes, when the direction
Of your fair cottage in the field
You take, yon spot where such dejection
I knew, but where my grief was always healed.

But let me now explain and make my meaning clearer,
For this I know you will excuse,
The ditties I then sang hold dearer
As tributes paid to you, and to the village muse.

When by my cruel maid tormented,
Ere break of day my grief abroad I vented,
And rashly would not rest contented
Till in yon mead you oft frequented,
Whose glowing beauties you have taught
Me to discern, your face I sought.

Your paradise I roamed to find your shadow,
Sped through each wood, o'er every meadow,
By stream, by brook, my anxious hopeful face
Flushed by the morning's rays,—I sought nor found your
    trace.

Ill-humoured, ill at ease, upset through perturbation,
Poor basking frogs I slew from sheer vexation—
Aimless I strayed about, now caught
A butterfly, and then a brighter thought.

Thoughts not a few, as well as butterflies,
Did rise
Before my outstretched hand, arrested
As it would seize them, by the sound
Of footsteps, or of voices which suggested
Some ramblers in the wood around.

The verses thus by day repeated,
By night, when to my home retired,
I jotted down, and so completed
Rhymes good and bad as thus inspired.

Oft I returned, to find my hope still languish,
To this my fated scene of anguish,
Till fortune smiled, and all my griefs did vanish,
And a bright dawn dispelled the seeming gloom.
But scarce could I enjoy the fleeting pleasant season,
It was but all too near the tomb.
What I then felt I hide with reason,
For this my crude prosaic verse
Is ill attuned such feelings to rehearse.

Here then you have my lays, and as requital
For all I've suffered for your sake ;
When home you seek, in their recital
Some pleasure take—
And chant them there—where I did wander—
With glee, though grief e'er ruled my song ;
Then think of me, and say :—Down yonder
Beside the stream, he tarried long,
Unfortunate ! and oft—his tears with gladness blended—
The glowing prospect scarce did heed !
If hither now his footsteps tended
No further search he'd need.

But by my troth I think 'twere time to finish,
For after filling thus two sheets with verse,*
One feels his rhyming powers diminish,—
Though rest assured my news I will rehearse
In the like mode in future, if no worse
Reception these poor lines—than prose distinguish.

---

* The letter fills two sheets, written in a firm neat hand.

With warm regards my kind friends greeting,—
I pray you pass not Richter by.
Adieu !   And should the smiles of fortune constant vie
With my affection, how bright a future you are meeting.

GOETHE.

II.

MADEMOISELLE,

The answer has been long deferred,—shall
I beg of you to excuse me !   Certainly not, if I *might* do
so ; if I might say : Mam'selle, pardon me,—I was overwhelmed with very much business, enough to have made
even Hercules stretch his arm.   I really could not,—the
days were short,—my brain, owing to the influence of Aries
and Aquarius, was somewhat cold and damp,— and the
full string of commonplace excuses, not to let it be supposed I was lazy.   Indeed if I could make up my mind to
such subterfuges I would rather not write at all.   Oh !
Mam'selle, it was an impertinent condition of wayward-
ness innate in me, which chained me for four weeks to
my bed, and for four weeks more to my chair, all of which
time I would have as gladly spent confined by magical
enchantment in a cleft tree.   And at last these weeks
have passed by, and during the time I have studied fun-
damentally and seriously the chapter of contentment,
patience, and what not of subjects in the book of fate, and
am grown all the wiser for my contemplation.   You will
therefore excuse me if the present letter is more a com-

mentary on yours than a reply to it ; for although I have
derived much pleasure from the perusal of your letter,
I have also much exception to take to it, and—*Honneur
aux dames*—but indeed you have done me injustice.

We must understand each other better, before we proceed further. Assume, then, that I am dissatisfied with
you ! And now I will commence, and go on from
beginning to end, in the style of an old chronicler, and the
letter will grow to be as long as the dissertation of a parson
on a short simple text.

You know, then, of old—at least it is not my fault if
you do not know it—you know that I look upon you as a
good girl who, if it suited you, have it in your power to
reconcile an honourable man with your sex, even though
he were as irritated as Wieland. If I am wrong, that
again is not my fault. For nearly two years I have
frequented your house, and have seen you almost as
seldom as a nightly enquiring Magus hears a mandrake
whistle.

To speak then of what I have seen—the Church does
not judge of that which is not revealed, said Paris—I can
assure you that I have been enchanted by it ; but indeed
philosophers of my stamp generally carry Ulysses' bundle
of charmed herbs, along with other trinkets, in a *sachet* in
their pockets, so that the most powerful witchcraft does them
no more harm than a drinking bout, followed next morning by a splitting headache, but leaving the eyes clearer
than before. Let this be well understood in order that
there may be no misconception.

You are fortunate, very fortunate ; if my heart were not
just now dead to all sensation, I would tell you how ; indeed

I would sing it to you. The most possible of all Gessner's worlds; at least so I imagine. And your mind has formed itself according to your good fortune; you are tender, sensitive, a connoisseur of beauty; this is good for you and for your companions, but it is not good for me; still you must be good for me if you would be a perfect girl. I was once ill, and again became well, well enough at least to reflect with comfort upon my last wish. I slunk about in the world like a ghost, which after death is now and again drawn to those places which formerly attracted him when he could enjoy them in his bodily presence; with woe-begone looks he creeps to his treasures, and I meekly to my girls, to my friends. I hope to be commiserated; our self-love always hopes for something, either love or pity. Mistaken spirit, remain in your tomb! You may stand and wail ever so pitifully in your white sheet,—he that is dead is dead; he that is ill is as good as dead; avaunt ghost, avaunt! if you don't want people to say you are a troublesome ghost. The stories that led me to these reflections do not belong to this letter. Only one of them will I narrate to you circumstantially, if I can manage to recall it correctly. I came to a girl,—I could have sworn it was you,—she received me with shouts of laughter at the idea that any man in his twentieth year could be so ridiculous as to die of consumption! Indeed she is right, thought I; it *is* laughable, although as little so for me as for the old fellow in the sack, who was almost killed with a beating which made an audience almost die with laughter.* As however all things in this world have

---

* Molière's Les Fourberies de Scapin, III., 2.

two sides, and a pretty, agreeable girl can easily make one believe that black is white ; and as I am at any rate easily persuaded ; the thing pleased me so much that I allowed myself to fancy that it was all imagination, and that one must be happy, so long as one is pleased, and so forth ; and then she told me how happy *she* had been in the country, how she had played at blindman's-buff, and cock-shy, and fished, and sang, so that I felt as pleased as any girl does in reading Grandison ! there's a fine specimen of a man, such an one you would like, thinks she.

How gladly would I have joined in, and have made my illness worse. Let a man be as bad as he may, Mam'selle, there is nothing so bad but that fate may derive some benefit therefrom,—your mercilessness during the last few days towards the poor doomed one, gave him fresh strength. Believe me, you alone are to blame that I left Leipzig without any especial pang. Joy of heart and heroism are as communicable as electricity, and you possess as much as an electrical machine has sparks.—I will see you again to-morrow !—Such a farewell to a poor wretch one is about to chain to the galley, by my faith, is not the most tender. So be it ! It gave me renewed strength, and yet I was by no means satisfied with it. Between ourselves, greatness of soul is generally combined with want of feeling. When I consider the matter, you acted quite naturally ; my departure must have been a subject of indifference to you ; but to me it was far from being so. I should certainly have wept had I not been afraid of spoiling your white gloves, an unnecessary precaution, for I saw at last that they were of silk and knitted, and then I could have wept

again, only it was too late to do so. But let me conclude.
I left Leipzig, and your spirit accompanied me with all
the sprightliness of its being. I arrived here and commenced making observations for which time had failed me
before. I looked about for friends, and found none ; for
girls, they were not so specific as I like ; and in the midst
of my grief I complain to you in beautiful rhyme, and
wonder, will she commiserate you, and comfort the unhappy swan with a letter ! Then came a letter ! Well,
it is true that refreshed my spirit ; for you cannot imagine
the drought which causes one here to pant for agreeable
entertainment ; but comforted I certainly was not. I saw
you meant to say that poetry and untruth are twin sisters,
and that your correspondent might perhaps be a well-
meaning man, but that he was also strongly imbued with
a poet's notions, who, from his preference in favour of
chiaroscuro brought out his colours more brilliantly, and
his shadows more darkly than nature does. *Bon.* I am
willing to give you credit where you are right. But it
is a little too bad to suppose things to belong to me
which I as little possess as the alchymist's stone. *A sound
head,—a good heart !* now it will be some little time before
I allow myself to be persuaded that these belong to
me ; but teachable disciples ; worthy friends ; these I have
failed to find, when I have caught such birds of paradise
I will write to tell you. You were therefore wrong to write
me out a recipe for a species that exists in Leipzig only,
seeing that this must of necessity vex me, as you can well
imagine. You are most unreasonable ; you have made my
heart indifferent about leaving L., and now you wish to
make me forget it altogether ! Oh you know yourself

and your countrywomen too little !   Any one who has
seen Minna played in Frankfort, knows better what
Saxony is. You are therefore wrong ! This I again repeat,
although for the instant I know not why ; for I have
written so much about it that I really have quite forgotten
what I was thinking of.   My opinion is that the whole
affair was an impartial, disinterested reminder of a certain
young lady ; that a really good heart includes also compassion ; that the feeding of the poor or of birds is no
evidence of the highest degree of susceptibility ; that
laughter is no better remedy for real misfortune than for-
getfulness is ; that when we are ourselves satisfied we cannot
with a good grace hold a discourse upon contentment with
a hungry man ; and lastly, that the most delightful letter
does not possess a hundredth part of the charm of a conversation.   Now you might have cast all this and much more
in my teeth and not by any means in such choice language,
to my utter confusion, and I should never have ventured to
make any, even the least, of these impertinent observations.
If young ladies only knew what they could do if they
wished to !   It is well that it is as it is, and I for my part
shall be content that they do not know all our weak points.
But a truce to this subject about which I have written so
much, because I hope never again to write about it.

Whilst referring to this, I may add that this new year's
time I have written a farce shortly to appear, under the
title of " A Comedy in Leipzig."   At the present time
all farces are contraband in Parnassus, as are all ideas in
the Louis Quatorze style.

Be your connexion with fate what it may, I shall stand
on a par with it ; and your motto might pass muster, and

even seem right and proper, were it not that it is taken from Rhingluff,* or what on earth you call him. Twenty poets have said the same thing just as well, or even better; and why should the man with the barbarous name receive all the honour; for, between ourselves, I am none of his friends? I know nothing further of him; but his verses, which I do know, give the lie to the venerable beard and majestic presence Herr Geyser † attributes to him. I will swear that in the flesh he looks younger. Are the songs bad, then? Who is likely to ask such heartsearching questions? Really I do not know what to reply. Mam'selle, if you desire it, you shall have my opinion respecting all sorts of things; tell me your own, and it will afford the most agreeable and most fruitful materials for our correspondence; but experience produces distrust. I speak frankly to you, as I would speak to but few in Leipzig, only do not let anyone see how I think. Since Clodius has evinced a more friendly disposition towards me, a great stone has been rolled away from my heart. I have always endeavoured to guard against giving offence. Rhingulff, doubtless, is

---

* K. Fr. Kretzschmann had published in Zittau "The Song of Ringulph the Bard, when Varus was Slain" (1769) which was highly praised in the New Library of Belles Lettres, 1769, VIII., I., p. 76. Later appeared "The Wail of Ringulph the Bard" (Zittau, 1771). In the Frankfort Journal Goethe ridiculed him thus:— "Herr Kretzschmann appears here in the altogether unexpected light of a patron, standing with a golden sickle under the consecrated oak, and, as an old bard, initiating the stranger Telynhard. Can any one tell who has consecrated him as Rhingulph, for the sake of Klopstock and Gerstenberg?"

† The copperplate engraver, afterwards Oeser's son-in-law.

in Leipzig; perhaps you know him. I know nothing; for I have lost all connexion with all noble spirits. I think of R. as of all poems of this description. Thank God we have again peace! Of what use is all this cry of war? Yes, if it was a poetical style, with a fund of wealth, of allegory, sentiment, and so forth. Then, indeed, there would always be fish to land. But nothing besides an eternal thunder of battle, the fire blazing from the warrior's eyes, the gilt hoof splashed with blood, the morion and plume, the spear, a few dozen monstrous hyperboles, and a perpetual ah! ha! when the line cannot be completed, and when it draws its slow length out—all this together is unbearable, Gleim, and Weise, and Gessner in one short poem, and enough to satiety of all else. It is a thing that fails altogether to interest; a wish-wash that only serves to pass the time. Forced pictures,—because the versifier has not seen nature; eternal repetitions,—for a battle is always *the* battle; and the situations are old used-up ones. And what does the victory of the Germans concern me that I should listen to the shouts of joy? Why, I can shout myself. Make me feel something which I have never felt—make me think of something which I have never thought of—and I will give you praise. But noise and shouts instead of pathos,— that does not suit me,—tinsel, and nothing more. Then there are in R. pictures of rural innocence which might be apt if applied to Arcadia; under the oaks of Germany no nymphs were born as under the myrtles in Tempe. And what in a picture is most insufferable is its want of truth. A fable contains its modicum of truth, and must contain it, or else it is no fable. And when the subject is so

hashed up one grows afraid. Our friends think, then,
the outlandish costume must produce effect ! If the piece
is bad, of what use are the fine clothes of the actor?
When Ossian sings in the spirit of his times, I can
willingly employ a glossary explanatory of his costumes,
and can willingly give myself much trouble to comprehend
it ; but when modern poets strain their wits to present
their poems in an old dress, it does not suit my humour
to strain my wits to translate their lucubrations into
modern language. Gerstenberg's " Skalde " I should
long ago have gladly read, but for the glossary. His is
a lofty spirit, and he has a principle of individuality.
One should not judge from his " Ugolino." I would
take this opportunity of observing that grace and lofty
pathos are heterogeneous, and no one can unite them so as
to produce a masterpiece of a noble art ; certainly a subject
of lofty pathos is not adapted for painting, that touchstone of grace ; and poetry has by no means any occasion
to enlarge its bounds, as Lessing maintains. He is an
experienced advocate of his cause; rather a little too
much than too little is his mode of thinking. I cannot—
I may not further explain myself ; you cannot but understand me. When one thinks differently from acknowledged great minds, it generally is a sign of a small
spirit. I have no desire to be at the same time one
and the other. A great spirit goes wrong as well as a
little one ; the former because it ignores all bounds, and
the latter because it takes its narrow horizon to be the
whole world. Oh ! my friend, light is truth, yet the sun
is not the truth, although light flows from it. Night is
untruth. And what is beauty ? It is not light, and not

night. Twilight, an offspring of truth and untruth—a middle thing. Within its empire is placed a finger-post so ambiguous, so much awry, that a Hercules amongst philosophers might well be misled by it. Here I must stop; for when I come to this subject I begin to ramble, and yet it is a subject for which I have a preference. How I should enjoy a few delightful evenings with your dear father. I should find so much to say to him. My existence is at the present time devoted to philosophy. Locked in, solitary, pens ink and paper and a couple of books form all my apparatus. And, by this simple way, I arrive at a knowledge of truth, often as far or farther than others with all their library knowledge. A very learned man is seldom a great philosopher; and he who, with much labour, has thumbed the pages of many books, is too apt to despise the easy, simple book of nature; and yet nothing is true which is not at the same time simple, although, certainly, this is but a poor recommendation for true wisdom. Let him who follows the simple path go on his way in silence; humility and prudence best become our footsteps on this path, all of which will eventually meet with due reward. For this I have to thank your dear father; he first moulded my soul in this fashion; time will reward the diligence I exercise to carry out that which has been commenced by him.

When I once begin to chat, I lose myself, as you do; only I cannot so soon find my way back. In saying I have chatted much, this remark applies more to the present letter than it does to yours. I was, perhaps, a little too abrupt.

Be encouraged by me to write! You do not know

how much you do for me in occupying yourself for me occasionally. And were it only on account of its singularity, you ought to keep up an interchange of letters with a correspondent in the Empire.

One or two trifles before I close. My songs, of which a portion have had the bad fortune to displease you, will be printed at Easter, set to melodies. I might, perhaps, have taken the liberty of dedicating a copy to you with my autograph, were it not that I know that you are easily moved by some trivialities to invective, as you yourself mention in the commencement of your letter, which I think, by the way, I have well understood. It is my misfortune that I am so frivolous, and that I look at everything on its bright side. Is that my fault? Throw them into the fire, and do not look at them when printed; only keep me in favour. Between ourselves, I am one of the resigned poets; if the poem does not please you, we will write another.

I should like to write something about Wieland, did I not fear prolixity. It would afford materials enough for another letter. You also have a good deal to tell me, you say in your last letter (which was the first). Spend an hour every week, I will gladly wait a month, and then I hope a friendly packet will console me. You would do me a particular favour if, amongst other things, you would give me some information about the newest agreeable and good works; here the first information reaches us quite three months after the fair. Although I have now almost wholly renounced modern literature, and my rhymes will only flow after some small excitement, I should not like altogether to forsake neology all at once. One always retains some desire to read the scribbled critiques which in Leipzig often pass muster for learning.

I should be glad to pay you a visit at Easter ; or, I tell you what,—do you come here to me, or send me your papa. We have room for all of you, if you will come. I am really quite in earnest. Only ask Master Jung,* he will tell you this is true. And our table expands when we have guests as well as your own. I hardly expect you will accept this invitation, the Saxon girls are somewhat nice on such points. Well, I will not force you. But if you make me angry, I shall come myself and invite you in person. Will you then not accept?

I remain, your most devoted

Friend and servant,
GOETHE.

FRANKFORT, *13th February, 1769.*

III.

FRANKFORT, *8th April, 1769.*

Well, what great crime is it if I beg of you to gossip a little? How is it you abuse an honourable man without afterthought, as a villain, because he tells a girl who knows how to employ his tongue, in a voluble and agreeable manner, that he knows how to value this pre-eminent gift of her sex? Your vehement blame does not affect me in the least, and you would have done better not to have grown angry.

---

* See page 92.

And so I have an evil idea of the fair sex? Well, in a certain way, yes! But you should understand me, and not always interpret my words in a bad sense.

I well know what I have experienced, and I hold the experience for the alone genuine knowledge. I assure you that for the few years I have lived I have acquired but a very moderate idea of our sex, and to say the truth no better an one of yours. Do not take offence at this. You have followed my example; and even you, do you not give me cause to continue in my obduracy? You will show me your sex from another point of view! Oh! had you left matters as they stood, bad as they are, you would not have made bad worse. How advantageous is, then, this new point of view. Let us see! That every young, innocent heart is thoughtless, credulous, and therefore easily seduced lies in the nature of innocence. Do you deny this? Do you call that, then, blame if one states the case as it really exists? You contradict me, and wish to defend your sex. That not all girls are frivolous, you yourself have proved; that I must confess. But you have helped me to a dangerous argument : the wiser portion is also distrustful. For distrust is the temper of all your letter. How have I deserved this? Oh! the suspicion lurks in your own heart, and therefore *nonchalante*, upright, honest passages in my letters must be malevolent railleries. My letters are in your hands, and I appeal to them ; you will find no malice in them, except what you seek out of them.

The opinion of a young lady on works of taste is to me of greater weight than the critique of a critic ; the reason of this is patent, and all your eloquence shall not serve to pervert my probity. What do I say when you confess that the lines from Rhingulff were inserted as an artifice? That you can well imagine. I will say you know well how to place your mouse-trap, and that I am glad I have allowed myself to be caught. You can see how open I am. Had you been frank, and had you asked me, I should have told you neither more nor less. Had Herr Gervinus * not been with me here, I should not have known how the matter stood. By his account I learn that the bard was well received in Leipzig, and that he gave universal satisfaction; and I can well see that he has pleased you too, and that I have written evil of your friend. Let it be so! What I have written I have written. Put it down to the account of envy, or of my want of feeling, that the bard does not please me. It is all one to me. Enough, I can feel nothing where nothing has been conceived. And a republican spirit does not deny himself; Saxony has tempered his roughness and his boldness, but has not been able to make him join in the concert of praise. I am indebted to your father for the sense of the ideal; and the distorted attractions of the French will as little rouse me to ecstacy as the dull nymphs of Dieterich, however naked and sleek they may be. Every style has its merits, reckoned by its own standard. I am your most obedient, Mam'selle, on all points; we will not fall out on this account. In future, be not so severe against authors, but at the same time do not be so severe against me. How shall I reconcile myself with your sex if you continue as you have

---

* Fried. Gervinus, of Zweibrucken, studied at Leipzig in 1768.

begun. And yet if you cannot act otherwise, just scold on ; you are still pretty, whether you are friendly or cross.

Your trees in Delis* will now soon be budding, and so long as they are green I need hope for no letter from you. Meanwhile, I will compel you sometimes to think of me ; my spirit shall think so intensely of your bushes, that he will appear to you before you expect him, and my letters in prose and verse shall make you more observant of the attractions of a country life, in spite of Hirschfeld, the anatomist of nature, should no other subjects present themselves to me. Herr Regis can hardly be satisfied with us ; I am really sorry that so agreeable a man should have found so unpleasant an *accessit* to us on the first occasion. I am—I do not myself rightly know what— but still now, as of old, with all my heart,

Your friend and admirer,

GOETHE.

Several letters to Frederika Oeser are missing. Schöll, however, has published, from copies retained by Goethe, two written from Strasburg, which, as I believe, were also addressed to her. The first bears the superscription " To Mam'selle F."; the abode in Sesenheim recalled to him the days which he had passed in similar intercourse in Oeser's country house at Dölitz; the second, without any superscription, follows immediately thereafter on the

---

* Dölitz.

same sheet, and in this the reference to Leipzig is clear.
Kitty is mentioned in this, of which there can be no
doubt, and Fränzchen, most probably the young friend
who had acted Francisca in Minna von Barnhelm, referred
to in a letter to Kitty (p. 58). The tone of these it is
true shows a marked difference from the preceding; we
perceive that Goethe has grown healthy and more mature,
and the breathing of the newly opening love which
inspires him is perceptible; in other respects however the
manner of these letters accords completely with the
character of his relations to Frederika Oeser, and the
train of thought peculiar to these relations is evident in
a marked degree. These letters are therefore here subjoined.

———

IV.

14th October, (1770).

To Mam'selle F.

Shall I again tell you that I am still alive and well, and
as pleased as one in a tolerable condition can be, or shall
I hold my peace, and rather not do anything beyond
thinking of you with shame for my silence? I think not.
To receive forgiveness is as sweet to my heart as to
deserve thanks; indeed it is yet sweeter, for the feeling
is a more unselfish one. You have not forgotten me,
that I know; I have not forgotten you, that you know,
notwithstanding a silence the length of which I do not

care to reckon. I have never so vividly experienced what that implies to live delighted, without one's heart being engrossed, as now, here in Strasburg. An acquaintance with agreeable people,—a lively, intelligent society about me helps me through one day after another, leaves me little time for thought, and no leisure for sentimentality; and when one has no feeling for anything, one certainly does not think of his friends. In fine my present existence may be compared to a sleigh drive, exhilarating and musical, but as little satisfying to the heart as it is to the eyes and ear.

You will hardly guess how it comes that just now it should so unexpectedly occur to me to write to you; and, as the reason is worth relating, I will mention it to you.

I have been spending a few days in the country with some most agreeable people. The society of the amiable daughters of the house, the beautiful scenery, and the bright skies awoke in my heart each slumbering feeling, each recollection of all that I love; so that I have hardly arrived here again before I sit down to write to you.

And from this you can see how readily one forgets his friends in prosperity. It is only volatile, deplorable felicity that makes us forget self, and that obscures the memory of loved ones; but when our perception is genuine, and we taste the quiet and pure joys of love and friend-ship, then by a peculiar sympathy each interrupted friend-ship, each half expiring tenderness of feeling starts again into fresh life. And you, my dear friend, whom amongst many, I may so name pre-eminently, accept this letter as a fresh evidence that I shall never forget you. Farewell.

V.

SAARBRÜCK, *27th June, (1771).*

If everything, my dear friend, were written down, which I have thought of telling you during my journey to this lovely neighbourhood, whilst enjoying all the alternations of a splendid summer's day in the sweetest repose, you would have a good deal to read, something to sympathize with, and not a little to laugh at. To-day it is raining, and in my solitude I find nothing more attractive than to think of you; of *you* all, that is to say, and even of Kitty, of whom I well know that she will not belie herself, and that she will feel towards my letters, as she did towards myself, and that she—but enough, anyone who has seen a sketch of her only, knows her already.

We were on horseback the whole day yesterday, and night was approaching as we neared the mountains of Lorraine, with the Saar flowing at our feet through the lovely valley below—when I looked to the right over the verdant abyss and the river as it flowed grey and still in the twilight, whilst on my left the deep shade of the beech woods on the mountain seemed to overhang me, and the fluttering songsters flitted silently and mysteriously around the dark rocks showing through the copse, my heart felt as still as the scene around, and the previous exertions of the day seemed to pass from my memory like a dream, which one must make an effort to recollect.

What a blessing it is to possess a light free heart! Courage impels us to meet difficulties and dangers; but great joy is only to be attained after great exertion, and that is perhaps the greatest objection I can raise to love; we hear it said it makes courageous—by no means! So soon as our heart grows tender, it is weak. When one feels it beating warmly against his breast, with a choking sensation in the throat, and strives to express the tears from his eyes, then as they begin to flow one is seized with unutterable bliss. Oh! then we are so weak that we are fettered by chains of flowers, not because they through any magic charm have become strong, but because we tremble lest we should tear them asunder.

The lover who is in danger of losing his sweetheart it is true grows courageous; but that is no longer from love, but from jealousy. When I talk of love I mean that agitation of feeling, in which our heart appears to float, constantly hovering now on one side and then on another around one spot, whenever any attraction has caused it to leave the ordinary path of indifference. We are like children on their rocking-horses, always in motion, always at work, but never progressing. That is the truest picture of a lover. How dire is love when one is so tortured, and yet lovers cannot exist without torturing themselves.

Tell my Franzchen that I am still devoted to her as ever. I am very fond of her, and was often angry with myself because she tortured me so little; when in love one wishes also to be in fetters.

I know a good friend whose sweetheart often did him the kindness to make her lover's feet her footstool at the dinner table.* It happened one evening that he wished to rise before she desired to let him leave ; she pressed her foot upon his in order to detain him by thus coaxing him ; unfortunately her heel fell upon his toes, he suffered much pain in consequence, but still he recognized too highly the value of such a mark of favour to withdraw his feet.

Amongst a considerable number of letters and reflections of Frederika Oeser which we have had the opportunity of perusing, unfortunately there were none found which she had written to Goethe. In order to give a livelier view of his correspondent it may not prove uninteresting to subjoin a fragment from a letter she addressed to a friend in Dresden, dated 21st January, 1770 :—

" I was as you know the favourite of my father, and his constant companion, even in his business. A thousand little tricks which I played my phlegmatic brother Hans betrayed a designing head, and often a small sympathising tear at the troubles of a Yorick, or a tender heart at the exasperation of a Beatrice's hard task, at the same time however, there was observable a goodly portion of ambition. But suddenly came that cruel war which tore me, perhaps for ever, from my beloved native town ! We fled before its fury to a count's palace,† where we spent three

---

* See the song written in Leipzig entitled " True Enjoyment," p. 142.

† Dahlen, a residence of Count Bünau.

years removed from all disturbances. Here, dear N., your
friend became a little peasant girl, who preferred digging
potatoes or going to country fairs! My father was most
of the time absent from us, we expected every month to
start off again, we therefore engaged no tutor except a
writing master whom his grown-up pupil still daily honours
by a *remarkable* handwriting;* my father's travelling
library was all I had to kill time in rainy weather, and I
read very diligently ; it was under such sad circumstances,
and during such times that I formed my conceptions of
the great world. From my earliest years I had heard
frequent regrets expressed at my disfigured features, I
knew, therefore, even in my ninth year, that I was not
pretty (a great knowledge for young girls !) but only half
recognized my misfortune and learned to console myself
for it. " If you have no beauty of feature, take care to
acquire other more beautiful virtues " (said I to myself),
" you must grow more talented than the rest of the world,
and learn everything better than girls who are pretty need
to learn it, for this must certainly be the next way in which
one may learn how to be so fortunate as to please. There
are none but good and sensible people in this world. And
when you grow up, you must be able to show yourself in
their company without disadvantage ; when this or that
important question is put to you, you must not find yourself embarrassed to return a proper reply." In short,
dear N., my world was a larger rendezvous for remarkable
things than Roland's discoveries in the moon ! and never

---

* Her handwriting is very distinct, firm, and decided in
character.

can more ambition have flickered in a young bosom,—at the same time ambition without pride; I was almost entirely unimpressionable when I was praised for anything, particularly when I found myself deceived in my anticipations, and learnt to know the Leipzig world as my world. I learnt to understand it and myself better, and as I at first from ambitious motives had fixed upon certain examples as my standard (always be it understood as to the acquirement of talents, for my heart had its peculiar ideas) which I found I could never reach, I at length sought to use this knowledge as the surest means of preserving me from more than ordinary vanity, and it thus became easy for me to cure myself tolerably of this inordinate passion. I now followed wholly the inclinations of my honest, good heart, I became almost indifferent to the world around me, in which I heard much of evil and saw much that was unprofitable. I gradually learnt to recognize my failings, and to have all the more consideration towards the weak points of my friends, who, I discovered, were only too good! I gave myself up entirely to the bent of my inclinations, particularly to my taste for books, in which I followed the advice of persons of discernment, but yet I only read such books as improved and pleased me ; and in the large, open, but indispensable book of human experience I learnt at length to turn over a few pages. And so I grew to be the girl I am ! whom you very well know, dear N., and who will hardly ever be able entirely to cure herself of her deficiencies and of her great faults. How is such a girl fitted to express rational decisions respecting this or that question, since she has her heart, and not her understanding to thank for the beauties she feels, and also knows no rule by

which she could demonstrate the opposite of one passage
or another?   Will you listen to these opinions of my feelings?   If so I am ready to communicate them to you on
each occasion which may present itself, but for the reasons
why I so feel, you must not ask me!   I might perhaps
answer *you*, but should not know how to answer *myself*."

GOETHE'S LEIPZIG SONGS.

The songs of which mention is so often made in these letters, and which Goethe also referred to in his work, " Truth and Poesy," as having been published without his name, and as being but little known, were afterwards included by him with the remainder of his smaller productions. These " buds and blossoms which the spring of 1769 brought forth," as he writes to Mad. von Stein, appeared under the following title :—

NEW SONGS

SET TO MELODIES

BY

BERNHARD THEODORE BREITKOPF.

LEIPZIG:

PUBLISHED BY BERNHARD CHRISTOPHER BREITKOPF AND SON.

1770.

It is evident, however, from our letter (p. 74) that the collection was already printed in 1769. Tieck was the first to call attention to " this oldest book of songs," and in the sixth volume of the New Annual of the Berlin Society for the Cultivation of the German Language and Archæology he reprinted these songs, and Vickoff subsequently included them in his Exposition of Goethe's Poems, vol. I. p. 45.

Some of the poems were also communicated to the " Almanack of the German Muses," for 1773 (2, 3, 7, 16) and for 1776 (4, 6, 10, 13), and also to the Leipzig Journal "The Muses" for 1776 (3, 7, 11) with a few inappreciable variations evidencing an earlier composition. As was surmised, they were certainly taken from copies existing from the time of Goethe's residence in Leipzig.

Amongst the remains left by Frederika Oeser was preserved the original written book of songs by Goethe, the same collection referred to in the rythmical letter, (p. 112) with the title,

SONGS

WITH MELODIES

DEDICATED

TO

MADEMOISELLE FREDERIKA OESER,

BY

GOETHE.

This contains only ten songs, of which nine appear in the collection published;* the tenth is not included, but this is to be found in " The Muses," referred to above, and in the index of that work Goethe is given as the author. Like the songs, the melodies also exhibit a few differences in the written copy from the printed one, but all of an unimportant character. Amongst the same remains there was also found a copy (not, however, in

---

* They are—in this order—11, 7, 13, 3, 5, 4, 12, 6, 10.

Goethe's handwriting) of the Marriage Song, in which the
original expressions were evidently retained.

As the Leipzig songs could not well be omitted in this
work, they are here inserted along with the hitherto unpublished poem.

1.—THE NEW YEAR.

What ho !   Who buys my modest wares
For new year's mottoes who here cares
    His fate to foretell ?
If here and there a shaft do go
Wide of the mark,—one glove we know
    Fits twenty hands well.

Sweet youths !   Still flick'ring prove your loves,
Billing like tender turtle doves
    Constantly cooing.
Your life is yet to dulness nigh,—
Wait till this year has fleeted by, —
    Rash grows your wooing.

Ye to whom Cupid's ways are known,
With whom the spark has fiercer grown,
    For you I tremble.
Beware, my children, cease your play.
This year ! but not another day
    Dare to dissemble.

Young married man, young married wife,
Probe not too deep your partner's life
    Now ye are wedded,—
For jealousy racks many hearts,
And double trouble aye imparts
    When deep imbedded.

Thou widower yearn'st, when deep distressed,
Thy sainted spouse to join in rest
    Through death's dark portals.
My worthy friend, stay—not so fast !
That which thou seek'st, with heart downcast,
    Thou find'st 'mongst mortals.

Ye, who to woman's love averse,
In sparkling cups your fancy nurse
    And seek to inspire—
'Tis true that wine oft clouds the brain,
Yet the ills in matrimony's train
    Mount ten times higher.

The Muses grant that at spring-tide
With joyous verse in fullest pride
    Your hearts I gladden.
Join in my songs ye maidens fair,
Then shall I wander free from care,
    Nor doubts me sadden.

2.—TRUE ENJOYMENT.

In vain, oh Prince ! her heart assailing
    A maiden's lap with gold thou heap'st,
Nought but her free gift is availing
    To yield the bliss which then thou reap'st.
Gold wins thee voices there's no telling,
    But not a single heart it buys.
No ! would'st thou virtue,—'tis by selling
    Thy heart alone thou hast such prize.

What is the joy that in embraces
  Of harlots vile thy lust attains?
Thou art an abject, void of traces
  Of aught that's pure, and folly reigns.
She kisses thee with venal motive,
  A gleam for gold her eyes diffuse.
Thou wretched one!   An off'ring votive
  Love asks, which vicious lusts refuse.

If strange to virtue, yet the features
  To man belonging do not lose!
For feelings of desire all creatures
  As brute beasts foster, nor abuse;
But man refines these, and the teaching
  Should not prove grievous, but assure
Thee increased joys, without impeaching
  Thy better nature when 'tis pure.

Although from sacred ties exempted,
  Oh youth! restrain thyself, for we,
By indiscretion though not tempted,
  May freedom taste, nor yet be free.
Let one alone inflame thy passion
  If all her heart with love o'erflow,
And so shall tenderness' fair fashion
  Than duty stern, more binding grow.

With throbbing heart make thy selection,
  And do thy love with love allure,
Whose beauteons form her soul's reflection,
  Thus ecstacy like mine secure!
I of this heart have long been master,
  I chose a trusting child to mate,
And naught we lack but that the pastor
  Our wedded bliss should consecrate.

Anxious alone to give me pleasure,
  Only for me her beauty blooms
Her passion burns, in richest measure,
  To others coyness she assumes.
And lest our ardour time should weaken,
  No claim importunate she heeds ;
Her favour ever proves the beacon
  To which my grateful heart she leads.

Contented easily, enjoyment
  I owned whene'er with smile so sweet
Beneath the table she employment
  As footstool gave my willing feet ;
The apple reached which she had tasted,
  Or glass, impressed with recent sips,
Or bared her bosom as she hasted
  To shun the kiss reft from her lips.

When in some chatty social hour
  She breathes forth thoughts with love that burn,
The cherished words my heart o'erpower ;
  For words, not kisses, then I yearn.
What depth of soul and innate meekness
  Her ever growing charms display !
She is perfection, and no weakness,
  Save love for me, her thoughts betray.

By homage at her feet prostrated,—
  Clasped to her breast, by love impelled,—
'Tis then, oh youth ! desire is sated.
  Seek wisdom—in like thrall be held—
Snatched from her side by death's embraces,
  To join th' angelic choir on high,
Thine shall be all bright heaven's fair graces,
  Translated with nor pain nor sigh.

3.—NIGHT.

Gladly I this cot forsaking,
  Home of my own loved one's choice,
Through the woods a pathway breaking
  Shun the sound of human voice.
Moonbeams through the oaks are playing
  Zephyrs sweet her haunts betray,
And the beeches gently swaying
  Shed their odours o'er the way.

Now my heart is wildly thrilling,
  Melts my soul with glad delight,
Rustling sounds the groves are filling.
  Oh thou beauteous, lovely night!
Oh what bliss! scarce apprehended!
  Yet bright heav'ns I render ye
Back a thousand nights more splendid
  If my maid grant one to me.

4.—THE SQUALL.

AFTER THE ITALIAN.

I did my sweetheart once pursue
  Into the wood's deep shade;
Around her neck my arms I threw—
  "I'll shriek!" she threat'ning said.

Aloud I cry, "The wretch I'll kill
  Who ventures e'en a word."
"Hush!" whispers she, "my darling! still!
  Or else you will be heard."

5.—THE BUTTERFLY.

Where we oft caressing stood,
　As a butterfly I flutter,
　　Gladsome blissful hours recounting
　'Midst those scenes our joy which utter,
　　Over meadows, at the fountain,
Round the hill, and through the wood.

There I watch a tender pair
　From the maiden's locks bright shining ;
　　Earthwards from her wreath down glancing
　All I see for what I'm pining,
　　And the image most entrancing
Melts my grief into thin air.

On her lips but smiles are found ;
　Love entwined they joys are lasting
　　Gracious gods have deigned to lavish.
　How his lips are boldly hasting
　　Bosom, mouth, and hands to ravish !
And I flit with glee around.

Then she sees me, butterfly,—
　At her sweetheart's ardour trembling
　　Up she jumps, and off I hurry.
　" Come !" she cries, with mien dissembling,
　　" Come and catch him, for 'twill worry
Me to lose him when so nigh."

6.—JOY.

How oft in dreams thou sawest us meeting,
And 'fore the altar vows repeating,
　Which made of us a wedded pair.
How often from thy lips when waking
Sweet kisses thou hast found me taking
　In moments thou wast not aware.

The joys all pure we then have tasted,
Our bliss, which all too quickly hasted,
  Then with enjoyment quickly fled.
Of what avail is present pleasure ?
Like dreams have fled the joys we treasure,
  Forth like a kiss our bliss has sped.

7.—A YOUNG GIRL'S WISH.

Oh ! that I could see
A husband for me.
How nice it is—ah !
To be known as mamma.
No need then for sewing,
To school no more going.
Have maids in one's power,
Who cringe and must cower,—
Choose gowns that are striking,
Made up to my liking,—
With drives be delighted,
To balls be invited,
Nor ask for permission
Papa and mamma.

8.—EPITHALAMIUM.

TO MY FRIEND.

Within the chamber Cupid's hidden,
  And true to thee keeps watch and guard
'Gainst wanton guests whose tricks unbidden
  The bridal bed's peace would have marred.
Thee he attends, his flambeau beaming,
  Its golden rays and flick'ring glare
With rolls of mystic incense teeming,
  Your fullest bliss his only care.

H

How yearns thy heart, when the clock's dial
  Warns noisy guests to bid good-bye,
That of those lips thou may'st make trial
  Which, silent, soon will naught deny.
Then swift, for fullest consummation
  Ye seek the sanctuary bright,
And Cupid's mild illumination
  Smiles still and softly on the night.

How thrills her bosom with th' implanted
  And oft repeated kisses warm ;
All trembling thy desire is granted,
  For boldness now takes duty's form.
With Cupid's aid she quick undresses,
  Whilst thou art faster far than she.
The rosy god then coyly presses
  Both eyelids to, lest more he see.

9.—JUVENILE EXPERIENCE.

In all large towns the smallest boys
  Soon learn more than they need ;
O'erdone with books, they scorn vain toys,
  But tittle-tattle heed
Of love, and phrases buttered
'Twere better left unuttered ;
And many scarcely twelve years told,
Look wiser than their sires of old
When erst their wives they took.

The girls too from their earliest days
  For admiration pine ;
When small, they deck in borrowed rays,—
  Full grown, at balls they shine ;

And proud beyond all measure
In love they find no pleasure.
Their highest thoughts they yield to dress,
These cares, alone, themselves oppress
And others they ignore.

But quite another tale is told
  In villages around ;
The youngster there in heat and cold
  For bread must till the ground.
The hind o'erdone with labour
Won't bore his fairer neighbour ;
And he besides who nothing knows,
Of nothing thinks, for nothing glows ;
And such is rustic life.

Yet peasant maidens who in rest
  And quietness are bred,
Are anxious often to be blest
  In ways their mothers dread.
And frolicsome they dally
Their stolid swains to rally.
Refreshment from their labours light
They find in toils that joy excite,
And therewith are content.

10.—JOYS.

Around the fountain bubbling
Is fluttering and doubling
  The water butterfly,
Whose hue is ever troubling
  The eye to specify.
Now red and blue, then blue and green.
Oh ! that I could but seize it
To view its wings so sheen !

Upon the bank it sought repose,—
I seized the wand'rer for inspection
  Ere yet he rose.
I now regard his varying hue,
And lo ! a dark and dingy blue.
Like fate attends thee by thy joy's dissection.

11.—LOVE'S GRAVE.

AFTER THE FRENCH.

Weep maidens here by Cupid's grave,—he here
  Succumbed to chance, by nothing dire o'ertaken.
But is he really dead ?   I will not swear 'tis clear.
  A nothing, a mere chance, his life afresh may waken.

12.—LOVE AND VIRTUE.

When to the girl our love who heeds
Her mother lessons sternly reads
Of virtue, duty, modesty—
All which our maiden will not see,
  But takes delight, with yet more vicious
And increased warmth, our lips to seek,—
'Tis less to love is due this freak
  Than to a spirit most capricious.

But when the mother does succeed
And makes the tender heart to bleed,
And, by her lessons, sees with joy
The maiden shun us, cold and coy,—
  The heart of youth she fails t' unravel,
For a girl acting in this wise,
Shews fickleness in virtue's guise,
  At which we've justly cause to cavil.

13.—INCONSTANCY.

In the purling bright brook I lie quite excited
With wide spreading arms, by each ripple delighted
  Which amorous washes my wild longing breast,
Then frivolous dashes along, downwards rolling,
Another soon follows, caressing, consoling ;
  By each changing wavelet I feel then so blest.

Oh, youth ! hence learn wisdom, let not your heart languish,
Nor waste precious moments bewailing your anguish,
  If, fickle, a maid from your sway strive to burst,
Call back the old times which so joyous were reckoned,
You'll kiss just as raptured the breast of the second
  As ever the bosom you kissed of the first.

14.—TO INNOCENCE.

Brightest virtue, tend'rest feeler,
  Purest fount of charity !
More than Byron, than Pamela,
  Prize so rich by rarity.
'Fore another flame there's danger
  Lest thy feeble light's forgot.
Felt most there where thou art stranger ;
  Who thee knows, he feels thee not.

Goddess sweet ! of yore not scorning
  Ere our fall with man to dwell,
Still thou'rt seen in early morning,
  As the dewy meads can tell.
Poets, who their muse are nursing,
  View thy shape at break of day ;
Phoebus comes the mist dispersing,
  Melts thy form in mist away.

15.—THE MISANTHROPE.

A. At first we see him seated
   With smooth unwrinkled face ;
  When lo ! his visage heated
  To passions deeply seated
   And visions stern gives place.
B. You ask us is his case
  Chagrin, or love defeated ?
C. Alas ! we both can trace.

16.—THE RELIC.

I know, oh youth ! how sweet thy pleasure
When thou can'st seize, as valued treasure,
A string or scrap, too small to measure,
 Of any dress thy loved one wore.
A veil or necklace, rings, or garter,
Thou wilt not for a trifle barter.
 I'm not content unless I've more.

Next to my life most highly rated,
My maiden's pledge, with heart elated,
I'll lay beside thy treasures, fated,
 By contrast, mean t' appear. Oh ! how
I laugh to scorn thy toys, and glowing
Tell of her gift of ringlets flowing
 Which once adorned her beauteous brow.

E'en though thou, sweetheart, far dost wander
I do not wholly lose thee yonder ;
But see, and handle, and grow fonder
 Of this thy fairest ornament.
How like the fate of these fair tresses,
And my poor self ! We spent caresses
 Round soft lost cheeks we now lament.

Both round her form all closely twining,
Anon upon her cheeks reclining,
And with desire thence often pining
    Upon her swelling breast to lie.
Oh ! rival, who no envy bearest ;
Thou relic, treasure, sweetest, fairest,
    Bring back delights long fleeted by.

17.—IRRESISTIBLE LOVE.

Full well I know, and oft deride,
    The fickleness ye girls display.
Ye love, as if at cards, to side
With knave and king each after other ;
As both are trumps, the trick they cover—
    And thus ye gain in either way.

Yet am I in a wretched plight ;
    My face my sorrows does betray—
The slave of love, a foolish wight !
The griefs I mourn I'd temper gladly ;
But ah ! they rack my heart too sadly,
    And jeers will not drive love away.

18.—THE JOY OF LOVE.

Sip, sweet youth, that bliss entrancing
Daily from thy love's eyes glancing,
    Night by night her vision see ;
Fare as well as fondest lover.
Greater joy will round thee hover,
    If by fate ye parted be.

Powers eternal, time and distance !
Scorning, like the stars, resistance,
  Still, oh still, my throbbing veins.
Grows more delicate my feeling,—
Needs my lighter heart less healing,—
  Joy supreme triumphant reigns.

Ne'er in thought of her forgetful,
Free in soul, no longer fretful,
  Calmly taking every meal.
My scarce mark'd infatuation
Transforms love to adoration,
  Warm desire to frenzy leal.

Drawn up by the sun's full splendour,
Breathed on by the zephyrs tender,
  Ne'er did lightest cloudlet float
Calmer than my heart elated.
Free from fear, with unabated
  Cordial love on her I dote.

19.—TO THE MOON.

Sister of the first born light,
Gentlest form in garb of sorrow !
Clouds their silver lining borrow
  From thy charming face so bright.
Softly though thy course be run,
  Thou dost rouse from caverns dreary
  Souls departed sad and weary,
Me, and birds that dread the sun.

Bared beneath thy fitful gleams
Lies a field all bounds despising !
Grant that to thy side uprising
  I may revel 'midst thy beams.
Then though doomed afar to roam,
  Through my maiden's casement peering,
  Am'rous looks, no hindrance fearing,
I may cast around her home.

  Dimly floats my wanton sight
Gloating o'er her rounded shoulder,
Lower sink my glances bolder,—
  Naught is veiled from soft moonlight.
But how prurient grows my mind !
  Longing for joy's sweet fruition,
  Hung aloft by such ambition,
One could stare till grown quite blind.

20.—DEDICATION.

Behold them then ! You have them there !
Such verses free from art or care
  As bubbling brooks inspire.
In love and joy, with throbbing heart,
I've played a youthful joyous part,
  And thus have tuned my lyre.

He sing them then who sing them may !
Upon a brilliant vernal day
  Some youth may use a number.
The poet from afar approves,
Whilst dietetic quiet moves
  His heavy lids to slumber.

With look, askance half, and half sage,
As nascent tears o'ercloud his page,
  Your joy in bursts he praises.
List then to these his parting strains ;
Like you of joy he drank the drains,
  And learned its fleeting phases.

You sigh and sing, and melt and kiss,
And shout, nor dream your transient bliss
  So near yon gulph for mortals.
Flee meadow, brook, and sunshine bright,
Steal, e'en though 'twere by winter's light
  Soon to the nuptial portals.

You laugh and jeer, and cry, the fool !
The fox, his tail lost, has grown cool,
  And fain would cut his brothers'.
The fable's moral here does fail,
The faithful fox who lost his tail
  Points out the traps to others.

TO VENUS.

Sea-born Venus ! mighty Goddess !
  Beauteous Venus, hear my prayer.
Ne'er thou saw'st me
In my cups 'fore Bacchus' altar
  Prostrate on the earth laid bare.

Ne'er the goblet have I tasted
  That my maiden did not fill.
'Midst carousals
I e'er cared a rich libation
  O'er thy roses first to spill.

Then, but not till then, was pouréd
  On this heart, thy loyal shrine,
From the beaker
Glowing golden drops enflaming,
  And I kissed my maid divine.

Thou alone my heart did'st quicken,
  Goddess grant me some reward.
Deep of Lethe
Must I drink when death o'ertakes me ;
  Rid me from yon draught abhorred.

Spare me Goddess kind—let Minos
  Judge my death amends may make—
Mem'ry only !
Thoughts of joys long since departed,
  Joys renewed to life awake.

GOETHE'S LETTERS

TO

CHR. G. AND J. G. E. BREITKOPF.

I.[*]

GOD GIVE THEE GOOD EVEN
 BROTHER GOTTLOB.

That you are an honest, hearty good fellow, and that
you are distinguishing yourself, so says all the world that
comes from Leipzig; and highly delighted I am that you
are not in any way changed, unless it be to your own
advantage; for you were of old a jolly lad, with shrewd
sense, and thoughts such as those of a man who compre-
hends his subject, and ideas such as do not occur to all.
Pay us a visit soon. The girls here are all on your side.
I have given them all sorts of accounts of you, and there
are some bright chits among them who fancy there is
perhaps something to be made of you. Write me, my
dear brother, and let me know in what circumstances you
are now placed.

I am living tolerably,—pleased and quiet. I have
half-a-dozen angels of girls whom I often see, and with
none of whom I have fallen in love; pleasant creatures
they are, and they make my life uncommonly agreeable.

Extracted from Fragments of a Goethe's Library.

He that had not seen Leipzig might find himself in right good case here; but Saxony—Saxony! Ah!—ah!—that is full flavoured tobacco! Be one never so hearty and strong in that accursed Leipzig, he burns away as quickly as a bad pitch link. Well, well, the poor little fox will doubtless recover by degrees.*

One thing I must say to you, and that is, beware of lewd habits. It happens to us men folk with our powers, as to maidens with honour, when once virginity has gone to the deuce, it is off. It is true it may be in a measure *quack*-silvered; but all that helps but a little.

Adieu, my dear brother. Keep me in your heart, and do not forget me. In spring I go to Strasburg. Who knows whether we shall hear anything of each other there. Write me before then; and if brother Bernhard will not do so, let him give you any message he may have for me, and add it to your letter. Greet Stocken and his lady, and tell him he made right pretty things.

GOETHE.

II.†

The confidence I have in your kindness induces me to address you respecting a small literary matter which interests me.

In the year 1752 an edition of " Reineke Fuchs " was

---

* See above, p. 20 and 68.

† The following letters are addressed to the father, John Gottlob Immanuel, and to the firm.

printed by you. This work is illustrated with copper plates, which are really the cause of my now writing. As they are worn out, and in some places have been touched up again, it is to be supposed that they have served for one or more earlier editions. Now, I very much wish to discover and, if possible, to possess the earliest of these, as I attach a high value to the works of Aldert Van Everdingen,* by whom they were engraved. To whom can I apply with better hope than to yourself, certain that at the least I shall obtain some reliable information from your kindness. You will excuse, for the sake of our old regard and friendship, the liberty I take. Honour me with an early reply, and rest assured that I at all times remain yours respectfully,

GOETHE.

WEIMAR, *20th Feb., 1782.*

III.

In reliance upon the former good understanding which existed between us, I venture to recommend to you the young man who is the bearer of this letter. He wishes to settle in Leipzig, in the hope of meeting there a better fate than has hitherto been his lot. I trust he will not be burdensome to you. Be good enough to allow him

---

* "If you can discover any of Everdingen's etchings send them to me. Since I have known this man I do not care to look at the works of any other."—Letters to Merck; Mad. Von Stein.

occasionally to visit you, and to open his mind to you.
Procure for him, if possible, a few acquaintances and
connexions, in order that he may be enabled to earn a
little by literary occupations. His name is Vulpius, and
he is known to me as a well conducted young man.
Pardon my request, and rest assured of my continued
friendship and respect.

J. W. GOETHE.

WEIMAR, *31st August, 1789.*

IV.

You had the kindness some short time ago to send me
three of Bach's sonatas for artists and amateurs, amongst
them the —— piece, promising at the same time to
forward me the remainder later. I have not, however,
as yet received them. Should you not have discovered
the three missing pieces, or perhaps not be able to find
them, I beg that I may be obliged with information
respecting them, in order that I may look about for them
elsewhere.

I enclose a few impressions of my coat of arms, as
requested by you.

With particular respect,
Your most obedient,

GOETHE.

WEIMAR, *Oct., 1790.*

V.

Not having received the missing sonatas of Bach, nor indeed any further information from you, I take the liberty of returning the three pieces of the collection, now of no further service to me, along with my best wishes for your health.

J. W. GOETHE.

WEIMAR, *4th Feb., 1791.*

GOETHE'S LETTERS

TO

PHIL. ERASMUS REICH.

I.

Frankfort, 20th Feb., 1770.

My dear Sir,

There are mixed emotions which Mendelssohn can so correctly draw, and Wieland so sweetly depict, but of which we others must forbear to speak. Of such it was that I was overcome on the receipt of your esteemed letter, and the very agreeable gift which accompanied it.

Nothing was new to me. For that Wieland stands so high as an author, and you as an editor, so kindly inclined moreover towards me, I have known since you and Wieland have been known to me; but to such an extent! and under such circumstances! that was indeed all new to me. My thankfulness you can readily measure by the value of your friendship, the excellence of the book, and the delight which in this Frankfort dearth of good taste must be felt to such a lively degree, on receiving so quickly a new work. Hence I gladly abstain from a profession of acknowledgments; for certainly you would be heartily tired of listening to oft-repeated thanks, did not your especial kindness impose respectful silence on all you oblige.

Oeser's discoveries gave me a fresh opportunity of blessing myself that I have had him for my instructor.

Dexterity or experience no master can communicate to his disciple, and a few years' practice can in the fine arts produce but moderate results,—moreover our *hand* was only his secondary aim ; he strove to penetrate our very *souls*, and we must have been soulless not to have been benefited by him.

His instruction will influence my whole existence. He taught me that the ideal of beauty is simplicity and repose, whence it follows that no youth can be a master. Fortunate is it when we have not to be convinced of this truth by dire experience. Commend me to my dear Oeser. After him and Shakespere, Wieland is the only man I can acknowledge as my true instructor ; others had shown me that I erred, these exhibited to me the way to do better.

I do not suppose that you desire to learn my opinion respecting the " Diogenes." To appreciate and keep silence is the utmost that I can do at present ; for I hold that even a great man should not be praised except by one as great as he. But I have been much vexed on Wieland's account ; and I think with reason. He is so unfortunate as frequently not to be comprehended,—the fault possibly is occasionally his own, but sometimes it is not, and it is then annoying if people retail their misunderstandings to the public as explanations. Only recently a critic wrote " the speech of the Man in the Moon* is a subtle satire on the philosophy and follies of former ages." How could such an idea occur to anyone ? Yet indeed he has found a companion in the person of the translator

---

* Diogenes 34. Op. XIII., p. 141.

of Agatha. *Tableau des mœurs de l'ancienne Grece!* Some such is his title.* I verily believe the good man took the book for a work on archæology.

I know not whether W. is also annoyed at this; he certainly has cause to be so.

When you write to your friend, this great author, or see him, be kind enough to make him acquainted with an individual who, it is true, is not man enough to be able properly to value his inestimable services, but yet has a sufficiently sensitive heart to honour them, and who with feelings of the greatest respect also calls himself

Your most obedient servant,
GOETHE.

II.

HONOURED SIR,

It affords me much pleasure immediately on the commencement of a new year to have the opportunity of reminding you of your former favours towards me. Lavater, under the following circumstances, has charged me to transmit to you the accompanying manuscript of the commencement of his work on physiognomy. The translation of the introduction is committed to my care;† on

---

* Histoire d'Agathon, ou tableau philosophique des mœurs de la Grèce, imité de l'Allemand de M. Wieland. Laus., 1768.

† Goethe was to have the introduction translated into French by Gotter. (Lavater's letter to Reich, 20th Jan., 1775.)

I

the other hand, you are yourself asked to have the fragments from page seven, and onwards, translated by Herr Huber.   At page 17, where a cross in pencil will be found marked, as also at page 21, some additions may possibly follow.   Should these however not make their appearance, it may be pointed out to the translator that these marks have no further importance.   Kindly advise me of the receipt of these papers, and if at the same time you can give me any hints to forward the completion of this work, I will avail myself of them with all diligence; and as the transmission of the manuscript is to be committed chiefly into my hands, I shall frequently have the honour of assuring you of the great respect with which I name myself,

Honoured sir,
Your obedient servant,
GOETHE.

FRANKFORT, *2nd January, 1775.*

III.

Herewith I send the addenda to be inserted in the places marked, I trust they may reach you in good time; if not, be good enough to advise me thereof immediately.

The sequel will already have reached you, or you will immediately receive it.

FRANKFORT, *23rd Jan., 1775.*

IV.

FRANKFORT, *14th Feb., 1775.*

Your last valued letter I duly received through Herr Jonas, and yesterday the proof-sheets came to hand, which I will immediately forward. I have already written to Lavater respecting the vignettes. The Judas after Holbein is not a vignette, but a large plate, and I have no doubt the Christ is also; although I have not yet seen it, but of this you shall hear more at a future time. Possibly Herr Jonas has written to inform you that we have taken at once the precaution suggested in your last. As the Book Commission requires a formal notice, this will be prepared in Budingen by Herr Bruder, who will therein clearly demonstrate that in the case of the 4th and 5th parts of Gellert's works,* the Imperial ordinance has been broken, and I have advised that there should be demanded of the Commission a requisition to the magistrate, throwing upon him the onus of at least proceeding in the first instance against Schiller. As regards a depôt here for Saxon books,† I have too little insight into the affair to be able to form a sound opinion on the subject; it would be a difficult matter to find a bookseller for the purpose, who would be willing to bind himself. What I can do, I will however do with pleasure. Have the kindness to give me further information and instructions on this point.

---

* Gellert's " Moral " had been pirated by Göbhardt, in Bamberg.

† This refers to Reich's suggestion to found in Frankfort au establishment for the sale of north German publications.

By yesterday's post some additions to the ninth number of Physiognomical Fragments were sent you, along
with an enclosure for Professor Oeser, which I beg you
will be good enough to hand to him.

GOETHE, Dr.

V.

Quite correct, the 21st article is on Apollo. A—C I
have received. At the end of part 16, I have intentionally
omitted one article, as you will perceive from the termination of the part in question having been struck out. I
trust this may not lead to mistakes. Part 17 follows
immediately afterwards.

GOETHE.

14th March, 1775.

VI.

A, B, C, D, are the four first articles on physiognomy,
the remainder will be all printed and bound up separately ;
these, therefore, will of course be so also. That Lavater
should have desired me to send one of the impressions
with the copy, was, I fancy, merely to show the composi-
tor, practically, that question and answer stand opposite
to each other on two pages, and that the table will then
be bound up between them. But I will write immediately
about this, and look after the other vignettes. I was much
struck with the Trenck affair.

G.

31st March, 1775.

VII.

You will have received by this time the vignettes 00. For the two others take in God's name a pair of unimportant ones. N.B.—Cancel the end of each article if it refers to the missing vignette. The portrait of the Margrave will doubtless soon make its appearance; I hear it has been engraved afresh. But I have written to Lavater about it.

G.

A friend writes me the enclosed, can you advise me thereon? Or yourself make use of the book?
5th April, 1775.

VIII.

Circumstances compel me to leave on a journey, I consequently cannot complete the parts, P P, Q Q, R R. Be good enough, therefore, to omit these from the accompanying notice. On the other hand I send you appendix P P, and the last of the articles on Physiognomy.

G.

19th April, 1775.

IX.

The sheets of the Phys., up to E E, are to hand; I await the copies, and shall then be able to discharge this other lot.

Will you write to Göbhardt, at Bamberg? If not I will do so. He has not the slightest right to the book, unless he has received the commission from Herr Pfeffels.

At your convenience, a line in reply.

G.

Frankfort, *11th May, 1775.*

X.

I beg of you, dear Herr Reich, at your earliest convenience, to let me know the latest date up to which I have again to send you more MS. The reason is this. The work is now with me, out of Lavater's hands, and quite ready; but I should like to make a few additions, and have indeed commenced to work upon them. Still, if it *must* be so, the whole can be sent you at an hour's notice.

Farewell.

G.

Frankfort, *28th May, 1775.*

XI.

I must trouble you, my dear Herr Reich, to do me a little favour; kindly have the undernoted vignettes of the Physiogs. struck off separately, the impressions cut close round the mark of the plate, and forwarded to me by post.

1 p. V Portrait of the Margrave.

2 ,, 43 Boy with tresses.

3 p.   56 Three satyrs.
4 ,,   84 Judas' kiss.
5 ,,   91 Saviour's face.
6 ,,   95 Face distorted with laughter.
7 ,,   97 Friend of brandy.
8 ,, 109 Two double heads.
10 ,, 111 *Ayes trois choses.*

Yours,

GOETHE.

FRANKFORT, *29th Aug., 1775.*

XII.

My best thanks for your early attention to my request
for the vignettes. May I ask you to try to obtain the
following works of Hamann and send them, or such of
them as you can hunt up, to my usual address at Frankfort by the stage, and charge me with the outlay.

1. Clouds.   An imitation of Socratic memorabilia.
2. Pastoral on the school drama.
3. *Essai à la Mosaique.*
4. Authors and critics.
5. Authors and readers.
6. Last opinions of the Knight v. Rosenkreuz, respecting the origin of language.
7. Two critiques and addenda.
8. Addenda to Socratic memorabilia.
9. Letter of the Witch of Kadmonbor.
10. *Lettre perdue d'un Sauvage du Nord à un financier
    de Pe-Kim.*

11. *Lettre provinciale neologique d'un Humaniste au
Torrent de Kerith.*
You will thereby for ever oblige,

Your most obedient,

GOETHE.

2nd Nov., 1775.

XIII.

I hope you duly received the Phys. papers sent off to
you on 5th Jan. Herewith some more, and in a few
days you shall have the remainder of the first section.
Be good enough always to send me a table of contents,
and to advise me of anything noteworthy.

Please send me also Hamann's "Hierophantic Letters."

GOETHE.

WEIMAR, *15th Jan., 1776.*

XIV.

In my next I will send you the sheet forming the close
of Part 22. Be good enough to advise me how many sheets
are printed, and how far you have got in the MS. I
have still much in hand, and only fear the second section
of the work may grow to be too voluminous.

GOETHE.

WEIMAR, *10th March, 1776.*

XV.

Herewith I send you Titlepage, Dedication, Conclusion, and Table of Contents, and congratulate you on the completion of the second edition. A pleasant journey to you. Shall we not see you before you start?

G.

WEIMAR, *25th April, 1776.*

XVI.

Herr Lenz left the accompanying with me before starting on his journey, and thought I would be able to enclose the MSS. he therein refers to, but I do not find them amongst my papers. I should be glad therefore if you did not proceed to press with the piece,* until I receive further advice from him.

GOETHE.

29th Nov., 1776.

XVII.

The continuation is no further advanced. I have not been able to take it again in hand here. The Dedication remains as before, to the Landgrave of Hesse Homburg.

—　　　　　　　　　　　　　　　　　—

* The " Soldiers " and the " Englishman," by Lenz, were published by Weidmann in 1776 and 1777 respectively.

In regard to Lenz, I beg you will act as if I did not exist.
I may say that I have had no part in the matter, and intend to take none.

G.

13th Jan., 1777.

XVIII.

Many thanks for the Fair Catalogue, and oblige me
with a copy of the Excise regulations of the Electorate
of Saxony,—also, if possible, of the Prussian. I have for
some considerable time had lying by me a few dozen songs
with melodies, from Kayser of Zurich. I know they are
not pleasant stuff, and therefore have said nothing about
them before. He reminds me of them again, however, and
I would therefore ask if you can use them, or find a
publisher to dispose of them. They have always been
played and sung with approbation,* where I have shown
them. If Klinger is in Leipzig,† and you would be kind
enough to say a word to him about them, he might possibly look about for somebody who would take them in
hand.

GOETHE.

WEIMAR, *28th April, 1777.*

-----

* These are "Songs with accompaniments for the piano." Leipzig and Winterthur, 1777.

† Klinger was from 1776 to 1778 theatrical poet to Seyler's company, which played in Gotha, Dresden, and Leipzig. In Kayser's
collection of songs is one by Klinger.

XIX.

I send the first sheets of the " Physiognomy," the remainder shall follow as they come to hand. Will you be good enough to forward me a few " Regulations for Pawnbrokers," if you can obtain any ; and at the same time make out an account of what I am at present indebted to you.

WIEMAR, *25th Nov., 1777.*

XX.

Should young Herr Tobler, of Zurich, a son of the well-known choir leader,* have called upon you before this letter reaches you, I doubt not but that even without my introduction you will have given him a favourable reception, since his own merits sufficiently commend him. You will find this none the less so should he present himself to you after this letter comes to hand. I beg your accustomed attention in his favour for my sake also, and, should he be in quest of a publisher for some of his successful translations from the Greek, I trust you will give him your aid, either by word and deed, or, as circumstances may require, by good advice alone.

Professor Garve is at this time with us, and desires to be warmly remembered to his Leipzig friends.†

I commend myself to your friendly remembrance.

GOETHE.

WEIMAR, *30th May, 1778.*

---

* Letters to Madame v. Stein, II., p. 69.
† Letters to Merck, II., p. 186.

XXI.

My best thanks for the beautiful books sent to me,* they will journey with me to Eisenach, where a rural assembly is to take place, and whither the Court is to proceed. Possibly a quiet hour may present itself in which to enjoy " Solitude."

With warm remembrances,

GOETHE.

WEIMAR, *24th May, 1784.*

XXII.

SIR,

Receive my liveliest thanks for the sequel of the brilliant edition of a brilliant work.† If anything be wanting it is the portrait of Dr. Oberreit,‡ which should have adorned the front of the third volume. I hear that we may soon look for the pleasure of seeing you here.

GOETHE.

WEIMAR, *23rd May, 1785.*

XXIII.

SIR,

I beg you will do me the kindness to have the best edition of my works in four volumes got up in nice

---

* Zimmermann on Solitude.   Leipzig, 1784 and 1785.
† By Zimmermann.
‡ Oberreit at that time in Jena, the opponent of Zimmermann.

English binding with green edges, and sent to me carefully packed.

I much regretted that I had not the opportunity of
seeing you during your recent stay here, and of assuring
you by word of mouth of the great regard with which I
subscribe myself,

Sir,

Your most obedient servant,

GOETHE.

WEIMAR, *22d Aug., 1785.*

EXTRACTS FROM LETTERS

OF

CORNELIA GOETHE.

During the preparations for the celebration of the Goethe Festival, there came to light, in Leipzig, a number of letters written by Cornelia Goethe to one of her young friends, which had lain neglected amongst the effects left behind by the latter. The publication of extracts from these letters was imperative after Goethe's remark respecting his sister: " Only by the most exact details, by endless particularities, breathing out her whole character and giving evidence, by their nature, of the depths from which they spring ; it is only by such means that it is possible, in a degree, to give some perception of her remarkable individuality ; for the fountain can only be judged of by the channel through which it flows." To quote these letters in the present work, is the more necessary, inasmuch as they refer to that period during which the majority of Goethe's letters, as here given, originated. Trivial though the views we here gain may be they yet contribute to render clearer and more decided the presence of his so dearly loved sister, and of the relations they held towards each other.

The friend to whom these letters are addressed was named Katharine Fabricius, daughter of the Syndic Fabricius at Worms, who was councillor of the principality of Leiningen ; she married later a merchant of

leaves are written on some days, and the contents are tame and unimportant; that little of note occurred, of which she complains, was scarcely the sole reason, the relation between them seems gradually to have grown less intimate.

In the earlier and more important part of the diary, the narrative is copious and lively. The little occurrences connected with Cornelia and her friends are given with full details, and an especial preference is evinced to introduce parties as talking, and to communicate whole conversations. In between, are presented animated expressions of sentiment and passion, meditations upon herself, and moral reflections. There can be no question that the whole would appear to much greater advantage, and exhibit more freedom and ingenuousness had it been written in German; however, under any circumstances, there can be detected a lurking literary design in the form assumed by these delineations. That peculiarity of Goethe, to give to his own experiences and feelings an artistic utterance, had certainly some influence upon her; and as he communicated to her all he wrote, whether in satisfaction of his inner longings, or in pursuit of his studies, it is only reasonable to assume that this may have aroused in her the intention to seek, by similar means, comfort and relief. That in her case the same result was not attained, need not cause surprise. At the same time she had another ideal, which inspired her to make this attempt—Grandison.

"Il y a longtemps que j'ai voulu commencer cette correspondence secrète, par laquelle je vous apprendrai tout ce qui se passe ici; mais pour dire la vérité j'ai toujours eu honte de vous importuner avec des bagatelles qui ne valent pas la peine qu'on les lise. Enfin j'ai vaincu ce scrupule en lisant l'histoire de Sir Charles Grandison ; je donnerois tout au monde pour pouvoir parvenir dans plusieurs années à imiter tant soit peu l'excellente Miss Byron. L'imiter ? folle que je suis ; le puis je ? Je m'estimerois assez heureuse d'avoir la vingtième partie de l'esprit et de la beauté de cette admirable dame, car alors je serois une aimable fille ; c'est ce souhait que me tient au cœur jour et nuit. Je serois à blamer si je désirois d'être une grande beauté : seulement un peu de finesse dans les traits, un teint uni, et puis cette grace douce, qui enchante au premier coup de vue ; voilà tout. Cependant ça n'est pas et ne sera jamais, quoique je puisse faire et souhaiter ; ainsi il vaudra mieux de cultiver l'esprit et tacher d'être supportable du moins de ce côté là.—Quel excellent homme que ce Sir Charles Grandison ; dommage qu'il n'y en a plus dans ce monde." Goethe therefore had not far to go in search of the fair worshippers of Grandison (pp. 98, 111). It would at the same time be a mistake to suppose that the journal is a sort of romance, or is even adorned with romantic expressions ; it bears the impress of truth to the core.

The sensation it produces is on the whole painful and touching. In general a modest earnestness, at times bordering on the sublime, is evinced, combined with a gloomy, restless mood, devoid of inward satisfaction. The characteristic attributed by Goethe to his sister is fully confirmed, alloyed however with many traits of a girlish disposition when addressing her confidential friend, which might scarcely have been expected of her,—instanced for example occasionally in those parts of the diary where she evinces an interest for dress and ornament, pleasures, and scandal, as well as a certain disposition for satire.

The life she leads, as she herself frequently complains, is monotonous in the extreme, and affords her but few and simple means of distraction. Amongst these may principally be mentioned her walks, which she can only take in select company, if she will not expose herself to merciless tattle ; and she must be the more careful on this point, as she is strictly watched by certain parties, to whose good opinion she is certainly indifferent, but to whose animadversion she nevertheless does not wish to lay herself open. Amongst her pleasures may also be included the drinking of the waters. "Je ne vous ai pas encore appris (she writes on 28th July, 1768) que je bois les eaux à l'allée,—nous avons là une compagnie tout à fait charmante des dames et des chapeaux, dont le plus aimable est Mr. le Docteur Kölbele, que vous connoissez, par son oration du mariage qu'il tient une fois en votre présence,—où il nous compara nous autres femmes, à des poulets. Maintenant il nous donne des leçons sur la philosophie morale. Cependant rien n'est plus plaisant que quand il veut exercer la galanterie qui dort depuis longtems auprès de lui. Nos dames qui sont les plus gaies du monde la lui apprennent de nouveau. Elles se font mener par lui, porter le parasol, verser leur verres, ah, ma chère, il execute tout ça avec des gestes si modernes, qu'on le disoit être arrivé immédiatement de Paris. Nous avons aussi de la musique composée de dix instruments, savoir de cors de chasse, hautbois, flûtes, un contreviolon et une harpe. Vous pouvez vous imaginer quel bel effet ça fait dans la verdure. Nous chantons aussi souvent pour plaire à notre charmant Docteur, car quoiqu'il soit très sérieux, il aime nonobstant de voir la jeunesse enjouée. Ce chanson s'accorderoit bien sur lui : Es war einmal ein Hagenstolz, il s'est même bien plû à l'entendre." This is clearly that same Kölbele of whose large feet Goethe avails himself in his portrait of Gottsched (p. 46)*. Now and then visits are paid to the gardens of Herr Glötzel, and of her uncle on the opposite side of the Main ; she also on one occasion ascends the church tower with a party of friends, and gives with much complacency an account of the prospect, of the telescope, and of the large bells. Her father was no friend of picnics ; she therefore does not take part in an excursion made by her young female friends to the Forsthaus, a place of rural enjoyment still standing in Frankfort Wood, on the left bank of the Main below the town, which Goethe probably had in his eye in his hunting lodge in Faust.

An agreeable source of distraction indoors was the piano, with which, as Goethe tells us, she was further advanced than he. "Je jouerai un air sur le clavecin (she once writes when much excited) "que ces vapeurs passent." She speaks with much sympathy of the unfortunate death of the pianist Schobert, who expired in the orchestra of Prince Conti, at Paris, poisoned by mushrooms. (1st Oct., 1767). "Il a composé XV. ouvrages gravées en taille douce, qui sont excellentes et que je ne saurois me lasser de jouer. Toute autre musique ne me plait presque plus. En jouant des sentiments douloureux percent mon âme, je le plains ce

---

* Johann Balthasar Kölbele, Doctor of Laws and advocate, was also an author and converter of the Jews. He died in 1778.

grand auteur, qui à la fleur de son age avec un tel génie a fallu périr d'une façon si misérable et inopinée." Her reading is but little touched upon ; besides Grandison mention is made of the "lettres du Marquis de Roselle," by Elie de Beaumont (Paris, 1764.) " Je vous ai envoyée (she writes, on 14th March, 1768) les lettres du Marquis de Roselle, lisez les avec attention, ou y peut profiter beaucoup, le vice y est montré sous l'apparence de vertu dans toute sa forme. Le Marquis qui n'a pas l'expérience du monde, donne dans les filets de cette fausse vertu, et s'y enveloppe de façon, qu'il coute beaucoup à l'en tirer. Que tous les jeunes gens y prennent un exemple, qui comme lui ont le cœur droit et sincère et ne se doutent nullement de la tromperie que cette sorte de femmes exercent avec eux. C'est là une grande cause que notre jeunesse est si corrompue puisqu'un vice engendre l'autre. Relisez plusieurs fois la lettre où Mdme. de Ferval parle de l'éducation de ses enfants. Si seulement toutes les mères en usoient de même, certe qu'on ne verroit pas tant de filles insupportables comme vous en connoissez et moi aussi."

The social intercourse consists chiefly of afternoon visits, previously announced to each other, which ended punctually at eight o'clock (ten o'clock was bed time) ; besides this, in winter, formal parties held, it would appear, every Tuesday alternately, at the house of one or other family, and every Friday a concert in the saloon of Herr Busch, where the *élite* of the city met. It is true that she complains sometimes of *ennui* experienced at these assemblies, but she does not appear by any means indifferent to these pleasures. She writes—"Je vis à présent d'une façon très tranquille, mais cette tranquillité n'a point des charmes pour moi ; j'aime la variété, l'inquiétude, le bruit du grande monde, et les divertissements tumultueux." The winter has, in consequence, slipped by, she scarcely knows how, when Simonette Bethman is betrothed to Herr Metzler ; she hopes a ball may be given on the occasion, although she was usually prevented visiting balls, on the score of her health. We become better acquainted with not a few out of the circle of " sensible and amiable girls " she had assembled around her, and over whom she lorded it without being imperious. The diary shows us that, although she enjoyed the respect and esteem of all her young friends without a single exception, she did not stand in intimate or close relations with any. She complains to Katharine Fabricius that she has no real female friend in Frankfort, and the language which she uses respecting her acquaintances confirms this. Her pretty and lively cousins Antoinette, Charlotte, and Katharine make themselves very agreeable, Leonora de Saussure amuses her by her witty remarks at a tedious party ("la méchante Leonore fit quelques remarques, aux quelles je ne sûs resister ; ces dames s'imaginèrent je crois, que nous tenions un peu de la lune : n'importe ce sont des fades créatures "), Caroline and Lisette von Stockum are admired as great beauties ; but not a sign of greater intimacy is visible. She relates of a certain Miss B. that she is inconsolable for the departure of her lover T., who from unfortunate circumstances was compelled to turn playactor in Brunswick ; but thinks her grief will not last longer than that of a young widow, who the first day is anxious to die with her husband, consoles herself on the second, and on the third day looks about for another match; she reports shortly after that she has already found another lover; a little later, however, she finds her again inconsolable, because she has lost a ring which T. had presented to her; Mdlle. S. makes herself quite unbearable by her love of dress and her coquetry. Inexplicable in view of her general character is her true and constant affection for a certain undeserving W., whom she cannot forsake, although she knows and deeply deplores her faults, so that in this respect we cannot but entertain regard for her; for true constancy to any one whom she has once learned to know and esteem she recognizes in others, and admits that this she holds for one of her good characteristics.

Her most unfavourable description is given of a cousin of Katharine Fabricius,—she is silly and tiresome, conducts herself in a constrained and ridiculous manner, prides herself on reading many books of which she understands nothing. " Ha, ha, riez,—elle eut dernièrement sa grande compagnie, j'y fus; qu'elle scène misérable, —ah, ma chère, Vous connoissez celles qui la composent,— nous parlâmes d'économie, de la lecture, des arts, des langues. Qu'en dites Vous? Pour moi, j'eus si mal d'une conversation, dont je ne pouvois détourner la fadeur, qu'il me falloit bien de temps à me remettre. Je pouvois là à loiser examiner la caractère de chacune et j'entrevis clairement, que c'est l'éducation, qui les rend si sottes. Elles font les dévotes forcées, ne regardent point d'homme, parce qu'on leur défend absolument de converser avec tout autre, que celui qui sera leur mari; d'éviter toute connoissance particulière avec qui ce soit; et que si elles parlent très peu, se tiennent bien droites et font les précieuses qu'alors elles sont accomplies. N'est ce pas là une éducation bien pitoyable et peu digne d'être imitée? puisque au lieu des filles spirituelles on ne trouve que des statues, qui ne prononcent autre chose que oui et non." She has a lover named Steinheil, who later takes his departure; she soon consoles herself for this. Her name would appear to have been Baumann, in which case she is the young lady who, with her head dress " en forme de pyramide ou pour mieux dire à la rhinoceros," was paying a visit to Cornelia when her brother entered the room. " Elle prit une de ses mines, que Vous connoissez, la tête levée et les yeux baissées et ne parla pas le mot." We here recognize that kind of conduct which so grievously offended Goethe after his residence in Leipzig, and Cornelia plainly states that which Goethe did not trust himself to utter (p. 110). If all the other young girls varied greatly from this type, yet Cornelia's account makes it very conceivable that he did not run much risk of losing his heart in his intercourse with them.

The only girl she mentions with lively interest, and about whom she is perpetually concerned, is Lisette Runkel, who appears as a pretty, charming vision. At first she speaks of her as a dear friend, and sensible girl, with ardent tenderness. However, after a time she exhibits great vanity, and a love of dress and coquetry, which is as little suited to her slender means as the arrogance she commences to assume. We learn at length that B., the wealthy possessor of the inn, "The King of England," a widower of some six and forty years of age, is paying court to her, and that she now, in hope of marrying him, acts the great lady. She has made a journey with

him in his phaeton to Darmstadt, where, at the court
festivals, she has played a brilliant part, thanks to her
beauty and her splendid attire. "Elle étoit vêtue en
Vénitienne, une juppe de satin bleu doublée en argent, un
corset de la même couleur et un survêtement de satin
cramoisi, le tout garni de pelisse brune et de dentelles
d'argent. Ses cheveux pendoient flottants, ils étoient
noués en façon romaine et entrelacés de perles et de
diamans. Sur le milieu de la tête il étoit attaché de la
crêpe blanche, qui pendoit jusqu'à la taille, et de là par
terre étant serrée au milieu avec une riche écharpe
d'argent." She excited universal attention, the princes and
princesses crowded round her,—Prince George danced with
none other, and would suffer no one else to approach her.
The death of the Landgrave, however, put an end to these
festivities. Notwithstanding the estrangement which arose
between Lisette and Cornelia in consequence of this conduct, they still met, and the former occasionally exhibited
real attachment for Cornelia. On the occasion of a visit
she paid to her, bedizened like a princess, she informs her
that the match with the widower, who had made her the
offer of his hand, was broken off, and later discloses to her
that a wealthy young merchant of Amsterdam, named
Dorval, had seen her on a visit to Frankfort, had become
enamoured of her, and that they were engaged. The two
friends are now reconciled. Cornelia, who relates everything in fullest detail, is highly delighted at Lisette's
good fortune; who, to crown all, now has a legacy left
her; she takes the liveliest interest in her engagement;
extols the ardour and constant tenderness of Dorval, who
must be one of the most excellent of men, and reads his

letters to Lisette with such attention, that she is able to
write down a great part of them from memory; she finds
them, it is true, somewhat overdrawn and romantic in style,
but still so excellent, that they might well be printed.
This good understanding lasts, however, but a very few
months; Lisette's conceit and coquetry grow too obtru-
sive; during Dorval's absence, she is surrounded by
swarms of admirers, whom she permits to pay court to
her, and conducts herself altogether in a manner which is
not by any means amiable. The widower gives a brilliant
ball, of which Lisette is to be the belle; Cornelia, as well
as her cousin Katherine, is prevented taking part in it by
indisposition; the least they can do, however, is to deck
out the sister of the latter in such a way that she shall
eclipse Lisette's diamonds. She feels that she is no longer
to be considered a true friend. " Vous et Mdlle. Meixner
Vous êtez mes seules amies en'qui je puis me confier. Je
croyois en avoir une éternelle en Lisette, mais son terme
a peu duré l'applaudissement général du grand monde l'a
gaté. Fière de ses conquêtes elle méprise tout le monde
et quoique Dorval est uniquement aimé, l'encens de tant
de cœurs lui plait au delà de l'expression, elle s'en
vante partout et triomphe secrètement de Vous abaisser
par ses charmes. Jugez, ma chère, si avec ces sentiments
elle peut être amie fidèle. Il y avoit un tems où peu
connue du monde elle ce crut heureuse par mon amitié,
mais ce tems n'est plus, et je vois par là, que c'est le train
du monde." A formal rupture at length ensues. " Que
direz Vous, ma chère, si je Vous apprends que Miss
Lisette et moi nous sommes totalement brouillées et d'une
façon qui ne sera pas à remettre. Si j'avois le tems je

Vous ferois part de toute l'histoire, mais elle est trop longue : il suffit à Vous de savoir, que la mère et la fille m'ont accusée de médisance et de trahison, et que j'ai trouvée ces termes trop viles pour m'abaisser à une justification. Cette affaire m'a causée une révolution de quelques jours, mais elle est passée et j'ai reprise ma tranquillité, qui a l'air de durer longtems, si un accident nouveau ne la chasse."

There was, however, another cause for this rupture. In the house of the Runkels, Cornelia had made the acquaintance of a Mr. G., an honourable, good-natured, but as it would appear, a somewhat awkward man, who during the whole of this period appears as her faithful, indefatigable lover, but who is treated by her with the utmost coldness. He is alluded to under the cognomen of " le misérable " or " le miséricordieux, qui fait tout par miséricorde, Vous m'entendez bien." In her first letter she relates how she has turned her back on him with supreme contempt, and later she rejoices that Lisette —" elle devient tous les jours plus sage et naturellement plus grande," hates and despises him as much as she herself. We then learn the cause of her indignation. " J'eus jusqu'ici une très mauvaise opinion de lui, croyant toujours qu'il étoit coupable et qu'il avoit raisonné de moi d'une manière peu décente, comme je Vous l'ai appris." Her conduct towards him for a year past having been so marked, he had complained of it and learned what had been laid to his charge. Indignantly he declared this to be a calumny ; " cette méchante vipère de Rst inventa tout ceci par haine ou par jalousie," and implored an interview with Cornelia, in order that he

might justify himself. " Je le vis, il se justifia, con-
vaincue de son innocence je le remis dans mes bonnes
graces ... et voilà la paix faite — hahaha! C'est bien
court me direz Vous, je m'attendois à une description
particulière. Pardonnez moi ... je ne saurois; de peur
d'étouffer de rire. Ma chère si Vous aviez été dans un
coin, Vous n'auriez pas subsisté ... Représentez Vous
notre situation, la sotte figure que nous fîmes en nous
abordant. Suffit." This ridicule accords but indifferently
with the moral reflection with which she introduces her
story—" mon principal but est de faire réparation
d'honneur à une personne, que j'aie noircie dans Votre
esprit étant alors préoccupée des rapports malins qu'on
m'en avoit faites. Il est vrai, mon enfant, nous avons
touts le défaut de croire plutôt le mal de de notre prochain
que le bien; c'en est un grand je le confesse,"—but yet
this mood remains predominant, and the worthy G.,
notwithstanding all his pains, derives but small benefit
from the " bonnes graces." To justify himself completely
he seeks to arrange a meeting between himself, Cornelia,
and Rst, "pour lui dire, qu'elle est la plus infame
créature et de la forcer d'avouer la verité en ma présence;"
a meeting, however, which the latter naturally seeks
equally to avoid. He is untiring in his efforts to meet
Cornelia, at parties or at concerts, that he may have the
opportunity of unburdening his mind, but in vain ; if she
cannot avoid him she answers him very curtly and keeps
him at arms' length—"j'étouffe de rire" is almost invariably the expression with which she winds up. At
length, however, a favourable opportunity presents itself

to him to escort her home with her cousin Katharine.
" Enfin notre carosse arriva, nous descendîmes, il se
faisoit gloire de me mener par toute la foule, mais moi
j'en étois choquée.   L'aimable Cathérine vit ma peine,
fachée de ne pouvoir y remédier, elle me serra la main
en me conjurant de prendre patience.   Nous la menâmes
chez elle et enfin me voila seule avec cet homme.   Chère
Miss, me dit il en mettant sa main sur la mienne, ce
procédé Vous paraitra peutêtre libre;   mais j'ai taché
depuis longtems à Vous parler sans temoins, l'occasion
est si favorable et Vous me pardonnerez cette liberté.
Ce commencement me paru trop ridicule pour ne pas
éclater ; il ne s'en apperçoit pas et continua."   He begs
of her to be candid, tells her that he had incautiously
divulged to Lisette Runkel and her mother the impression that Cornelia had made upon him, that they had
sought, and were still seeking to prejudice him with
Cornelia through Rst.   " Je fus prédestiné à être malheureux et je le serai tonjours, si Vous ne me rendez pas
Votre affection.   Dites moi, Miss, me hairez Vous sans
cesse? prononcez une seule parole et je sui le plus
heureux des mortels.   Si ça Vous rend tranquille, Monsieur, je la prononcerai.   Je Vous assure de mon estime
et de mon amitié.   Soyez heureux, c'est ce que je
souhaite de tout mon cœur.   Je n'y tiens plus, ma chère,
j'étouffe de rire."   Her attention now hereby aroused,
she discovers that Lisette and her mother endeavour to
prevent an interview between her and the said G., and
that to frustrate this they invent appointments in her
name, under the pretence that they are thereby doing her

a favour; upon this falseness and deception she pronounces herself very decidedly, and now herself prompts an invitation to a visit at which he shall also be present. " En entrant chez Lisette j'y trouvai sa mère et une dame de leur connoissance ; après le café nous jouâmes quadrille. A six heures Monsieur se fait annoncer et entre dans le même instant. Il nous salue généralement, puis se postant vis à vis de moi il me regarde pendant un quart d'heur entier. Il n'ose approcher de moi, mais Madame l'en prie d'un ton monqueur et il s'assied entre nous deux filles. Je lui parle avec beaucoup de complaisance, Lisette me comtemple d'un air jaloux et Madame qui se trouve piquée s'en veut venger en me raillant de ma distraction et de mon inattention pour le jeu ; je fis semblant de ne pas comprendre ce qu'elle vouloit dire." To the great annoyance of both, G. accompanies Cornelia home, and on the way fresh explanations arise. " Que m'apprit-il là, ma chère ? des inventions infernales pour nous désunir, des mensonges ouvertes ; enfin que Vous dirai-je ? je vis, mais trop tard, que je lui avois foit tort pendant le cours de quatre années, que ma credulité en étoit la cause, et qu'il n'a commis aucune faute que celle de me trop estimer. No suis-je pas la plus blamable des filles ? Grondez moi, ma chère, car je le mérite." As they reach her home he has still much, indeed the most important matter to say to her. " La porte s'ouvrant alors j'entre le cœur dechiré par mille pensées diverses Ne me plaignez pas, je le mérite." This compassionate tone lasts however but a short time. Before his departure she once more sees G., whom she no longer designates by his nickname after their explanations. " Ma chère, si Vous aviez entendue ce discours Vous auriez fait des éclats de rire ; pour moit j'étois si serieuse, que l'occasion le demandoit."

This repugnance to this poor G., it may be observed, is a purely personal one ; ordinarily Cornelia does not show herself so unimpressible ; " she stood as much in want of love as ever a human being."*　Goethe tells us of a love passage between her and a young Englishman who was being educated at Pfeil's establishment,† and who was very intimate with Goethe and his sister, practised English with them, and conceived a passion for her, which she returned.　According to Goethe's report, this relation existed before he left for Leipzig, and must have continued during the whole period of his absence, for he tells us that it was brought to a close in October, 1768, unless we assume that a second Englishman won her affections, which is hardly probable.　At the same time Goethe is possibly not exact in his chronology, seeing that he with some show of reason, in his narrative of Frankfort events, reports certain circumstances as occurring during this period, which happened later on.　The probability is that he made the acquaintance of the young Englishman before leaving for Leipzig, whilst the affection of this person for Cornelia (who at that time was fifteen years old) originated at a later date, and Goethe on his return found the connection between them more developed.

In the opening of her journal she particularly confesses herself so much interested in Grandison, because he is an Englishman. " Si je puis croire, qu'il y a encore quelqu'un

---

* Goethe's Works, XXI., p. 151.　　　† Ib., p. 18.

qui le ressemble, il faut qu'il soit de cette nation. Je suis
extrèmement portée pour ces gens là, ils sont si aimables
et si sérieux en même tems, qu'il faut être charmée
d'eux." On the afternoon of the same day, follows a
half admission. " Je viens dans ce moment de la table,
et je me suis derobée pour Vous entretenir un peu ;
Vous ne devez rien attendre de prémédité dans ces lettres,
c'est le cœur qui parle et non pas l'esprit. Je voudrois bien
Vous dire quelque chose, ma chère Cathérine, et cependant
j'appréhends . . . mais non, Vous me pardonnerez ; ne
sommes nous pas tous ensemble susceptible de foiblesses ?
Il y a ici un jeune Anglois, que j'admire beaucoup ; ne
craignez rien, mon enfant, ce n'est pas de l'amour, c'est
une pure estime que je lui porte à cause de ses belles
qualités,—ce n'est pas ce Milord dont Mdlle. Meixner Vous
aura parlé sans doute, c'est un import . . . st st ! il est
aussi Anglois, et n'aime-je pas toute la nation à cause de
mon seul aimable Harry ? Si Vous le vissiez seulement,
une physionomie si ouverte et si douce, quoiqu'avec un air
spirituel et vif. Ses manières sont si obligeantes et si
polies, il a un tour d'esprit admirable ; enfin c'est le plus
charmant jeune homme que j'ai jamais vu.* Et, et . . .
ah, ma chère, il part dans quinze jours, j'en suis fort
affligée quoique ce ne soit pas une douleur pareille à celle

---

* Goethe relates of him :—" He was tall and well formed, like
herself, only yet slimmer ; his face, small and contracted, would have
been really beautiful, had it not been so much disfigured by the
marks of small-pox ; his manner was easy, firm, at times indeed
almost reserved and stiff; but his heart overflowed with kindness
and tenderness, his soul was full of generosity, and his affections as
lasting as they were decided and unobtrusive."

quand on aime. J'aurois souhaité de demeurer dans la même ville que lui pour pouvoir lui parler et le voir toujours, je n'aurois jamais eu une autre pensée, le ciel le sait, et il est . . . . mais j'en serai privée, je ne le reverrai plus. Non, non, je ne puis le quitter tout à fait, j'ai une pensée en tête, qui s'exécutera, il faut que ça soit, oui en verité."

This plan is the following. She has made the acquaintance of a young artist from Paris, who is gifted with the talent of taking the portraits of persons in his company, quickly and secretly ; she has arranged matters with him, and thinks of having a musical party at her father's house on Sunday. " Harry sera invité parce qu'il joue admirablement du violon ; et le peintre viendra pour faire une visite à mon frère et agira comme s'il ne savoit pas qu'il y a de la compagnie. On fera alors très bien ses affaires et justement quand le plus aimable des hommes joue sur son instrument—je m'y perds ma chère." She is happy in anticipation of success. " Plus ce jour desiré s'avance," she writes on the Friday . . . "plus mon cœur palpite. Et je le verrai donc ! je lui parlerai ! mais à quoi ça me sertil ? Hé ! bien folle, ne l'auras tu pas puis pour toujours— du moins son image, et que pretends tu de plus ? Ah, ma chère, je suis pleine de joie ; Vous en aurez une copie, surement Vous ne me donnerez pas tort de l'aimer— Qu'ai je dit ? effacerai-je ce mot ? non je le laisserai pour Vous faire voir toute ma foiblesse. Condamnez moi.— Aujourdhui je n'écoute que le plaisir, je danse par toute la maison, quoique quelquefois il me vienne une pensée qui me dit de me modérer et qu'il peuvent arriver plusieurs obstacles. Mais je ne l'écoute pas, en m'écriant dabord :

Il le faut." On the following day she sends out the servant to invite the ladies, and impatiently awaits his return. "Un rêve qui j'ai eu cette nuit m'inquiète. J'entendis dire une voix : Tu ne le verras plus !— — Ah, ma chère, que ferais-je ? le domestique est de retour et les dames ne viennent pas—malheureuse—tout est fini. Mon orgueil est bien puni maintenant.—Il faut que ça soit—j'avois bien sujet de dire anisi.—Ayez pitié de moi.—Je suis dans un état à faire compassion—il m'est impossible de poursuivre—pardonnez moi toutes ces folies." Some days later she writes more composedly :—" La fin de ma dernière lettre étoit très confuse, pardonnez le moi, je ne savois ce que je disois et une sorte de saisissement s'empara alors de mon âme. Je m'étonne quelquefois de moi même, j'ai des passions si fortes, que dabord je suis portée à l'excès ; mais ça ne dure pas longtems et c'est là un grand bonheur pour moi, car il n'y auroit pas le moyen d'y subsister. Pour maintenant je suis assez tranquille, espérant que dans cinq jours il y aura encore un dimanche —taisons nous de peur que si nous manquons encore une fois, on aura sujet de se moquer de nos dessins. Vous le feriez, surment, n'est ce pas, ma chère? et je le méri-terois. S'il part dans cette semaine . . . ne donnons point de lieu à une idée si choquante, la seule pensée me fait frémir." This fear proved, however, to be well founded, for he actually took his departure within a day or two. " Vous attendrez," she writes, " surement des ex-clamations douloureuses, si je Vous dis, que mon amiable Anglois est parti, qu'il est parti sans pouvoir me dire le dernier adieu, que je n'ai pas son portrait, qu'enfin toutes mes mésures ont manqués.—Mais, ma chère, je me com-

porterai comme il me convient ; quoique ça Vous étonnera
après ce que je Vous ai déjà écrit.—Mon cœur est insensible
à tout.—Pas une larme, pas un seul soupir.—Et quelle
raison en aurois-je aussi ? aucune je pense.—Cependant,
ma chère amie, y avoit-il jamais un souhait plus innocent
que celui de voir toujours son image? j'avois toujours un
extrème plaisir à le regarder, et j'en suis privée maintenant—mais ça ne fait rien—vous voyez toute mon
indifférence—l'état de mon âme approche à l'insensi-
bilité."

This appears to be the only instance in which there is
any talk of an actual passion on the part of Cornelia, but
in her intercourse with men generally, she exhibits a
peculiar susceptibility, a wavering between prudish diffi-
dence, and the desire and secret hope to make a favourable
impression on them,—a state of mind which she herself
does not comprehend, and which causes her passionate
emotion and embarrassment.   A marked instance of this
is presented in the following little occurrence :—

Mercredi, ce 26 Octobre 1à 2 heures après diné.
" Dans ce moment mon frère est allé voir deux jeunes
Seigneurs de qualité, qui viennent de Leipzig, où il a eu
connoissance avec eux.   Je le priai de me les décrire, ce
qu'il a fait avec plaisir.   Monsieur de Oldrogg* l'ainé,
me dit-il, a environ vingt six ans, il est grand, de belle

---

* Johann Georg v. Olderogge studied in Leipzig from 1764, his
younger brother Heinrich Wilhelm joined a year later; they were
natives of Livonia.   Goethe mentions (XXI., p. 65) that several
Livonians belonged to his section of the University.

taille, mais son visage a des traits peu flatteurs, il a beaucoup d'esprit, parle peu, mais tout ce qu'il dit, montre la grandeur de son âme et son jugement élevé; il est très agréable en compagnie, pousse la civilisation jusqu'au plus haut bout, supportant avec condescendance les personnes d'un mérite inférieur, enfin il possède toutes les qualités requises pour rendre un cavalier aimable. Son frère aura vingt ans, il a la taille moins haute que l'ainé mais ses traits sont d'une beauté charmante, comme vous aimez à les voir vous autres filles, il est beaucoup plus vif que l'autre, parle souvent, quoique quelquefois mal à propos, il a le caractère aimable, mélé avec beaucoup de feu ce qui lui va très bien; encore un peu d'étourderie, mais ça ne fait rien. Il suffit á toi de savoir que c'étoient là les cavaliers les plus distingués de toute notre académie.—Je suis charmée de cette description, ne l'étez Vous pas aussi, ma chère? car je Vous assure que quand mon frère loue quelqu'un il faut qu'il ait beaucoup de mérite.

"a six heures du soir.

"Il est de retour; pensez, mon enfant, demain ils viendront chez nous; je suis curieux de les voir, mais j'ai honte de me présenter à eux. Voilà une de mes grandes foiblesses, il faut que je l'avoue; Vous connoissez mes pensées là dessus, et Vous me pardonnerez si je rougis en pensant de montrer à des personnes d'un tel mérite une figure si humiliante et si peu digne d'être vue. C'est un désir innocent de plair, je ne souhaite rien—Ah, ma chère, si Vous voyez les pleurs—non, non je n'en verse pas, ce n'est que—ce n'est rien."

" Jeudi, à 10 heures du matin.

" Si je pourrois Vous déployer l'état présent de mon âme, je serois heureuse, du moins je comprendrois alors ce qui se passe en moi. Mille pensées mortifiantes, mille souhaits à demi formés et rejetés dans le même moment. Je voudrois—mais non je ne voudrois rien. —Je Vous envie presque, ma chère, le repos que Vous goutez étant contente de Vous même, ce que Vous avez sujet; au lieu que moi—je ne saurois poursuivre."

" à 2 heures après midi.

" Que ferai-je? Je me suis habillée pour sortir et je n'en ai pas le courage. Je m'en irai; il m'est impossible de les voir; voyez la folle, comme le cœur lui bat. Vingt fois les escaliers furent descendues et autant de fois mes pas me ramenèrent dans ma chambre. Mon frère m'a demandé si je sortois aujourdhui et je lui re-ponduc qu'oui, ainsi je ne saurois reculer — Adieu, je m'en vais pour la dernière fois, prenons courage; vite, point de grimaces. Ne suis-je pas bien ridicule?"

" à cinq heures.

" Me voilà revenue, je me suis trouvée mal, je crains à tout moment une foiblesse.—Je vais me deshabiller.—Ils sont là, ma chère, et pensez, il est arrivé justement un de mes cousins qui étoit depuis quelque tems à la cour, il est aussi auprès de ces Seigneurs, s'il lui venoit en tête de me voir.—J'ai été surprise, mon frère est entré et j'ai caché vitement ma lettre; ah, ma chère, il a été envoyé de mon cousin qui veut me voir absolument, il a déja fait mon éloge à Messieurs de Oldrogg—je me suis excusée, disant

que je me trouvois mal ; mon frère étoit effrayé en me·
regardant, car je suis pâle comme la mort. Je n'y
saurois aller—que vais-je devenir ? j'entends la voix de
mon cousin qui s'écrie : il faut qu'elle vienne—il entre
ah, ma chère, sauvez moi !"

"à 7 heures.

" J'y ai donc été ; hébien sotte, qu'avois du besoin de
craindre ? Je suis si gaie maintenant—écoutez moi, je
Vous dirai tout ce qu'il se passa."

She relates how her cousin led her almost forcibly in a
state of half unconsciousness into the room, where after
paying the first compliments, she had seated herself as
far as possible from the light, in order to avoid the looks
of the strangers, and gradually with some exertion
regained her composure. After a few more compliments
her cousin leads the conversation to her brother. " Ma
chère cousine je ne vous ai pas encore communiqué la
joye que j'ai ressentie en trouvant à mon retour ici un
cousin si aimable ; on a sujet de Vous féliciter d'un frère
si digne d'être aimé.—Je suis charmée, Monsieur, que
vous aites convaincu à présent combien j'avois raison
d'être affligée de l'absence de ce frère cheri ; ces trois
années ont été bien longues pour moi, je souhaitois à tout
moment son retour.—Ma sœur, ma sœur, et maintenant
que je suis là personne ne désire de me voir, c'est tout
comme si je n'y étoit pas.—Point de reproches, mon
frère, Vous le savez Vous même, que ce n'est pas là ma
faute ; Vous êtez toujours occupé et je n'ose Vous
interrompre si souvent que je le voudrois. — Mais, ma

-chère cousine, comment .va donc la musique? Vous
excelliez dejà l'hiver passé, que ne sera ce maintenant!
Oserois-je Vous prier de me faire entendre vos nouveaux
progrès? je suis sur que ces Messieurs en seront charmés.
Il faut Vous dire, ma chère, que je me portois mieux à
tout moment, et je commencois à recouvrir toute ma
présence d'esprit. Je me levai d'abord et lorsqu'ils virent
que je marchois vers mon clavecin ils se postèrent tous
autour de moi; le cadet se mit de façon à pouvoir me
regarder à son aise pendant que je jouois. Je le surpris
quelques fois. Je fus deconcertée un peu sans savoir
pourquoi, je rougissai—mais, ma chère, pourquoi me
regardoit il aussi? cependant j'exécutai assez bien mon
concert. Mon cousin me ramena à ma chaise et en me
demandant ce qu'il devoit faire encore pour m'obliger je
le priai de reprendre sa place, Vous saurez qu'elle étoit
vis á vis de moi. Je vois á quoi ça aboutit, s'écriat-il,
Vous voulez que je m'éloigne, c'est Vous Monsieur, dit-il
au jeune d'Oldrogg, qu'elle a élu pour être toujours près
d'elle. Ah, ma chère, que le cœur me battoit, je ne sus
que dire; le jeune d'Oldrogg étoit en peine pour moi, je le
vis à l'émotion peinte sur son charmant visage. Il me
regardoit timidement comme s'il eut craint de m'offenser.
Je ne pouvois me défendre le plaisir de le contempler, je
crus voir mon aimable Harry, je ne sais plusque ce
je pensois alors. Mon frère pour donner un tour à
la conversation parla de Leipzig, du tems agréable
qu'il y avoit passé et en même tems il commença à se
plaindre de notre ville, du peu de goût qui y regnoit, de
nos citoyens stupides et enfin il s'émancipa que nos
demoiselles n'étoient pas supportables. Quelle différence

entre les filles Saxonnes et celles d'ici, s'écria-t-il.* Je
lui coupai la parole et m'adressant à mon aimable voisin,
Monsieur, lui dis-je, ce sont ces reproches, qu'il faut que
j'entende touts les jours. Ditez moi, je Vous prie, si c'est
en effet la vérité, que les dames Saxonnes sont tant
supérieures à celles de tonte autre nation?—Je vous
assure, Mademoiselle, que j'ai vu le peu de tems que je
suis ici beaucoup plus de beautés parfaites qu'en Saxe;
cependant j'ose Vous dire, ce qui porte tant Ms. Votre
frère pour elles c'est qu'elles possèdent une certaine grace,
un certain air enchanteur.—C'est justement, interrompit
mon frère, cette grace et cet air qui leur manque ici, je
suis d'accord qu'elles sont plus belles, mais à quoi me sert
cette beauté, si elle n'est pas accompagnée de cette douceur
infinie, qui enchante plusque la beauté même?—Juste
ciel, il sonne dix heures, il faut aller me coucher, je n'ai
pas soupée aujourdhui pour pouvoir Vous dire tout ça. Le
cadet prit un congé très poli de moi, il baisa ma main, la
serra à plusieurs reprises, je crus presque qu'il ne vouloit
plus me la rendre. Qu'avoit il besoin de se comporter
tellement? J'envie ces belles dames qu'il a vu ici, n'y
auroit il pas une douceur infinie de plaire à un tel homme?
Mais pourquoi dis-je cela? Vous voyez que le sommeil
m'égare."

On the following day she relates of the brothers
Olderogg that they came from a distance of some hundreds of miles, and that now after having completed their
studies they were about to make the "grand tour"

---

* See page 109.

through Europe, that her brother passed the whole day with them, and that she envies him his good fortune. On the Wednesday she then writes :—" Messieurs de Oldrogg viendront cet après-midi, je m'en rejouis—du moins je verrai encore une fois cet amiable visage, qui a tant de ressemblance . . . st, st.—On m'interrompt—c'est mon frère, que va-t-il dire ?—Ah, ma chère, plaignez moi —tout s'accumule pour me faire désespérer—ils partent ce matin—que ferai-je ?—Si vous vissiez ma peine, elle est au dessus de mes forces—tous les plaisirs que je me promets me manquent—à quoi suis-je encore reservée ? Ils passeront par Worms et y logeront à l'empereur Romain—Vous les verrez peut-être. Mon frère s'en est allé dans ce moment pour leur dire adieu—ah ! quelle pensée s'offre à mon esprit—non, non—adieu."

The passion with which she here expresses herself is not wholly to be explained by the resemblance existing between the younger of the Oldcroggs and her Harry. The departure of the latter takes place during their visit, and one feels almost tempted to attribute her composure under these circumstances, in part at least, to the interest excited in her by her brother's friends. Although we may well conceive that at this period she was in an unusually excited state, she still at other times exhibits a similar susceptibility and uneasiness, yet more deeply seated. The manner in which she speaks of the love affairs of her friends, shows us how much these occupy her thoughts and become as it were interwoven with her imagination. She admires the ardent affection and perfect constancy of Dorval, which, with a sympathetic feeling, she contrasts with Lisette's fickleness. In another in-

stance a somewhat similar illustration of this feeling is
exhibited in a remarkable degree.

Marie B., the daughter of a wealthy Protestant, becomes
engaged to a certain Mr. St. Albain, a fine looking young
man, of great talent and more solidity of character than
might have been expected of a Frenchman. Cornelia is
the confidante of Marie, and St. Albain on this account is
so very friendly to her, indeed almost markedly so, that,
were not Marie quite assured of her lover's heart, she
might well grow jealous. "Hier au soir il me mena en
carrosse chez moi. Il gardoit longtems le silence, puis
tout d'un coup comme s'il éveilloit d'un songe il me
demande avec empressement : Chère Miss, quand Vous
reverrai-je ?—Eh, lui repondis-je en riant, que Vous importe de me voir.—Ma aimable Miss, Vous ne savez pas...
Vous ne croyez pas...que dirai-je ? mais non, je ne dirai
rien...Miss, venez Vous demain au bal ?—Non je n'y vais
pas, on me l'a défendu par rapport à ma santé ; Miss
Marie y ira et cela Vous suffit. Hereux St. Albain, Vous
serez bientôt lié à cette admirable fille, que désirez Vous
de plus ? Moi ?...rien que...votre amitié...me la promettez
Vous ?—Oui, St. Albain, et voilà ma main pour gage, tant
que Votre charmante épouse m'honorera de son amitié,
Vous avez droit sur la mienne, je Vous estimerai toujours,
nous vivrons ensemble, en amis, nous nous verrons souvent
...Souvent, Miss ! est-ce bien vrai ? conservez ces pensées !
mais...Eh bien mais, qu'y a-t-il encore ?—C'est là que la
carrosse s'arrêta, il prit ma main. Vous ne viendrez donc
pas au bal ?—Non, Vous dis-je mais mardi prochain chez
Miss Philippine.—Adieu donc jusqu'à là, j'y verrais
sûrement, n'oubliez pas Votre promesse.—Non, non, Saint

Albain, je ne l'oublierai pas.—Que vouloit-il dire par tout cela, ma chère? Sotte que je suis, il s'est cru obligé de me faire quelques compliments et voilà tout. Je ne saurois Vous dire combien je l'estime et combien il mérite de l'être."

During this ball St. Albain overheats himself, becomes ill, and in a few days dies. Cornelia is beside herself with grief at the death of this estimable young man, at the thought of his bride and his parents. The day on which she had promised to meet him in company is the day appointed for his funeral. She gradually becomes more composed, but her silent grief relieves her, although it proves lasting. With great effort she represses her feelings, and attends a concert; the music fails to move her, she thinks only of St. Albain, and is afraid lest any one should speak to her of him; she imagines the distress of his disconsolate bride. To her astonishment, the latter enters the room in choice mourning, takes her seat close by her, and she hears her engage in most frivolous conversation; grief has evidently never affected her, and she is more cheerful than ever, and deplores the sad garments she is compelled to wear. She is beside herself, and with difficulty conceals her indignation, as all eyes are directed towards her; in her heart she deems St. Albain fortunate that he did not marry this woman, who is so unworthy of him, and whose friend she ceases to be, now that she has learned to know her. Later, as the before-mentioned G. accompanies her home in the carriage, St. Albain again enters her thoughts. Were he but at her side! But she has promised herself not again to speak of him.

In these various traits we see the earnest longing of a

sensitive heart for love, the innate consciousness of a
capacity and need for a true and constant affection, combined with this antagonistic peculiarity that she has no
confidence in herself, and is consequently prevented from
satisfying this longing, whilst at the same time she
indulges in vague, fantastic dreams. Hence we see her
heart in a state of continual tension and disquiet, through
which however we still discern her noblemindedness and
unaffected modesty. In all of these her effusions, we fail
to detect even the slightest sign either of impropriety of
thought, or of consciousness of her superior power of
mind; she is only painfully sensible that she does not
make that impression, which for a woman is the natural,
and therefore only satisfactory one. From her own
descriptions, which in this respect afford a touching, we
might almost say a dignified candour, as well as from
Goethe's account of her characteristics, we learn one
essential reason for this unhappy disposition, namely, a
sense of her inability to inspire love, owing to her want
of personal attractions.*

Goethe, describing his sister, says :—" She was tall,
well and delicately formed, and possessed something
naturally dignified in her demeanour, which melted into a
pleasing tenderness. Her features, neither striking nor
beautiful, evidenced a being which was not, and could not
become, reconciled with itself. Her eyes, whilst not the
most beautiful that I have ever seen, were yet most pro-
found, beneath which a great deal might be looked for,

* Goethe's Works, XXI., p. 15. See also Eckermann's Conversations, Vol. II., p. 331.

and when expressing regard or affection, burned with an
incomparable lustre ; and yet their expression could not
properly be deemed tender, like those glances proceeding
from a heart alive with longing and desire ; although
coming from her very soul it was overflowing and
rich, but seemed only anxious to impart and not to
receive.

" But that which peculiarly disfigured her appearance,
so as to make her at times look positively repulsive, was
the fashion of the time, which not alone exposed the fore-
head, but contributed to make it apparently or really,
adventitiously or premeditatedly, larger. Possessing the
most feminine and purest arched brow, and at the same
time a pair of thick, black eyebrows and prominent eyes,
this combination of striking features formed a contrast
which, if at first sight not repugnant to a stranger, was
at least not attractive. This she soon perceived, and the
feeling grew to be more painful to her the nearer she
approached that age when both sexes take innocent
delight in making themselves respectively more agreeable
to each other.

" To no person can his own figure be hateful, the
ugliest as well as the most beautiful has a right to rejoice
in his existence ; and since kindness is forbearant, and one
views kindly his own reflection in a mirror, we may maintain that every one regards himself with satisfaction, even
though disposed to be captious. My sister, however,
possessed so sound an understanding, that it was impossible she could be blind and silly on this point ; she was
perhaps more aware than was necessary that she stood far
behind her playmates in mere external beauty, without

feeling to her consolation her infinite superiority to them in power of intellect."

The portrait of his sister,* which Goethe had hastily sketched on the broad margin of a proof sheet of Goetz† in the year 1773, clearly exemplifies his description of her. The resemblance of the brother and sister, which in their earlier years was so great that they might almost have been taken for twins,‡ is unmistakeable; this is particularly the case when compared with the portrait of Goethe painted by May in the year 1779. The strongly marked features, however, impart an uncouth and harsh expression to the female face, which is at the same time deficient in frankness and decision of character. That her unbecoming style of dressing the hair should have so justly displeased Goethe, there can, as we see, have been no question.

We may gather from her letters how correct was the judgment Goethe formed of his sister. Although so intimate that they mutually communicated to each other their little joys and sorrows, as well as their love affairs,§ it is no more than natural that the girl should, on certain points, have been more unreserved towards her friend than towards her brother. She does not shrink from

---

* This was found amongst Friederika Oeser's papers.

† It was almost impossible for me to make use of good, white and perfectly clear paper for my drawings; I preferred gray, old leaves, sometimes written on upon one side, as if my want of skill had caused me to avoid the touchstone of a white ground.—Goethe's Works, XXI., p. 11.

‡ Goethe's Works, XXI., p. 14.

§ Letters to Merck, Vol. I., p. 169.

avowing that which she herself occasionally blames, as foolish vanity, her vexation at her unfavourable appearance (pp. 189, 207, 211.) One morning she is surprised whilst performing her toilet in her chamber, which was also used as the reception room, by a visit paid to her father by a newly arrived representative of Baden-Durlach ;* and in the utmost embarrassment, she retires in very awkward manner.

" Je repris mes forces en venant dans le froid, et lorsque je me regardai dans une glace je me vis plus pâle que la mort. Il faut Vous dire en passant, que rien ne me va mieux que quand je rougis ou pâlis par émotiou. Tout autre que Vous me croiroit de la vanité en m'entendant parler ainsi ; mais Vous me connôissez trop pour m'en croire susceptible et cela me suffit." A few days later she sees him at a concert, and finds him so amiable, that she would select him for her model, had she to paint the god of love ; at the same time she thinks of the miserable figure she presented in his eyes. She overhears him holding a lively conversation with the Marquis of Saint Sever, about a beautiful girl who has made a great impression upon both of them. Fortunate girl ! she thinks. It is Lisette v. Stockum, whose beauty had previously drawn from her the expression,—" Quel aventage que la beauté ! elle est préférée aux graces de l'âme." A little after, the Resident turns to her, and politely converses with her ; now she is happy and content.

---

* Fredk. Sam. v. Schmidt, Lord of Rossau and Hullhausen, was appointed Representative for Baden-Durlach, on the 14th November, 1768 (Fichard, Frankfort Archives, Vol. II., p. 362) ; the visit took place on 11th December.

Another time she writes :—" Je vous prie de ne plus me faire rougir par Vos louanges que je ne mérite en aucune façon. Si ce n'étoit pas Vous, ma chère, j'aurois été un peu piquée de ce que vous ditez de mon extérieur, car je pourrois alors le prendre pour de la satire ; mais je sais que c'est la bonté de votre cœur qui exige de Vous de me regarder ainsi. Cependant mon miroir ne me trompe pas s'il me dit que j'enlaidis à vue d'œil. Ce ne sont pas là des manières, ma chère enfant, je parle du fond du cœur et je Vous dis aussi que j'en suis quelquefois pénétrée de douleur, et que je donnerois tout au monde pour être belle."

She therefore surrenders all belief in happiness to be found in love. " Qu'en ditez Vous, ma chère, que j'ai renoncé pour jamais à l'amour. Ne riez pas, je parle sérieusement, cette passion m'a fait trop souffrir, pour que je ne lui dise pas adieu de tout mon cœur. Il y eut un tems, où remplie des idées romanesques je crus qu'un engagement ne pût être parfaitement heureux sans amour mutuel ; mais je suis revenue de ces folies là."

In yet harsher terms, and with cruel indifference for self, she thus gives utterance later to her utter hopelessness. " Quel don dangereux que la beauté ! je suis charmée de ne pas l'avoir, du moins je ne fais point de malheureux. C'est une sorte de consolation et cependant si je la pèse avec le plaisir d'être belle, elle perd tout son mérite. Vous aurez déjà entendue que je fais grand cas des charmes extérieures, mais pént être que Vous ne savez pas encore que je les tiens pour absolument nécessaries au bonheur de la vie et que je crois pour cela que je ne serai jamais heureuse. Je Vous expliquerai ce que je pense sur ce sujet.

L 2

Il est évident que je ne resterai pas toujours fille, aussi seroit-ce très ridicule d'en former le projet.   Quoique j'ai depuis longtems abandonnée les pensées romanesques du mariage je n'ai jamais effacée une idée sublime de l'amour conjugal, cet amour, qui selon mon jugement peut seul rendre une union heureuse.   Comment puis-je aspirer, à une telle felicité ne possédant aucun charme qui pût inspirer de la tendresse.   Epouserai-je un mari que je n'aime pas?   Cette pensée me fait horreur, et cependant ce sera le seul parti qui me reste, car où trouver un homme aimable qui pensât à moi?   Ne croyez pas, ma chère, que ce soit grimace; vous connoissez les replis de mon cœur, je ne Vous cache rien, et pourquoi le ferois-je?"

This painfully acquired resignation of spirit, holding fast the lofty sentiment of the true happiness of love in all its purity, whilst relinquishing all hope of it from distrust of self, caused by an inconsiderate acerbity of mind acting on a passionate heart, affords a spectacle which we find the more affecting when we realize how this sad presentiment was later actually fulfilled.   We hence see more distinctly how it was she found no satisfaction in the match with Schlosser, to whom we can certainly ascribe no blame ; no, the cause lay more deeply seated in her own disposition, and the continual severe reflexions on self must have gradually overpowered her capacity to give herself up to him unreservedly.   There can be no doubt but that we here already see evidence of the morbid condition which, later, rendered her very existence burdensome and lamentable.   She complains repeatedly of the state of her health ; she is becoming hypocondriac, violent and passionate at times, and then dull and indifferent. This gloomy mood, which is at the bottom of all these descriptions, is evident in her remarks penned upon her birthday—

" Mercredi, ce 7 Decemb.(1768).

C'est aujourd'hui le jour de ma naissance où j'ai dix-huit ans accomplis.* Ce tems est écoulé comme un songe, et l'avenir passera de même, avec cette différence qu'ils me restent plus de maux à éprouver que je n'en ai senti. Je les entrevois."

It is not surprising that Cornelia never mentions her parents, since, as Goethe tells us, she opposed all the austerity of her character to her father, who pestered her with his pedantic pedagogy, and put a stop to, or embittered, so many of her little innocent pleasures, thereby greatly distressing her mother, for whom, however, she does not appear to have entertained any very great warmth of feeling.† On the other hand her brother is frequently mentioned, even at the time that her descriptions are devoted to her own most private affairs. He had returned from Leipzig, in a state of suffering, and in a condition which awakened the anxiety of his friends.‡ On her birth-day (1768) he was seized with a violent colic, which caused him the most intense pain ; and his friends in vain sought to afford him relief and ease ; she could not much

---

* Nicolovius gives the 8th December as her birthday (J. G. Schlosser, p. 36). She was one year younger than Goethe (Goethe's Works, XX. p. 77.)

† Goethe's Works, XXI., p. 150.

‡ See pp. 54, 94, 114.

longer have endured seeing him in a state which tore her very heart, whilst she could not help him. He remained in this terrible condition for two days, when he somewhat improved ; yet even then he could not hold himself erect for a quarter of an hour at a time ; but she hopes that, if the pains will only cease, he will soon recover strength.* His condition excites universal sympathy; wherever she appears in society her friends crowd around her to learn the state of his health. In the beginning of January, 1769, on his restoration to health, Councillor Moritz gives him an entertainment to celebrate the happy event. Not long afterwards, however, he suffers from a relapse.

As the brother and sister shared all things with each other, so it proved with their interest for their friends. Cornelia communicates to her brother certain letters of Katherine Fabricius, which excite so lively an interest in him, that without having seen her he enters into a correspondence with her, and undertakes the replies for Cornelia ; she gives up to him, all the more gladly, the task of writing the official letters to her, since she is engaged upon the journal ; her friend, she thinks, will certainly find pleasure in her brother's letters, and she begs of her to reply to him, especially as it will afford him an agreeable distraction during his illness,† and he takes such pleasure in her letters that her younger sister, at his earnest request, handed over one of her letters to him. The better she

---

* "An imperfect digestion, at times almost bereft of power, produced such symptoms that I began to entertain the most serious fears for my life, and thought that none of the remedies employed would prove efficacious."—Goethe's Works, XXI., p. 156. Compare page 50.

† See p. 123.

learns to know him, the more she will become convinced
of his candour, and that he only writes what he really
thinks, which he also says of himself.* She again con-
fides to her the fact that her brother is no longer on the
same terms with his friend Müller as before; their principles are too divergent, for her brother's philosophy is
based upon experience, Müller's only upon theory. He
has also exhibited much coldness at her brother's illness,
and she now sees clearly that his principles are not
adapted to practical life and the world. We see from
this that Goethe's experience, to which Behrisch took
so muc hexception, and about which he gave himself such
trouble,† made a great impression upon Cornelia, to which
he refers with no little pride.‡ A remarkable proof of
Goethe's influence over his sister is to be found in her
handwriting. This is at first clear and firm, but gradually
grows light in character, freer, and approximates more to
his, to which at last it bears the greatest resemblance.
Unfortunately she speaks less of his works than we could
have wished; he draws charming heads for her, of which
she promises to send a few to her friend; he reads to her
all he writes, and she listens to him with rapt delight.§
As she writes (16th Nov. 1768) he is just engaged upon
a new comedy. Whether by this she means the "Cul-
prits," which he was continually revising at Frankfort,||
or the farce mentioned above (p. 119) or something else
—who can tell?

---

* See p. 127. † Goethe's Works, XXI., p. 111.
‡ See p. 126. § Goethe's Works, XXII., pp. 128, 149.
Goethe's Works, XXI., p. 105.

GOETHE'S LETTERS

TO

FREDERICK ROCHLITZ

I.*

You are, I feel assured, convinced of the cordial interest I take in the strange change of fortune which has so unexpectedly befallen you. This web being broken, do not delay to spin others, even were it at first only for the purpose of distraction. I shall be much delighted by an occasional letter from you. It is true I am not the best and truest correspondent, but yet we might sometimes find sundry points to interest us in the dramatic art, in which you have already given such pleasing proofs of your power.

And with this view I repeat my desire that you will compete for the prize offered,† for, in so doing, a little world will be aroused in your imagination, drawing away your attention from other thoughts which at times will obtrude themselves upon your mind.

The new short piece I think of bringing out anony-

---

* Goethe's letters to Rochlitz have come as a legacy into the hands of Herr Keil, who has authorised their publication. But few of them are in Goethe's own handwriting, and such are denoted by an asterisk. Goethe frequently, however, added a few words at the close before signing the letter.

† See Schiller's letters, Vol. VI., p. 54. Körner's, Vol. IV., p. 237; and Goethe to Schlegel, p. 45.

mously, not that I consider it of less merit than the former, but to see more clearly what sort of effect it produces.

I shall make a few unimportant alterations, and shortly afterwards let you know my reasons for doing so.

You will herewith receive a discharge for the money sent. Our officials will doubtless enjoy a good holiday out of the liberal overplus.

Much that I could write respecting your case, will occur to an accomplished man like yourself,—that which my long experience would lead me to say, I dare not write. Perhaps we may soon have the opportunity of meeting, when our hearts shall be opened to each other in mutual confidence.

May you with fully restored health enter upon the new century, and continue as before, to act your part with mind and talent in whatever may be man's fate, bearing me in friendly recollection.

GOETHE.

JENA, *25th December, 1800.*

II.

As is always the case at theatres, the representation of your short piece was deferred from time to time; it is, therefore, all the more agreeable to me to be able to tell you that it has met with a favourable reception, although at the same time I was not altogether satisfied with the cast. That I withheld the name of the author, excited on the one hand curiosity, and on the other, admitted of an impartial expression of opinion. On the next occasion it will work better; in the meantime an amateur company we have here has asked permission to use the piece, which may be considered a good sign.

I return you the original with thanks. The few alterations I have made, are confined to some heavy expressions which it is as well to avoid in the case of certain persons, such as soldiers, together with a few jests bearing upon philosophy, which I could not approve, for the double reason, that they either fail of effect, or that the general public are induced to jeer at that which they do not understand, but which they should at least respect.

Excuse this pedantry, but one only learns after a life-long experience the true value of those genuine maxims so seldom recognized, which raise us above the common.

May I now trouble you with a few commissions?

I am desirous of obtaining information respecting a man named John Leonard Hoffmann, who in 1786, published through Handel, at Halle, a treatise on the history of the harmony of colours. The dedication to Herr Gottfried Winkler, in which he calls himself a Franconian, is dated from Leipzig, where he resided for some time, and may have been intimate with Oeser. You may, perhaps, find the opportunity to learn some more particulars respecting this man, who for certain reasons has become of interest to me.

Then you will, perhaps, be kind enough to procure for me a *bound* copy of the " Musical Journal " for the year ending October, 1800. The first volume, up to October, 1799, I already possess. Your outlay I will at once gladly cover.

Do you happen to be acquainted with a song composed

by the conductor Himmel, in which the distress of a girl in love at not being able to give utterance to her feelings, is expressed? the refrain of each verse is given in a particle, such, for instance, as I know not *whence, whither, why.* It is a *plaisanterie* one may be glad to hear again in company.

The questions as to Wilhelm Meister, I should prefer replying to orally. In the case of works like this, the author may have proposed to his own mind what he pleased, but there will still always remain a necessity for a sort of confession, of which he can scarcely render any account even to himself. The style will always present certain defects, and the author may thank God that he was able to infuse so much of sentiment into his work that feeling and thinking men were found who laboured again to evolve his ideas. The critique in the " Journal of General Literature," is certainly very unsatisfactory to any one who has himself thought over the work, but still it is not without value, when regarded as a solitary expression of well-considered opinion. More might certainly have been expected of a critique, particularly of one so late in appearing.

I trust that your health is again re-established; I am gradually getting the better of the troubles which have afflicted me.

Let me beg you will remember me to our esteemed friend, Weise.

GOETHE.

WEIMAR, *29th March, 1801.*

III.

If you will be good enough to prolong the time given me for the piece until the new year, the explanation due regarding it shall without fail be sent you. My time, and that of my friends, has until now been much occupied with the decisions formed respecting the works at this year's Art Exhibition. The report thereon is to appear by the new year as a supplement to the " Journal of Literature." In the theatre, also, some bold, but successful attempts have lately taken up much of our time. " The Brothers," after Terence, by Herr von Einsiedel, and an abridgement of " Nathan," have been both repeated several times by request, and succeed better on each representation.

Of " Faust " I can only say this, that latterly I have been working at it a good deal; but how near it is approaching to completion, or even to a close, I really cannot say.

Farewell, and bear me in friendly recollection.

GOETHE.

WEIMAR, *17th December, 1801*.

I have yet a request to make, the fulfilment of which I hope for from your politeness. It is this. When the auction of Winkler's effects is over, I should wish to possess a catalogue containing a note of the prices realized. In the case of the Rostisch sales previously held, I addressed similar requests to Secretary Thiele and others; but have never been able to attain my object : I know not why. Through your connexions, you may perhaps help me to procure what I want. I will very gladly pay the person who takes the trouble whatever you think right.

IV.

Whether the opinion expressed by you in your last letter respecting the antithesis of recitation and of singing be true and correct, I will not venture to decide; thus much I will however say, that my own inclines much the same way. As soon as I find myself at leisure I will let you know my ideas on the subject briefly.

To-day I have the following small request to make :— Amongst others recommended for the post in our new Botanical Institute in the Prince's garden, vacant through the death of our friend Batsch, is Doctor Schwägrichen of Leipzig. We are tolerably acquainted with his literary career, as well as with his travels and other labours. I should now, however, be glad to learn somewhat as to his character, appearance, mode of life and academic repute.

In filling up this vacancy I have not only the general good in view, but also my own connexion with the Institute, which I have conducted since its formation, and my propensity for this branch of science renders it desirable that I should have as fellow-labourer a modest, communicative man, with whom I can have agreeable intercourse.

In my next a word respecting the opera.

Commending myself to your kind remembrance,

GOETHE.

WEIMAR, *9th Dec., 1808.*

V.

After closing the accompanying letter it has occurred to
me that you promised me from Berlin a few friendly words
respecting " The Natural Daughter." Looking at the eccentric charivari which our German public never fails to play
when a new production is laid before them, an author
finds it really necessary to obtain those opinions which are
favourable to him. I shall, therefore, be the more glad to
receive your letter as I really require some encouragement in the prosecution of the work.

G.

VI.

Sir,

After long silence I am again induced to write
to recommend to you our theatrical company, who intend
visiting Leipzig. You have invariably been extremely
kind to our excellent artists, who certainly take great
pains, even though they may sometimes fail to attain
their object.

I am assured, Sir, that you will attend the representations they give, and I should be glad if you communicated
to me later your observations. There is much I could
wish altered, but yet one cannot always find his convictions of what can be done satisfied, and gradually becoming accustomed to men and manners, suffers that to pass
which happens. On the other hand, a fresh and keen
eye detects many a weak point, and the good advice of a

stranger frequently works more easily and with greater effect to excite emulation than the long known and accustomed instruction of a manager.

I beg of you not to withhold your good advice from our players during their abode in Leipzig, the more particularly as the transition from a small theatre to a larger one always presents difficulties at first. Be good enough particularly to iusist that an actor must be clearly understood at all corners and ends of the house.

Various pieces of yours have been studied. Have the kindness to attend their rehearsal, in order that they may be played to your satisfaction.

I have yet a favour to ask in addition to my previous requests. Most probably in some short time hence a visit will be paid to Leipzig by an Englishman, Chevalier Osborn, an interesting man of large experience, mature age, and of the highest character. He is a Fellow of the Royal Society in London, and wishes to be introduced to the Leipzig *savants*. I have no doubt but that you will do him this service for his own sake as well as mine.

Yours very respectfully,

GOETHE.

WEIMAR, *3rd April, 1807.*

VII.

SIR,

Receive my warmest thanks for your friendly letter, of the contents of which I have already endeavoured to avail myself. Immediately on their arrival our managers will solicit your further valued counsel.

I have added a prologue in accordance with your desire. I shall feel obliged by your looking through it and deciding whether it is suited for the place, which at a distance cannot be so well perceived.

Our older actors, with whom you are already acquainted, know tolerably how they should conduct themselves; I would therefore more particularly commend to you the younger members of our company, whose improvement is of the greatest consequence to us in the existing condition of our theatre.

Mademoiselle Elsermann, a sprightly child, well conducted, will please you, and may perhaps entice you into advising her as to one or other of her rôles. She has brought with her from Berlin a slight mannerism, in regard to which she has already been enlightened however, and it is only occasionally that she requires a little reminder on this point.

Messieurs Lorzing and Deny are well-behaved people, not without talent, and most anxious to do well. As they now appear more in routine they will doubtless make favourable progress.

On the whole I am satisfied that their sojourn in Leipzig will prove beneficial to our company, more particularly if a few connoisseurs and friends will act as middlemen between them and the public, which is highly necessary to produce a mutually friendly feeling, and to avoid misunderstandings.

I hope all will go well, and that you will at least be content to assume the office of writer of the epilogue. For if a prologue may perhaps be written at a distance, it is indispensable that an epilogue should be produced on the spot.

At the end of the present month I proceed to Carlsbad, where I hope to find, if not perfect restoration, at least some alleviation of my old complaint, which exhibits itself again from time to time. I trust this letter may find you free from any attack. Health was never more necessary than at present.

Commending myself to your friendly recollection,

GOETHE.

WEIMAR, *12th May, 1807.*

VIII.

SIR,

You have afforded me a very great pleasure. For certainly the managership of a theatre is an office full of care, especially if one seeks to please both connoisseurs and the general public, and at the same time to perfect the actors, and fill the treasury. Your letter sets all the relative facts so clearly before me, that in reading it I thought I was present, and witnessed with my own eyes many a well-known circumstance. Pray continue to take the same interest in this institution which you have hitherto exhibited, even although matters should occur of which you cannot altogether approve. Guide and pilot this bark to the best of your ability.

Very gladly would I have communicated you to the views raised in me in perusing your letter, but one becomes so distracted and upset by this water cure as to be scarcely able to compose a sensible letter. Nevertheless be kind enough to favour me from time to time with some information which will afford me all the pleasanter entertainment .the more you enter into detail. For the moment I have reason to praise the effect of the waters. It is much to be desired that it may prove lasting. With my best compliments,

GOETHE.

CARLSBAD, *5th June, 1807.*

IX.

At last our theatrical undertaking in Leipzig has terminated fortunately, crowned with honour and advantage, and, what is equally pleasing to me, I see our actors after this episode, in better spirits, more anxious, and more diligent, so that I look forward hopefully to an entertaining winter for ourselves, and for Leipzig, to a reanimated summer amusement. For we have before us not a few pretty and indeed curious ideas, which we think of practising.

Receive, my worthy Councillor, my best thanks for your friendly co-operation. I well know how to appreciate the quiet, unpretending mode of treatment with which you knew how to second our efforts. If a mistake occurred with the epilogue,* it is perhaps my own fault, for I do not clearly remember whether I wrote to the management respecting this, or whether I allowed the matter to take its course, relying upon your influence as in the case of

---

* Madame Wolf delivered an epilogue, written by Mahlmann. See p. 235.

the first farewell.† Pray accept my thanks for that which you would have been glad to do had you not been constrained to keep silence.

I sometimes take up your letters again, and have often re-read them. They serve me as a leading-string in the daily labyrinth of the theatre, which truly is one of the most wonderous mazes ever discovered by a magician. For not alone is it most strangely planted, but the trees and bushes from time to time move their situation, so that one can never make a mark to show how the road lies.

Discriminating criticism is unfortunately not to be met with here in Weimar. Everything is viewed too much as a whole. Pieces, actors, performances, all are either only approved, or condemned, as prejudice or humour happens to prevail, and one therefore can never feel much elated at praise, or take censure greatly to heart.

It is therefore immensely gratifying to me that our actors have at least been made aware that a criticism exists which knows how to appreciate the shortcomings of favourite players, and the merits of those who are but indifferent actors, or of those who are even found fault with. I intend this winter to visit the theatre frequently, so as to sharpen my powers of observation and reflection for the purpose of a stricter examination. For I frankly admit that the public here, by their capri-

---

† On the 5th July, Mehul's piece, "The Wilder the Better," was represented, and a "Farewell" was sung at the close. The company proceeded then to Lauchstadt, and again opened in Leipzig on 4th August, terminating their representations there on 29th August.

cious favour or antipathy, made me often so ill-humoured that the more trouble I gave myself at the rehearsals, the less inclination I felt to attend the representations. Now, however, that a voice from without incites and encourages me, I shall for a time trudge along the even tenor of my way again, and perhaps be gratified with the result.

The favourable reception my pieces have met with has been particularly pleasing to me. I certainly thought that possibly a day might arrive when they would take, but looking at the condition of the German stage I did not expect to live to see it. It is gratifying that even the short pastoral which I wrote in Leipzig in 1768 should crop up and meet with commendation.

Again many thanks which I should have been glad to have paid by word of mouth had I not been afraid to spoil the good effects of the water cure by an all too hasty conviviality. I will now see whether I cannot employ the quiet period of convalescence in such a manner as to promote the future amusement of yourself and of your townsmen. Farewell, and if possible pay us a visit this winter.

GOETHE.

Weimar, *21st Sept., 1807.*

X.

That I did not reply to your former letter, and further abstained from bringing out the piece, must be ascribed

---

* See p. 31.

to doubts raised in my own mind, which indeed you had yourself in a certain degree created. In order that the piece may prove effective, it is indispensable to find a man well up in years, ordinarily termed the aged lover, but who should more properly be called the dignified old man. He must command the confidence of the audience, excite their interests, and be so far estimable that, as was the case at your private performance, when he is jilted by the actress ladies present might feel not disinclined to compensate him. I do not think that any one of our actors pretends that he can produce so powerful an effect, although up to a certain point we can imagine some amongst them capable of approaching it. I have, therefore, now that the piece is printed, placed it in the hands of a few persons, in order that they may read it, and I will send it to Herr Becker, that he may take it with him to Lauchstädt. I trust you will be able to run over, and take a little personal interest in the piece, so that it may be performed in accordance with your own wishes and convictions; and before my departure from Carlsbad, which will soon take place, I will arrange the needful opportunity for you. Farewell, and continue to bear me in friendly remembrance.

GOETHE.

WEIMAR, *2nd May, 1808.*

XI.

SIR,

You will herewith receive back with thanks your communication as to your " Antigone." It would in more than one sense be a matter of regret did you not continue this work. On the stage, too, I think it would command success. As soon as the piece is finished, pray send it to me. Whether and how such a production can be introduced on the stage is a matter which cannot be decided positively in anticipation, since many unforeseen impediments may interpose themselves, and I myself am, perhaps, less disposed than usual to bring out anything which may be considered singular. But still it is my wish and intention to put upon the stage, at the commencement of next year, your " Antigone," and I therefore beg you will let me have it by the beginning of December, if possible. With my best wishes in the meantime for your welfare, and commending myself to your friendly remembrance,

Yours,
GOETHE.

WEIMAR, *30th October, 1808.*

XII.

SIR,

Many thanks for the " Antigone,"* sent me. On a hasty perusal, it has pleased me very much, and from my first impression I am of opinion that it will be practicable to have it performed. I will avail myself of a quiet hour to compare it with the original, in order that I may see how you have treated it.

---

* Rochlitz's Antigone, a tragedy after Sophocles, in three parts.—Selections, Vol. II.

With the confidence I repose in you, I cannot, however, conceal from you that our theatre is passing through a crisis which renders it impossible for me to predict whether I shall be able to resume the managership which I have for the moment resigned, and I therefore must reserve entering upon more particulars respecting your piece.

I now have to trouble you with a request. I am under such obligation to Dr. Kappe,* that I cannot do less than pay him a compliment. My idea is to present him with a copy of my works in vellum. With your permission, I purpose sending it carefully packed, addressed to your care—it is only in boards, but I should be glad to have it tastefully bound in Leipzig, under your direction. What would be the cost of 12 volumes? I will at once remit you the amount. I beg you will let me have an early reply, and remain yours,

GOETHE.

WEIMAR, *8th December, 1808.*

XIII.

SIR,

I take the liberty of sending you the copy of my works for Dr. Kappe. When bound, kindly let me know the expense. Be good enough to ask Dr. Kappe whether it can

---

* Dr. Kapp, Goethe's companion at the University (see p. 16), formerly a surgeon in Leipzig, and later in Dresden, treated his case at Carlsbad.—Letters to Zelter, I., p. 266. See XIII., XIV., XV., XXI., Goethe's Works, XXVII., pp. 240, 299.

be left in Leipzig, or whether you should send it to him at Dresden. I will then write to him myself. By that time I hope to be able to give you further particulars as to the fate of our theatre, and write you about your " Antigone." It seems to me that you will now have to undertake the same labour with " Œdipus," and afterwards with " Colonus," for properly speaking, " Antigone " can only produce its full effect in connexion with both these pieces. To spare yourself a little labour, you might adopt Solger's works, only rendering these more suited for German ears. But of this we can talk further when we have first succeeded in bringing out " Antigone."

With kind farewell, and assurance of my interest and thanks,

GOETHE.

WEIMAR, *26th December, 1808.*

XIV.

SIR,

I herewith trouble you again with a request for a little favour.

A young actor named Fr. Wessel, attached to the Dessau company, at present in Leipzig, has made an application for an engagement here, and proposes taking up the bass in young serious, as well as comic parts, and he would also make himself useful in dramas. May I beg of you to give me some information about him, more particularly as to his voice and singing ; without, however, letting any one know of this enquiry.

M 2

You will perceive from this commission that I have been induced to reassume the direction of our theatre. Your " Antigone " is being written out, and will probably appear in January. Excuse my saying no more to-day.

GOETHE.

WEIMAR, *9th January, 1809.*

XV.

SIR,

I am deeply thankful for the detailed information sent me as to the actor and singer, Wessel. How instructive it would prove to see several members of a theatrical company criticised in like manner. How desirable would it be to hold the mirror up so clearly to those intending to become actors, always of course presuming that they would be able to bear so distinct a view of themselves. If you remember a certain Weidner, of the Dresden company, who was highly praised to me by some traveller, as leader of the chorus in the Bride of Messina, let me also have your opinion of him.

Accept my sincere as well as lively thanks for attending to the matter of the books. Enclosed is a letter for Councillor Kapp. The outlay follows by mail. To-day nothing more except my best wishes. Antigone is fixed for the 30th. Unfortunately it will not occupy the whole of an evening, and I must fill up with a short operetta. As yet no one either knows or suspects the author.

GOETHE.

WEIMAR, *22nd January, 1809.*

XVI.

Sir,

You will receive herewith nine thalers; should any further outlay be incurred, pray inform me of it.

I have heard the recital, and one rehearsal of Antigone. It will be well delivered, and will be properly played. It affords me a very great pleasure to see and enjoy in its progress, so to speak, this glorious Sophoclesic treasure. This evening is grand rehearsal; to-morrow the performance. What we call effect the piece is not likely to produce in our days; but I firmly believe that it will glide into the circle of those quiet, stately, representations brought forward from time to time, and that it will hold its place. More at an early date.

GOETHE.

WEIMAR, *29th Jan., 1809.*

XVII.

WEIMAR, *1st February, 1809.*

Let me say in a few words that on the 30th Antigone was favourably performed.* The effect it produced was that which I foresaw. The piece made a very agreeable and pleasing impression. Everybody was satisfied and half surprised, being hardly able to realize the clearness and simplicity pervading the piece. The intelligible

---

* Goethe's Works, XXVII., p. 270.

language employed was here of the greatest advantage.
The players generally spoke clearly and correctly, some
of them excellently, and particularly must I commend
Madame Wolff, as Antigone, and her husband as leader
of the chorus; others were in parts very good, and, as I
have said, we have every reason to be fully satisfied on
the whole. To-day it will be again represented, and I hope
the piece will insinuate itself more and more with the
audience. In regard to your treatment of the subject I
cannot speak otherwise than favourably; that it is judicious
the result has shown. I have eliminated a little of the
prescribed music in order that the recitative and declama-
tion should not be weakened. The very few alterations
I have made are not worth noticing. I must not omit to
mention Herr Urzelmann, to whom I appointed the rôles
of the warrior at the opening, and also of the messenger
at the close of the piece—he delivered his narration
exceedingly well. Thus much at present with my thanks.
As yet the name of the author has been kept half secret.

GOETHE.

XVIII.

SIR,

Excuse me for having omitted earlier to reply
to your letter already some time received. I have been
occupied here for some months with the composition and
publication of a novel, which will be issued from the
press in a few days.*

---

* Die Wahlverwandschaften.

As you have so worthily distinguished yourself in this branch, I should be glad to hear your opinion of my work, and that publicly, if agreeable to you. There are, as you are aware, several methods of criticising such productions; a concise opinion pointing out the main plot, would be very acceptable to me.

Kindly accept the small honorarium due to you, which the theatre committee will discharge at the ducal treasury. We are in so many ways indebted to you, that we cannot neglect, on this occasion, although little important, to attest our thankful acknowledgments to you.

With best wishes for your health, believe me with kind remembrance yours,

GOETHE.

JENA, *28th Sept., 1809.*

*XIX.

The confidence with which I solicited your opinion upon my last work has been most delightfully rewarded by your esteemed letter, for which I render you my most hearty thanks. It is not unreasonable that the friends of the beautiful and the good should pronounce a word of consolation in regard to this production, which gives evidence at least of continued honest effort, and which in some respects has cost me much trouble; indeed, when I reflect upon the circumstances under which the little work has been executed, it appears to me a wonder that it stands upon paper.

Since it has been sent to press, I have not read it con-

secutively ; I generally defer the consideration of the proof
as long as possible.   A printed work is like a dried fresco
painting, it admits of no alteration.   So far as I recollect,
and as you by your remarks bring before my mind's eye, I
think it would have been as well to have added a few
touches for the sake of connexion and harmony.   Since
this, however, is now out of the question, I console
myself with the reflection that the ordinary reader will
not perceive such defects, and that the connoisseur, by
making such demands, himself supplies these wants, and
perfects the work.

That you are such a reader, and discerner, I very well
knew, and now, moreover, experience.   Receive my double
thanks for your sympathy, and your communication ; and
receive thanks yet a third time for having given them
utterance at a period when many another, without rhyme
and reason, would have kept silence towards his friends,
and have busied himself exclusively with his own good
fortune.   May the good which is in store for you be as
clear to your sight as the views you have of the world and
of art, and prove as abiding as the constancy evinced by
you to your friends.   Rest assured of my continued
interest.

GOETHE.

WEIMAR, *15th November, 1809.*

XX.

SIR,

Again I trouble you with another request, with this
particular observation, that there is no hurry to attend to

the matter.   If the information I desire reaches me by Christmas, it will be in ample time.

Whilst engaged upon my " History of Colour," I meet again with a man as to the circumstances of whose life I have for some time been desirous of obtaining further information.*   His name is John Leonard Hoff-man, and his work is entitled, " Essay on Pictorial Harmony in general, and on the Harmony of Colours in particular, with comments on the Science of Music, and sundry Practical Observations.   Halle, 1768.   Published by Joh. Christ. Hendel."

The work is dedicated in June of the same year to Herr Gottfried Winkler, and it is dated from Leipzig.   From this, as well as from the manner in which Oeser is alluded to in the Introduction, it is evident that the author resided some time in Leipzig.   He appears to have been a right thinking man, of fine feeling ; exhibiting a tolerable ac-quaintance with both painting and music, and although not fully equal to his subject, he still deserves honourable mention in the History, on account of his elegant and happy remarks.   If you can procure for me any informa-tion respecting this person, you will confer an obligation on me.

If your friend could oblige with a few of his drawings for " Faust," it would afford me and our little society much pleasure.   They shall be returned very soon.

With best respects,
GOETHE.

WEIMAR, *20th November, 1809.*

---

* See page 220.

M 3

XXI.

Through Mademoiselle Longhi, of Naples, a beautiful and accomplished performer on the harp, I should be glad, my dear sir, to refresh myself in your memory, and I trust I may succeed.

I am convinced that you will show kindness to this young lady for her own sake, as well as for mine.

I am induced to write to you at present, not simply on account of her distinguished talent, which in itself is sufficient recommendation, but because the dear child is in the unfortunate position of having both her little fingers attacked by a rheumatic swelling, the worst evil, perhaps, which could happen to one who hopes, by her performances on the harp and pianoforte, to work her way to St. Petersburg. If our excellent friend Kapp,* to whom I myself am so much indebted, is in Leipzig, do me the kindness to interest him for this pretty Italian, not forgetting at the same time to convey to him a thousand compliments from me. I shall not, and need not say more, since only a brief introduction is necessary, and I am writing this letter at a late hour. If the present communication induces you to let me have again a few words from you, I shall receive them with pleasure. With best wishes,

GOETHE.

WEIMAR, *22nd April, 1811.*

---

* See page 242.

XXII.

Sir,

I can assure you that I greatly regretted not being able to welcome you when you passed through this place on your journey. To meet one another once again, and to have a long chat over sundry matters, after several years' separation, contributes if not to a better understanding, yet to a more confidential and unrestrained one. However, I will console myself with the certainty of your regard and good wishes.

You express the desire that I should furnish the worthy Baron von Truchsess with a copy of Goetz as dramatized, and I will tell you why I entertain serious objections to do so. When the piece was originally published, he took so much, and such lively interest in it, as in a certain degree to realize in his own person the character of the hearty old hero, so that it certainly would be far from agreeable to him to see various points omitted, remodelled, changed, and indeed treated even in quite an opposite sense.

This modification of the work can be excused only for its theatrical object; and must be allowed only in so far as that what the piece loses on the one hand, is compensated for on the other, by its visible presentation on the stage as a play. Being convinced that nobody would approve of the new work on merely reading it, since it is not to be expected that the reader can fully supply the lacking stage effect, I have hitherto hesitated to have the drama printed; and, indeed, have referred my most intimate friends here, who desired to see the manuscript, to the performance, from which they returned not altogether dissatisfied.

I am assured that both you and the worthy Truchsess-Goetz, will not take it amiss that I attach so much weight to these reasons, as to decline acceding to the request made to me. However, pardon me for this, and bear me in friendly recollection.

You will receive at Michaelmas a somewhat wondrous biographical volume. The completion of Wilhelm Meister's Journeyman's years, has been hindered by my own journeyings. This little book will, I trust, convince you, that you belong to those for whom I have written it. My sole object therein has been the diversion of absent friends and kindred spirits, for such are really the only persons one cares to invite to become witnesses of his past life and doings, and to interest in his existence.

Your truly attached,
GOETHE.

WEIMAR, *11th September, 1811.*

XXIII.

With many thanks, my dear friend, I return the treatise sent me. He who knows the German public, whose egotistical obstinacy you so well depict,—he who has learned to experience what an anxious apprehension they entertain for everything novel, which is in any degree problematical (however greedy they may be to pursue it), and therefore allow free play to their discontent, only to be rid of their fear,—he cannot fail to be thankful when a friend intervenes

as middleman, in order that the world at large may the
more readily fall in with that which appears to them
strange and marvellous.* During the last twenty years,
particularly, one has had need of all his patience; for
several of my later works have required ten years or more,
before they gradually worked their way into favour with
an extended audience,—for instance, my Tasso came to
be twenty years old before it could be played in Berlin.
Such a forbearance can only be expected of those who have
early accustomed themselves to that *dédain du succès*
which Madame de Staël thinks she has found in my
case.† If she means instantaneous vehement *succès*, she
is certainly correct.‡ But as concerns true effect, I
am by no means indifferent,—on the contrary, my belief
therein has been my guiding star in all my works.
As time fleets by it is always more desirable to experience this success earlier and more completely, seeing
that one has less time left to await with indifference that

---

* See a critique on the first part of "Poesy and Truth" in the
Library of the Rhetorical and Pictorial Arts, VIII., p. 261, the
writer of which "was well acquainted with Goethe during his residence in Leipzig, attended class with him at Ernesti's lectures,
and took lessons in drawing with him at Oeser's;" and was thus
enabled to observe "that Goethe at that time was combating the
German language—a result of his deficient unclassical home teaching
as a boy."

† De l'Allemagne II., 7. "On apperçoit le dédain du succès dans
Goethe à un degré qui plait singulièrement, alors même qu'on
s'impatiente de sa négligence." See also Goethe's Works, XXVII.,
p. 150.

‡ I went on my way quietly, without troubling myself about success."—Eckermann's Conversations, I., p. 147.

happy moment, and to hope for a future one may not live to see.*

In this respect you have made me a famous present in your treatise, and again evince thereby the continuance of your former long tried friendship. And yet I ought not to be much surprised that in this work you have known how to penetrate so freely my ideas, for you are one amongst those absent friends who hover around me in imagination, when I begin in solitude to recount all my old fables to myself; and I can truly say that my first and chief object is to make myself heard by them in an indirect way, since there are so many impediments to a direct communication with them.

I value highly your friendly reception of my Asiatic World's Beginnings. The lessons I have thence drawn are intertwined with my whole life, and will crop up in unlooked for manifestations ; and I may hope from your affectionate faith that you are convinced the first part was written with a conscious intention, and does not contain any, even the least and apparently insignificant idea, which is not hereafter at some time or other to bear a cognate blossom and fruit. It is true the public, when led to the margin of a cornfield, always bring their sickles with them, without reflecting that many months are wanting to harvest time, and indeed, that the whole of the field, although already green, must repose for a goodly season under a covering of snow and ice.

---

* " When I reflect on it more particularly, I here find the root of that indifference to—indeed contempt of—the public, which for a considerable part of my life adhered to me, and later could only be subdued by watchfulness and training."—Goethe's Works, XX., p. 53.

It would deeply interest me if you would let me know what you think of the Science of Colour. My labours upon this, as also upon other matters, meet with more and more delay. For on this subject the public is most easily misled, since, whilst granting me some merit in other respects, they will find a pardonable excuse for me, if I do not guide them aright in this matter, which can hardly be said to belong to my province. However I shall be happy when I am at last quit of this subject, which I have had so long in hand. You can yourself estimate the great strain on my mind which it has proved to work it out, and I hardly venture to give expression to the important remarks I make, when I consider the opinions of my opponents. But still it is no secret that nobody will be convinced against his own will.

Why, therefore, should I not desire to know the opinions of my friends, and particularly your views, which for so many reasons must be of value to me.

Commending myself to your continued regard, yours,

GOETHE.

WEIMAR, *30th Jan., 1812.*

XXIV.

As the approaching spring will in all probability soon entice me from Weimar to Bohemia, I will no longer delay again writing to you to refresh me in your memory.

The sheet respecting my theory of colour I herewith return you with thanks, and only regret you had not sent more of them. It is just this sort of ingenious impulsive expression of opinion which is of such inestimable value to me, and particularly in this instance where I see with delight that the ideas about which I have been engaged for so many years flash upon a friend's mind, and gradually succeed in obtaining a hold upon it.

This winter the theatre has distracted much of my attention from other matters. I must see whether the solitude of Carlsbad, which I may hope to enjoy in the month of May, will afford me the opportunity of devoting more attention to poetry, science or some such matters.

In the meantime farewell, and let me advise you not to allow yourself to be drawn into literary disputations, for we have need just now to husband all our powers for weightier matters.

The sketch for a painting I have brought under consideration at our court, and not without some hope of a successful result ; unfortunately we can now hardly enjoy all that we already possess, how then should we wish to possess more? If our prospects in the north should grow brighter, there may possibly be something to be done in that quarter.

Commending myself, with best wishes, to your friendly remembrance,

GOETHE.

WEIMAR, *7th April, 1812.*

XXV.

If you and yours, my dear friend, will join me to-morrow at dinner with my family circle, you shall be heartily welcome.

Come about twelve o'clock, in order that we may have time to inspect some works of art. I will send the carriage. With kind regards,

GOETHE.

WEIMAR, *Tuesday, 7th Dec , 1813.*

*XXVI.

If your visit, my worthy friend, leaves anything to be regretted, it is that it did not last long enough. Even our meetings with friends have their seasons, which develope themselves in due course.

May these delightful though short days bear fruit when we are removed to a distance from each other.

Select four sketches from the dozen:† it will delight me to know they are in your possession. These leaves bring to my memory the recollection of a bygone pleasure, and their absence will therefore be as precious to me as if it were a gain.

May your good angel protect you amidst the billows

---

* Rochlitz was in Weimar.—Goethe's Works, XXVII., p. 290.

† Four drawings by Goethe, now in the possession of Herr Keil.

which may surround you.　Remember me affectionately, and rest assured that I know how to value the attraction of your friendship.　With our kind regards to you and yours,

Goethe.

Weimar, *28th Dec., 1813.*

XXVII.

Sir,

　　I am greatly obliged for the catalogue forwarded, and beg permission, about Michaelmas, to trouble you with it again, along with a few commissions.

In the case of paintings, and still more in the case of sketches, everything depends upon originality.　By originality I understand, not exactly that a work is by the hand of the master to whom it is ascribed, but that in its conception it is so full of powerful ideas, as to deserve the honour of a celebrated name.

The numbers of the catalogue to which I direct my attention I will forward to you, with particular remarks as to what I hope or expect after comparison.　I beg you will afterwards be kind enough to examine the drawings, to decide which, if any, are worthy of commendation, and bid for them or not as the case may be.　You will thus confer a favour on me, and everything that you do in the matter I shall with pleasure unhesitatingly agree to, with the conviction that I could not have judged better myself. Payment for a proportionate sum shall at once follow.

I the more readily venture, my worthy friend, to trouble

you thus, since by your so considerate reception of my
biographical attempt you have courteously confessed yourself my debtor. Pray continue to accompany me on my
way with your good wishes and sympathy. The loss we
all have more or less sustained, and which, alas! has
struck you so heavily, can only be endured by our drawing
yet closer one to the other, and by the German learning
to perceive that he can only hope to find consolation from
his fellow countrymen. With these pious wishes and
intentions, we can scarcely bear to reflect upon the state
of the community which unfortunately threatens to break
up through these sad dissensions. May this good fortune
at least be spared to private individuals, that they continue
to esteem and regard each other.

Faithfully,
GOETHE.

WEIMAR, *27th February, 1815.*

XXVIII.

Unfortunately I have deferred replying to your friendly
communication of the 29th July, until after the holidays.
Had I already in the spring noted down the orders as I
had thought of giving them, there is no doubt but that
you would yourself, or through a friend, have executed
them to my entire satisfaction. As it was, however, my
journey detained me too long on the Rhine and on the
Main ; and on my first arrival here, I could not make up
my mind how to act, and thus I let slip unfortunately the
finest opportunity of adding some important works of

art to my collection. Notwithstanding these circumstances, I return you my most sincere thanks for the
trouble you have so kindly taken, and for your candid
explanation, in which 'I recognize anew, with particular
emotion, your oft-tried characteristics. I can assure you
then should a similar instance again occur, I shall be
perfectly contented if you, or anyone in whom you repose
confidence, undertake to act on my behalf. At present,
however, you would confer a particular favour upon me
if you would procure for me a priced catalogue. The
inspection of this, although it might here and there
produce an unpleasant feeling, would at any rate be instructive; and I shall heartily thank you for this, as well
as many other kindnesses shown me.

Pray make my respects to all our esteemed well-wishers
and friends.

Faithfully,
Goethe.

Weimar, *23rd October, 1815.*

XXIX.

Sir,

I received some time since your excellent gift,
which has served to cheer most agreeably many a dull
hour; the dreadful tale of that day of battle particularly
teaches us how we should not succumb to smaller evils,
since man endures the greatest and is often saved out of
them.

The development of your character and style appears
here in the most favourable light; it always produces a

great effect when a man understands how to pourtray worthily his saddest experiences.

It is true as old age creeps on, it is another affair. The weight of years might perhaps be borne though fleeting by as fast as of yore, but as they come to be burthened with so many inconveniences even from without, with which youth will not be troubled, one comes to feel doubly and trebly the want of power and endurance. If however we have enjoyed in our time the good, and have learned to bear with the evil, nothing more remains for us but to husband our powers, in order to be worth something to the last.

Retain your sympathy for me, and rest assured of mine. Remember me to your family and to Lohri Keil's.

Before closing a request occurs to me; if you can conveniently procure for me a really good pen and ink drawing by Guercin at a cheap price, either a landscape, head, or half figure, you will do me a particular favour. There were several of them in that auction sale which I missed.

Again, with kind regards,
Yours faithfully,
GOETHE.

WEIMAR, *10th Dec., 1816.*

XXX.

SIR,

I was greatly delighted to receive your kind letter, from which I see that you still retain a lively remembrance of me, and that you desire in the most

friendly manner to satisfy my inclinations, and will use
your endeavours to afford me instructive amusement.   I
therefore, thankfully accepting your offer respecting
Guercin's picture, beg that you will send it me, and let
me know how much I am indebted for it.

As to the gems, you need not repent having informed
me of them.   If one hopes to dispose of his wares, he
must exhibit and offer them.   The duke is not at present
inclined to make such a purchase, but I have another idea
respecting them.   We have good connections amongst
the jewellers of Hanau, partly on account of the Order of
the Falcon, and partly on account of the presents our
Princes are frequently compelled to make.   In manu-
factures like this, they have a hundred opportunities of
making use of such things for snuff-boxes, ornaments,
rings, &c.   If you will send me an exact description of
them, stating what the gems represent, what their size is,
enclosing perhaps plaster casts of a few of the largest, or
most highly valued, I will forward them without delay to
Hanau, as I have at any rate some orders to give there.
I shall be delighted if I can in this way meet your
views.

May I hope that you are in better health and more
cheerful.

Faithfully,

GOETHE.

WEIMAR, *20th March, 1817.*

*XXXI.

Sir,

In Leipzig, surrounded as you are by your own art treasures, and collections of others, it is impossible for you to form a conception of my state of mind in this ugly, if intellectual town of Jena, on all at once catching sight of so charming an apparition as the picture you have sent me as a most friendly gift. It has already moved me to look at it a hundred times, and I shall always keep it before my eyes, to remind me daily of your merit and of your regard.

In the meantime accept my hasty thanks, and excuse me if I did not at first accept your beautiful present in the spirit in which it was offered. He who has had almost unceasingly to contend with an unruly world, fails often to acknowledge in a becoming manner the warm press of a friend's hand; let me therefore remain doubly and trebly your debtor in an ethical sense.

Faithfully,

GOETHE.

JENA, *9th April, 1817.*

Herr Angermann had the politeness to hand me the small box here in person.

More in my next as to the gems.

XXXII.

Sir,

Your hearty and frank letter has given me the greatest pleasure.*   I had certainly counted on you ; but that you should so quickly, instantly, and unhesitatingly have expressed your opinion, calls for my warmest thanks. Our friend Meyer, whose examination and review of ancient and modern times you cannot fail to have detected in the bold treatise,† has, with myself, for many years past carried such thoughts in his breast, and it seemed exactly the fitting moment to make our appearance with an historical common-sense proposition, honouring talent but sharply pointing out digression, now that folly threatens to outdo itself, and that all our true contemporaries, especially the fathers and teachers of clever sons seized by the prevailing mania, are in a state of despair. Thousands upon thousands of right-thinking minds will certainly speedily unite; pure common sense and appreciation of art will make itself heard, and we shall come to the aid of those who, against their will, have allowed themselves to be carried away by the stream.

Of the excess of folly as you depict it, we certainly had not the faintest conception ; as we however contemplate at any cost hammering away continually on this subject,

---

* Goethe immediately communicated Rochlitz's letter to H. Meyer. —Riemer's letters from and to Goethe, p. 108.

† Art and Antiquity, I., 2 p. 7. Modern German, religious-patriotic art.

I shall be obliged by your favouring me from time to
time with information upon this point. Our desire is, as
you will have seen from our opening treatise, to spare
genuine talent, as you yourself also do, and have done,
but sharply and remorselessly to attack all false, diseased,
and at bottom, hypocritical maxims, and, as you recommend and wish, reiterate again and again that which is
likely to prove effectual. In this respect, as well as in
others, our coming third number will be most sincere.

Kindly keep me acquainted with anything which may
come to your knowledge as to persons and individualities;
I shall not make any use of such information without
first submitting to you our proof sheets. We must make
it a matter of conscience to work together. The mass is
large, but weak, and I think of having them on the flank
from one side or from both sides.

This will give you some idea of our intentions. How
refreshing to me is the pure, unrestrained expression of
your letter, even viewed merely as a philological utterance; and to what wretched, strange follies would German
men compel us! These also we shall assail, and the
enclosed pamphlet will show you what hope of success we
may entertain amongst honest young sympathizers in our
opinions.

If this work is already known to you, you may like to
possess it, and to communicate it to friends. It is necessary now to acquire a party in order to hold fast that which
is reasonable, since absurdity is acting so vigorously. Let
us remember that we are this year celebrating the jubilee
of the Reformation, and that we cannot more highly
honour our Luther, than by openly enunciating with

earnestness and power, and, as you rightly urge, by often repetition, even though it be attended with some danger, that which we hold for correct, and advantageous for the nation and for our age.

The picture you so kindly presented to me still affords me much pleasure. A really good work of art gives us always much to discover in it, and is ceaseless in the effect it produces on us.

I do not know whether I have before informed you that my predilection for the sixteenth century has seduced me to become the purchaser at Nuremberg of a considerable collection of Majolica ware, which having safely reached me affords a very agreeable sight. I may, however, observe that such mediæval works of art can only be appreciated in groups, which admit of their merits, as well as their defects, being seen. If you should meet with any articles of this description in Leipzig, you will do me a favour if you will give me notice of them.

The casts of the collection of gems I will return in a few days. I was moved to make my former suggestion,* on the supposition that it was a collection of cameos, which, as attire, ornaments, or fashionable decorations, may be used by those who are not, as well as by others who are, *dilletanti*. Intaglios are used almost wholly as seals ; and for this purpose the preference is given to interesting, or admired personages, of whom, especially after our modern ideas, there are doubtless very few in the line of the Roman emperors.

I herewith send the impression of a title-page ; soon

-----

* See page 262.

after midsummer I will perhaps send you the work itself.*
Not having much inclination at the present to take up any
fresh work, I have employed myself during my protracted
stay in Jena with the republication of some of my former
writings on natural history subjects, and with the examination and revision of an accumulation of manuscripts.   This
latter occupation shows to a frightful extent how we may
become interested, excited and fairly carried away by
a series of subjects of the most opposite character.   I
shall now be compelled to connect not a few fragmentary
writings by the relation of occurrences, so that the whole
may not appear too disjointed and peculiar.   And it is
just for these connecting links that I would beg for your
co-operation.   Pray let us direct our mutual attention
earnestly to this point in our correspondence henceforth ;
there are epochs during which it is advisable, indeed indispensable, to forge our iron in common.

It has interested and delighted me much to hear that
you have repaired Konnewitz†, and that you have made it
an agreeable residence for yourself and family.   I have
often had need to clear my faculties from a mass of ethical
rubbish and ruins ; indeed, day by day, circumstances
occur in which the natural powers of our imagination are
challenged to duties of restoration and reproduction.   May
our intellects be preserved to further our need.

---

* On Physics, by Goethe.   First Volume.   Stuttgard & Tubingen,
1817.

† A village two or three miles from Leipzig, where Rochlitz possessed a country seat.

But now I must close, since I must make an end.
Hoping for an early answer,

Yours faithfully,
GOETHE.

Jena, *1st June, 1817.*

XXXIII.

Sir,

You again make me your debtor by your frank
and well-considered letter, which evinces so much genuine
practical knowledge and penetration. I am delighted to
think that the hope of the friends of art in Weimar for
the active co-operation of like-minded men is so fully
accomplished. Discreet use shall be made later of your
communication; at present it is perhaps desirable to watch
the effect upon the public of our opinions, and to see how
a helping hand can be most suitably offered.

Let me now trouble you with a small request. In
Dauthe's Catalogue, p. 92, No. 81 (the page is enclosed),
I find the " Cartoons from Hampton Court." As the
words, " an excellent work," are added, I assume they are
good impressions, in which case I should like to possess
them. You would do me a particular favour if you would
commission some one of skill to ascertain whether the
impressions are really good, and to obtain them for me.
I would give ten or twelve thalers, or even more, for
them. I will at once refund your outlay, with thanks.

As I am probably going to Carlsbad at the end of
July, or perhaps beginning of August, I shall have the

pleasure of meeting you at Franzensbrunn, when I hope
to spend an evening with you, which I look forward to
with pleasure. If you will let me have a word from you
after your arrival there, to say how things are looking, it
will give me a foretaste of our meeting.

You will doubtless have received the little box containing the impressions of the seals which I sent you by
mail. I must now close, for I am much pressed to
arrange many matters, which if they cannot be completed,
must be at least furthered.

May we soon be permitted in person to renew and
refresh our delightful intercourse.

In hope,

G.

WEIMAR, *26th June, 1817.*

Enquiring P.S.

Is there not something in the remarkable collection
of the architectural writer Dedike of interest to a connoisseur? It is almost impossible for a collector to have
been hunting all his life after absurdities without something of value falling into his hands at one time or
another. Have you any friend capable of forming an
opinion on this who would be kind enough to bid for it?
Amongst the small bronze figures there may perhaps be
something, or possibly amongst the embossed *alto* or
basso relievos, which, if not antique, is yet a good
specimen of modern art. Perhaps amongst the plates
there may be some Majolica ware. As such things will
hardly fetch a high price, one can scarcely go wrong.

G.

WEIMAR, *27th June, 1817.*

XXXIV.

Excuse me, my worthy friend, for so long delaying to reply to your inquiry. I am now leading a somewhat roving life, and am playing *rouge-et-noir* between Weimar and Jena, being occupied at both ends, not, it is true, beyond my sphere, but yet not in the most pleasant manner within it.

Accept my heartfelt thanks for all your trouble and sympathy, as well as for your remarks about my doings and sayings. That which I prefer I must leave undone, and from sheer bustle and work derive no enjoyment; and least of all can I come to a decision as to what should be preserved, expedited, thrown overboard, or burnt. How long this is to last, and what the result will be, I know not. Continue to favour me with your help, and bear me in kindly recollection in your labours.

The engraving I send you, as you will yourself see, is by no means satisfactory. The good man looking out of the paper finds meditation an arduous task, and the observer cannot forbear a painful feeling on contemplating it. This fault, which the artists have themselves admitted on comparison, is certainly very disfiguring. The root of the evil lies in the original, which I sent to honest Bois-seres, and has grown from bad to worse by copying from a copy.

View it with forbearance for our good friends, who, with so much genuine goodwill, have sacrificed their art; for, as an engraving, it is really meritorious. I must myself be blind to the matter; for when I showed the

plate to some friends here, they took me sadly to task
about it. I have found a quiet hour here in Jena to
write thus much. If you should happen to have anything
to send me, or to enquire about, address me to Weimar,
and rest assured of my sympathy and thankfulness.

Faithfully,

GOETHE.

JENA, *24th November, 1817.*

XXXV.

Delay in printing the accompanying work is the chief
reason why your esteemed letter has not been replied to
long since. Kindly accept this copy, and on perusing it
think of past times.

Letters such as you desire I doubtless possess amongst
my papers. Unfortunately, I gave up to the flames in
1797 a bound-up collection of letters received, spreading
over a period of twenty years, which, whilst engaged upon
my biographical works, I earnestly wished back again.
Those more recently received, up to within the last few
years, are packed up in boxes lying in the attic, where it
is impossible at present to get at them. I have also a
fine collection of autograph letters, collected for the sake
of the signatures; these I will also examine, to see
whether I can find amongst them something for you.
But at present I must really ask you to have a little
patience. Besides many other extra and pressing matters,
I have to prepare my Divan for the fair, and to attend to
sundry other affairs.

One more confidential inquiry, to which please send me an early reply. Judging from the agitation existing in Jena, the Grecians there, twelve in number, are likely to take their departure. I know several of them; excellent, diligent, and unpretending men.* Do you think it likely they would meet with an engagement in Leipzig, if they were to make a proper application? Give me your opinion upon this point, seeing that you know all the great stars in the place. No one shall learn what you may confidentially communicate to me. Not a word as to the wonderful occurrences of the day : these events must be digested by every man for himself alone.

With faithful and unchangeable regards,

GOETHE.

WEIMAR, *4th April, 1819.*

XXXVI.

SIR,

Let me in a few words thank you for the information furnished. If you can conveniently show a little kindness occasionally to these young men, you will be performing a good deed. Letters of introduction, which they well deserve, I have not given them. On the other hand, I have commissioned a Stuttgard musician, named Kocher, to present my compliments to you : he has really won my regard by his musical performances, and by his

---

* Goethe's Works, XXVII. pp. 337, 353.

conversation. Pray pay him some little attention, and confide to me your opinion respecting him and his works; as in a strange art I allow myself to take an interest, but not to presume to be a critic.

A few days ago it occurred to me to speak to my friend Von Knebel in Jena about the letters you wish to obtain. He has been for many years in correspondence with all our German *literati*, and we may perhaps gain some booty from him.

With my heartiest good wishes,

Yours truly,
GOETHE.

WEIMAR, *15th April, 1819.*

XXXVII.

It is worth while to have lived, if one sees himself surrounded by such spirits and intellects; it is a pleasure to die, if one leaves behind him such friends and admirers as keep alive his memory whilst they develope and propagate his ideas. Accept my most cordial thanks for your glorious letter, which I prize as a most valuable testimonial. I will, in a short time, send you a copy of my " Divan," for which I am sure I may count upon a favourable reception.

Very probably my children will pass through Leipzig on a short journey; be good enough to show them over Konnewitz, in order that they may be able to give me an

account, from personal observation, of the restorations
carried out in your so pleasant, although for a time so
neglected, country seat.

Yours eternally faithful,

GOETHE.

WEIMAR, *18th April, 1819.*

XXXVIII.

SIR,

You will receive herewith a slight contribution
from the two first letters of the alphabet, taken from my
collection of handwritings, as an earnest of my good
intentions. These four letters possess at least this
interest, that they give us an insight into certain times,
circumstances, and characters, of which we now can
scarcely form any conception. Bodmer's handwriting presents, perhaps, the greatest difficulty to decipher; still it
is very interesting to see what books were then recommended to be read. If you find these letters worth copying
for future use, be kind enough afterwards to return them
to me. I will gradually examine the collection, and send
you more of them, some perhaps of greater importance.

With sincere good wishes,

Your thankfully devoted,

GOETHE.

WIEMAR, *27th May, 1819.*

XXXIX.

My worthy, excellent friend, you have always accompanied me with uniform pace and steadfast congeniality of disposition in my path through life ; and, notwithstanding the many discordant events I have had to put up with from without, have always gratified me by your pure, true, and genuine sympathy, so that I should be very ungrateful did I not avail myself of any opportunity that presents itself to express my deep thanks to you. Accept, therefore, as a whole, what has hitherto been offered only piecemeal,* and remember me now and hereafter, in heart, with affection.

Let me add one remark which may be permitted to an old writer. There are three classes of readers: one, which without opinion derives enjoyment ; a third, which without enjoyment forms an opinion ; and a middle one, which enjoying, judges, and judging, enjoys : this last may be said to reproduce a work of art anew. The members of this class, to which you belong, are not many, therefore they appear to us more precious and deserving. I tell you nothing new ; you have yourself on this point made a like experience, and entertain similar ideas.

Farewell, and be kind to my children, if on the way back from Berlin they should stay any time in Leipzig, of which I am yet uncertain.

Ever yours faithfully,
GOETHE.

WEIMAR, *13th June, 1819.*

---

* The edition of Goethe's Works, in 20 vols., was completed this year.

XL.

Nothing more agreeable could have reached me, my dear friend, before my departure for Carlsbad, than a letter under your own hand. The perusal of your former communication excited in me a feeling I experienced in many similar cases, namely, that no fear need befal me on your account. When, however, I had at last decided upon making the journey into Bohemia, I concluded, for my own satisfaction, to inquire of others how you were, when just at this moment I learn from yourself, of your own accord, the gratifying intelligence of your convalescence. Let me offer you my sincere congratulations, and hope that after such an attack you may enjoy lasting health. My many pressing occupations before my departure forbid my adding more; and I therefore defer, until my return, the reply to your friendly offer, for one must equally deliberate whether to accept or to decline such unexpected, well-meaning intentions. Meanwhile farewell, and receive my hearty thanks, both for the early information of your improvement in health, and for the immediate expression of your kindly disposed regard.

I trust that on my return I shall receive yet better accounts of your improvement in health.

Faithfully yours,

GOETHE.

JENA, 23rd Aug., 1819.

XLI.

It is full time, my worthy friend, to knock at your door and inquire in a sympathising spirit as to how you are occupied in order that we may seem to be alive to each other's well-being. Since August of last year I have imposed much upon myself, and much has been imposed upon me, so that now, although I have given place to no distraction, and enjoy the most perfect quiet, seeking to avail myself of every day and hour, I am still much in arrear. And thus experience creeps in to convince us that old age is capable of less than youth, and that we are no longer able so promptly to give over one occupation for another.

Accept a copy of my Divan as a token of intimacy and of respect. Having ventured into other regions, I have lingered longer there, as one does on journeys, and have spent more time and efforts than reasonable, and finally have spared no exertion to reach home at last. Let me hear from you as to yourself, and your literary and artistic occupations. Herr Weigel writes to me me with ecstacy of those evenings on which you afford your friends a sight of your treasures. Would that I could take part in them !

Faithfully,

GOETHE.

WEIMAR, *3rd April, 1820.*

XLII.

Your kind gift, my dear friend, I regard by no means as trifling ; for it tells me that you remember me, and that too, not only in the act of writing, but generally in circumstances where to will and to perform are in conflict. As I must now strive to live an unruffled existence, in a state of moving tranquillity, or tranquil motion, if an end is not to be put to all business (which more than once has threatened to prove the case) I always quietly take great interest in those who at an earlier or later period may have trodden the same path, entertained like opinions, or experienced a like fate with myself.

My thanks, therefore, for the elegant piece* which gave you occasion to write. Some years ago it would have been performed ere this ; as it is, however, I have handed it to the powers that be, who will gladly avail themselves of it, and are anxious for the continuation.

Pray take a kind interest in the enclosed.

Very faithfully yours,
GOETHE.

JENA, *3rd Oct., 1820.*

---

* "The Friends," a play in one act.—Selection, Part V.

XLIII.

Sir,

Pardon me if I let you know rather tardily, and in a few words, that the first volume of Wilhelm Meister's Journeyman's Years is actually in the press, so that it may appear at Easter.   For this wondrous retarded production I beg your favourable consideration and interest.

I will gladly devote many a quiet hour to the selection of your works,† from which, as ever, I hope to draw manifold delight.   Pray keep me in friendly recollection. I am overwhelmed with business on all sides.   In haste.

Yours truly,

Goethe.

Weimar, *18th Feb., 1821.*

XLIV.

If unbelief, as both the Old and the New Testament tell us, is the greatest of sins, indeed the unpardonable sin, you, my dear friend, have much to repent of, since you still continue to entertain doubts of the healthy working of your delightful writings.   On the contrary I can assure you that your valuable volumes have afforded me a vast fund of delight in my conversations with old friends and acquaintances, that your more recent works met with a most favourable reception, and that they have thus enabled me to pass many a pleasant hour.

---

* Selection from Fr. Rochlitz's whole works.—Züllich, 1821-22.

On your side give my Traveller a friendly reception in
its present modest and quiet shape. Since we Germans
are not permitted to enjoy life in the confidence of intellectual companionship, and to improve each other by actual
personal intercourse, may that which each has effected in the
quiet of his study unite in producing a common effect, so
that we may at least feel that we have lived neighbourly
towards each other, and have mutually promoted kindly
sentiments. Ever keep me in friendly remembrance.

Faithfully,

GOETHE.

WEIMAR, *21st June, 1821.*

Permit me to make an inquiry and request. Your
fellow-townsman, Fr. Peters, supplies pianos for 245
thalers in mahogany, and 200 thalers in walnut. You
doubtless know both the man and his wares, might I beg
of you to examine and try those he has on hand, and give
me your opinion of them, as I should much prefer deciding
in this way, rather than by taking a general recommendation. Excuse the trouble I am thus giving you, we
shall have all the more reason to be the more frequently
reminded of it in our family circle.

XLV.

SIR,

I lose no time in informing you that the piano you
recommended arrived safely yesterday,* was at once tested

---

* Goethe's Works, XXVII., p. 398.

by Herr Hartknoch, a scholar of our esteemed conductor Hummel, and approved by him, and by all his audience. Accept my best thanks, and rest assured that by many an enjoyment of the instrument we shall gratefully acknowledge the share you have had in procuring for me so valuable an acquisition.

I trust that your residence in the beautiful neighbourhood of Schandau may be rendered agreeable by good weather and good company. I hope for the same in Bohemia, whither I proceed shortly, more for the sake of change and relaxation, than for the sake of drinking the waters.

After we have both returned, let us hear from each other.

Faithfully,

GOETHE.

WEIMAR, *15th July, 1821.*

XLVI.

Both your letter and its accompaniment, my dear friend, have highly delighted me. He who from an innate disposition faithfully and lovingly works, and gives the world the benefit of his labours, may safely calculate upon a hearty reception. Your "Epoch in Roman History * has proved of the greatest assistance to me, inasmuch as,

---

* Outlines of a picture of Rome during the years 60—44 B.C.—Selections, Part IV.

whilst engaged upon Knebel's "Translation of Lucretius,"
I have just come to a period immediately preceding that
of which you treat; * by seeking, therefore, to realize
your ideas, and by carrying back your views a few steps
only, I derive the greatest advantage, one indeed which
may be likened to a personal conversation.

Your admirable and well known description of those
days of Leipzig's calamity, † I have read again; and again
been struck with the peculiar providence which moved a
man of your mind and sense to seize his pen at a moment
when our senses generally forsake us, and to depict in
words, bearing the impress of natural and well disciplined
talent, the unbearable evils of the present. In return,
you shall shortly receive a true sketch of my wonderful
military career; this hereditary world's disease I had to
pass through in my time; then I marched on to meet the
world's history; later, history has come to seek us on our
own hearths.

I am much pleased that you have appropriated to yourself from the last portion of "Art and Antiquity,‡ exactly
that part which I wrote under the happiest inspiration.
The mind of an author at once communicates itself fully
to a true reader, and I thankfully acknowledge the agreeable consonance of a friendly congeniality of feeling.

Has Zelter's melody "At Midnight" reached you?§ I
am much edified therewith as often as I hear it. Any

* Goethe's Works, XXXII., p. 276; XXVII., p. 387.

† See p. 260.

‡ The poem mentioned in "Art and Antiquity," III., 3, p. 170.

§ See Correspondence with Zelter, II., p. 453; III., p. 82.
Goethe's Works, XXXII., pp. 341, 354.

communication you may make to me respecting music will be highly esteemed by me.

May your noble energy be rewarded on all sides.

Truly yours faithfully,

GOETHE.

WEIMAR, *22nd April, 1822.*

XLVII.

SIR,

Your esteemed letter has filled me with hope and desire; for, as I am myself no longer particularly active, nothing rejoices me more than when friends, whose ideas and sentiments I know, favour me with confidential opinions and feelings which occur to them during their travels. I have, therefore, with pleasure seen that you have had much that is good and praiseworthy to say of Vienna and its doings.

I was this year again in Bohemia; found my old friends and delights; met with yet others, and much enjoyed myself amidst all: took part also in the arrangement of the newly opened museum of Prague, and hope next year to repeat a now accustomed mode of life.

I was sorry, therefore, to see your remark—" Since now the people, I mean the mass in general (Bohemia excepted, which does not wish for better times than it experiences, and would be scarcely worthy of them if it had them)."—I well know that everything is not as it should be there; but still your words seem to me too hard

and metropolitan in their tone. I may, therefore, well
ask you to explain yourself more precisely, in order that
on my return to that neighbourhood my attention may be
directed to the point; and, since I can hardly relinquish
my propensity in their favour, that I may yet be enabled
to test my regard, free from all prejudiced prepossession.

I should also be glad to have a more particular description of Paul and John.

May good fortune still continue to smile upon you!
The first clean copy I receive from the bookbinder shall
be sent to you. I know from your sympathy of old,
which is so dear to me, that I need not more particularly
recommend it to you.

Much good luck has happened to me of late. Dr.
Henning, of Berlin, has lately held lectures on my
" Science of Colour." I enclose his introduction, which
I think comprehensive, and not without interest for every
refined mind.

In hope of an early reply, and desiring to be still
assured of your continued sympathy,

Yours truly,
GOETHE.

WEIMAR, *20th September, 1822.**

---

* On 26th February, 1823, August von Goethe informed Rochlitz of the serious illness of his father, and expressed the hope that
all danger was passed in the identical words which he employed in
writing to Zelter.—Z. Correspondence, III., p. 292.

XLVIII.

Sir,

Your truly esteemed gift * has diffused the greatest pleasure through my whole family. Your most affecting picture of the Messiah awoke the irresistible desire to rekindle within me old expired feelings; and now, under the direction of worthy Eberwein, assisted by artists and amateurs, I have so much enjoyed this exquisite work that I have been enchanted anew with it, and must sincerely thank you again for this gratification.†

Since in this, as lately under the fingers of Madame Szymanowska,‡ the magnificent piano, which still retains its uniformity of tone, takes a leading part, you are present with us in the spirit during many a delightful evening.

Permit me thus openly to give expression to a few words as to our domestic festivals, since I am induced to do so at your instance; and allow me to add that I have reason to be mindful of the remaining contents of your volume referring to earlier works.§ May you meet with every success, and further favour me with the sympathy you have bestowed on me during so many years.

Ever yours,
J. W. Goethe.

Weimar, *2nd April, 1824.*

---

* For friends of Harmony, by Fr. Rochlitz, Leipzig, 1824.

† Eckermann's Conversations, I., p. 148; Zelter's Correspondence, III., pp. 404, 417, 421, 430.

‡ Correspondence with Zelter, III., p. 329. She was in Weimar in October, 1823.—Eckermann's Conversations, I. pp. 72, 77.

§ "Art and Antiquity," V. I., p. 154. Goethe's Works, XXXII., p. 334.

XLIX.

Sir,

I have occasion to beg your kind assistance in a matter which, although of small consequence, is yet not unimportant to me.

Weygand, the publishers, who first issued my "Werther," and subsequently some further editions, I forget how many, informed me a short time back of their intention to try another, and wished to obtain my consent, asking me for a preface, as they termed it.

I could have no objection to a reprint; whether I could find any introductory words was a matter I must leave to the disposition of the public.

They now tell me they have gone to press, and that they require from me my approbation in the shape of a preface of some sort or other, when they will leave it to me to name as my fee such sum as I may consider reasonable.

Now, in a case of this sort, no great profit is to be expected ; and yet any one might hesitate to give expression to what is only a reasonable expectation from want of the means of putting his demand forward in a manner satisfactory to himself or to his friends. You will perceive, therefore, that it might be disagreeable to treat in this instance directly, or, indeed, perhaps, to higgle; therefore it is I beg your assistance to act in this matter for me ; and I would make the following remarks on the subject.

I enclose fifty lines of rhyme, which I hope you will approve of. They might be shown these good people, without, however, giving them up until such time as the affair is finally arranged. Being yourself an author, and having had transactions with publishers, you can sufficiently judge of what is right and reasonable in this matter.

Of a contract for the future there was no idea fifty years ago, and I scarcely remember the former negociations; and after this lapse of time, in consequence of the great changes which have taken place in the book trade, the present may almost be looked upon as a new business. Pray have the kindness to hear what those interested in the matter have to say on the subject.

It is here a matter of honouring my consent to a new edition, which the accompanying poem (which may also possess a value) clearly admits, and of justifying it both before the law and the public. Be good enough, therefore, to make such necessary propositions on my behalf according to the information you receive, as you may deem proper; and, as I have already said, retain the poem until matters are arranged, when I should wish to add a few remarks on the subject of the title-page.

The usual bound, half-bound, and plain copies you will be good enough also to stipulate for, for me.

I must confess that after my recent letters thanking you for your moral and æsthetical communications, a letter like this on an economic and practical subject possesses an attraction for me. May it also contribute to the preservation in a friendly sense of that good understanding which has so long subsisted between us.

Your truly sympathizing and faithful

GOETHE.

WEIMAR, *30th April, 1824.*

L.

Sir,

Accept my sincere thanks for your kind intervention on my behalf; enclosed you will receive the needful to enable you to close this little business. An aged German author knows only too well that he is neither an Englishman nor a Scotchman, and that in such cases it is a matter only of the acknowledgment of an existing right, and not of the equivalent for labour performed. Again, therefore, my hearty thanks for your willingness to spare me an invidious feeling which such a case is most likely to raise.

I stipulate, then, for *fifty* full weight ducats such as are current in Austria, to be sent me immediately by the mail, and afterwards twenty-four copies on good paper, some nicely bound, according to the accustomed usage in Leipzig. I should be glad if the title-page and poem were at once struck off, and sent me for revision. If this is not convenient, perhaps you will be kind enough to undertake this duty, in order that the necessary justice may be done to the poetical part.

I conclude from my own feelings that your last volume would produce a beneficial effect. I will soon send you the newest number of " Art and Antiquity," and beg you will accept it as an unaffected token of my interest. I find time striding on more quickly than I could wish, but still hope to be able soon to produce something.

Ever faithfully,
GOETHE.

WEIMAR, *22nd May, 1824.*

LI.

If you, my dear and tried friend, should think it mysterious that a few pheasants reach you along with this letter, the following will serve as explanation.

A company of musical friends, after much varied enjoyment here one evening, remembered over a jovial meal that they were indebted to you for the greatest part of their pleasure, in having supplied us with such an excellent, well-toned instrument; your health was drunk, and the wish was expressed that you might share in the game we were enjoying. It was afterwards happily hinted that if you could not come to the birds, they could go to you. A sporting friend undertook to procure them, and now they go accompanied with our congratulations upon the return of a new year, and with the hope that you will partake of them with sympathizing friends, and whilst enjoying them not forget us.

Faithfully,
GOETHE.

WEIMAR, *18th January, 1825.*

LII.

Certes, my dear friend, the agreeable visit with which you favoured us was a pleasant proof that we have not mistaken each other on our paths through life ; it showed that, even when distant from each other, we were advancing together along parallel paths, so that when we

at last met again neither of us felt the other a stranger ;
you enjoyed yourself with me, and I am certain the feeling
was mutual.   You could become the friend of my friends ;
all happened quite naturally, without the slightest necessity for making any allowances, and so we could have
wished that you had protracted your stay for yet a few
days.   My daughter-in-law and children returned, Herr
Rauch made his appearance, and we should have been
heartily glad to have had you with us at the happy hour
of meeting again, and have let you also take a contented
part in the joyous reception they met with.   I should also
have been happy to have introduced Otillie to a music-
loving guest.

I must now close, with truest thanks for your kind,
prompt letter, and with cordial good wishes and regards
to your loved family, and further with the announcement
of a piece, for the contents of which we beg a kind
reception.

Ever yours,
J. W. GOETHE.

WEIMAR, *3rd July, 1829*.

LIII.

May the accompanying design and the Holy Trinity
grant to my dearest friend, by continued contemplation,
such pleasing reflections as the unfortunate charioteers
permit to me and my surroundings.   May these plates
ever remain before the eyes of a sympathizer as an
agreeable token of a renewed intercourse, which for all

future time must be attended with the most charming results.

With many remembrances and regards, and a hearty salutation,

Yours ever,

J. W. GOETHE.

WEIMAR, *5th July, 1829*

LIV.

Let us still exchange a few letters ; for it is the advantage of a personal intercourse, renewed after the lapse of long years, that by a mutual contemplation of existing circumstances a fresh interest arises; seeing that the spirit now discerns the direction it should take, and the mind can feel certain that genuine sympathy will be favourably met.

It is in this sense that I feel thankful that you are willing to point out to me those parts of the Wanderings which you wish to identify with yourself. A work of this description, although ostensibly a collective one, whilst it appears to have been undertaken as the means of uniting the most disjointed matters of detail, yet permits, indeed requires, more than any other, that each should appropriate to himself what seems good to him, what encouraged him in his peculiar position, and what might be productive of a beneficial harmony.

When, therefore, my dear friend, I again referred to the points you alluded to, it proved to me as an agreeable conversation with an absent friend, conducing to my own strengthening, by reflecting and holding up to me, as in a mirror, a like mind and like efforts. For this I may well say, that what I have laid down as my purpose in my writings has for me no evanescent character; but I regard it, when again brought before my eyes, as a something ever working on, and those problems which lie here or there unsolved, ever occupy my thoughts, in the hope that in the empire of nature and morals the true inquirer may yet be able to make many things clear.

That you should, by means of your intelligent and keenly discerning powers of observation, have divined the existing state of affairs in our circle at Weimar, particularly in relation to that which most nearly concerns myself, is, unquestionably, evidence of your having a thorough apprehension of the connexion, all peculiar though it be, subsisting between the several links of an exclusive social chain. I trust that your health and our intercourse, so highly esteemed by and of such advantage to us, may be preserved. All those who have been contemporaries in the culture of their minds, have reason to draw closer together, and to keep themselves in a certain degree to their own circle; posterity may perhaps desire something better, certainly it will look for something different.

Ever truly yours,
J. W. GOETHE.

In the Park Garden,
 Weimar, 28th July, 1829.

LV.

For some weeks past, owing to the pressure of my own occupations, and the influence of others, it has been altogether impossible for me to look after my friends at a distance, and hence I have not before replied to your esteemed and very welcome letter. I would beg of you at your convenience to continue your observations on my " Wanderings," and to let me know what effect this particular point has produced on you, what the other excited, and the relative bearing of the result. Such consideration at the hands of a friend is the greatest possible reward for the care and attention I have devoted to the work. The remodelling of the rudiments it contained, which had already appeared in another form, was for me quite a new undertaking, that I was alone induced to attempt from my love for sundry points of detail I desired to connect in a more graceful style, my delight in the subject keeping my attention always alive.

I already find myself rewarded in a really encouraging manner, on the part of many kind discerning readers, who, apprehending those portions of the work expressive of their own sentiments and feelings, exhibit a humane consideration for the author, as being himself but human.

Now, my worthy friend, it will afford me much delight to hear a few good words from you, who are so capable of taking a comprehensive, thoughtful, and analytical view of the subject. For it is always an important matter to an author to learn that his aim has not proved a mistaken one, but that his mental bolts and shafts have flown as far as, and have struck the mark at which they had been aimed, and for which they were intended.

Accept my bounden thanks for the copious account you have given me respecting the representation of " Faust." It is somewhat singular that this uncommon fruit should now, all at once, begin to fall from the tree. It has also been performed here, not by my instigation, although neither against my desire nor without my approbation of the way and manner in which it has been got up. You will do me a favour if you will let me know the sequence of the scenes as preferred with you; for I consider it desirable to observe in what manner it has been apprehended, so as to make the *quasi* impossible capable of being carried out in spite of all difficulties.

It is praiseworthy on the part of the Germans that they did not require the work to be distorted, so as to be able to tolerate it upon the stage. The French were obliged to metamorphose it, and to lavish much strong spice and pungent ingredients on the sauce. According to the information which we have had given us, we can understand how it was that the jumble should have produced so much effect there.

Thus much, and no more at present, in order that this letter may reach you speedily.

Ever yours,

GOETHE.

WEIMAR, *2nd September, 1829.*

LVI.

My most hearty thanks, my worthy friend, for the information so kindly furnished as to how it fared with my revised " Faust," both before and after its performance.   During the period of my management for so many years of a theatre, I have never favoured such a representation, although often requested, indeed I may say urgently demanded ; and in the present case I have only suffered it in the strictest sense of the word. Whatever may generally be the opinion entertained of the representation, that at Leipzig, particularly, has clearly verified the old saying, " You should not paint the devil on the wall."*

In respect to the friendly inquiry contained in your valued letter, I return the following candid reply.†   The return of the Count to Weimar, as I am informed, will take place in December, a month which, for some years past, particularly in my old age, has been very trying for me, as I must confine myself almost entirely to my room, and unfortunately can only be visible to my most intimate friends.   I cannot invite so worthy a guest at that time,

---

* On the occasion of the representation of " Faust " in Leipzig, the youth of the University gave expression to such violent approbation of certain parts, that it was found necessary for some time to prohibit its repetition in Dresden.

† Rochlitz had expressed the desire on the part of the Russian Privy Councillor Count Manteuffel, to pay Goethe a visit in Weimar, and begged of him to fix a time for the purpose.

as I cannot be sure of the state of my health for any day or hour.

This does not hinder me, however, at favourable moments, from receiving esteemed persons who may be staying here, on their journey through Weimar, and occasionally giving them interviews for our mutual entertainment. Should, therefore, Count Manteuffel visit Weimar at that time, during which the presence of both Courts, and a numerous and interesting assemblage of noted strangers afford an agreeable diversion, I should esteem myself fortunate in being able to pass any favourable hour granted me, in the society of such a man, in communicating to him anything on my part which might prove of interest to him, and on the other hand in enjoying some participation in the treasures of his experience and recollections. If you will be kind enough, my dear friend, to mention and arrange this, with my best compliments, you shall receive my grateful acknowledgments.

Your own visit happened to occur during that favourable time of the year when the rooms in my house admit of being used under pleasing circumstances, which afforded a well-intentioned host better opportunities for displaying his sentiments towards visitors.

With cordial good wishes commending myself to your remembrance, and awaiting a continuance of your communications,

Yours ever,

J. W. GOETHE.

WEIMAR, *29th Sept., 1829.*

LVII.

Yes, it was quite right, and well fitted to our confidential intercourse, that you should sit down without any decided object, and write for our common amusement. Moved by your much esteemed letter, I feel myself constrained to write, not so much in reply, as rather to respond in a few lines.

You have given utterance to many a good and valuable idea in regard to my general design in the " Years of Wandering," and the intention with which it was written. It fares, however, with such a volume as with life itself. It contains within it something necessary or casual, something intentional or undecided, at one time successful, at another baffled, giving the whole an air of endlessness which can hardly be grasped, nor be expressed in understandable or reasonable language. Those points, however, to which I wish to draw the attention of my friends, and to which I would especially direct yours, are the various, clearly defined individualities, which, particularly in this case, give a value to a book. You would therefore be doing me a special favour if you would let me know what has most struck you (as we say), what you admit as new or reanimated, what you have found to agree with your modes of thought and sentiment, what you have found repugnant thereto, and the impression the resulting harmony of feeling, or the reverse, has produced in you. The volume does not deny its piecemeal origin, but admits, and indeed demands more than another, an interest in its prominent individual details. By such means alone can an author divine with certainty that he has succeeded in exciting emotion and reflection in minds of the most different character. Upon these points 1 have received the most encouraging communications, and have learned how even youthful and female minds have been seized by the most delicate but fundamental features in the work. If you will be equally kind to me, you will earn my most hearty thanks. On a subject of this nature it is difficult to treat in conversation, we are always restrained by a certain timidity; in correspondence, however, there is greater freedom, and one can sometimes open his inmost soul to a confidant at a distance.

I defer for future communications much of mutual interest, calculated to produce decided effects. The Chancellor has just returned from Italy, and did well not to be hindered from making his way to Rome; he will announce his own return in full assurance of a kindly reception at your hands.

As there is still room I add a little more.

Act *circumspectly*, is the practical mode of speech for *know thyself*. Neither saying is to be regarded as a law, nor as a duty; it is fixed like the bull's eye in the target, which must be always aimed at, if not always hit. Men would be wiser and happier if they knew how to distinguish between an unattainable end and a positive object, and learned to watch how far their means really reach.

With this I must end; expressing at the same time my hearty wishes for your welfare, and my desire to know what entertainment you have proposed to yourself for the winter.

Truly,

G.

WIEMAR, *23rd Nov., 1829.*

LVIII.

In order that I may lose no time in replying, however briefly, to your delightfully refreshing letter, I now put upon paper that which I have for some time past had the intention of writing to you.

In those sad hours when we had given up all hope of the recovery of our honoured princess, although we were aware that she was still in existence and yet flattered ourselves at the slightest flickering up of a long tried constitution, Ottilie was in my room with me, and your latest volumes* lay on the table before us. She took up one of them and read in the pleasantly written biography of the wonderfully innocent demeanour of the eccentric organist ; then the critique on Reichard's poems, and the remarks which followed, all of which arrested our attention and excited our interest to that degree that I was much indebted during such days and hours to your truly lively representation.

I desire simply to inform you of this, and to add how much I have been delighted to see my " Italian Journey " so vividly reproduced by you. How would it be possible for·

---

* For quiet hours. Leipzig, 1828.

us to call up past events did we not possess the belief
and conviction that gifted spirits would arise to interpret
all that had been mentioned, moved by like feelings and
led by similar experiences to the same result.

And in this way I am well satisfied with both my older
and more recent productions. I have guarded myself as
far as possible from a didactic style, and have sought to
inspire my works with a poetic life. It is therefore highly
delightful to me to see that so worthy a co-operator and
cotemporary as you finds himself, and that which relates
to him reflected in my works; since, taking all in all,
this affords evidence of an honest striving after a noble
end, which, if never reached, has yet constantly been
held in view, and gives encouragement to renewed efforts
on the part of the author as well as of others, inducing
him to strike out a path, at times alone, at times in company with others, which, once travelled over, may in itself
be regarded as an end attained.

I must here close, in order not to be diverted into the
abstruse; although I feel I could hardly wander into any
region in which you would not be willing to accompany
me with approbation and contentment.

This letter is hastily concluded, in order not to lose a
single post. With my most cordial good wishes,

J. W. GOETHE.

WEIMAR, 6th April, 1830.*

----

* On the 15th November, Chancellor von Müller, by desire of the
father, communicated the sad intelligence of the death of Goethe's
son, of which he had had himself to inform his father, who received
the intimation with great calmness and resignation, and had
exclaimed, " Non ignoravi me mortalem genuisse!" whilst his eyes
overflowed with tears. A report of the state of Goethe's own health
followed later from the same quarter.

LIX.

Let us still, my dear friend, enjoy the pleasure of a speedy neighbourly intercommunication; such a half presence possesses peculiar attractions.* I am, in a word, in a tolerable, but not altogether in a presentable condition; I can receive letters, and revise works, but am hardly equal to correspondence; indeed I have not been able to get through the most pressing matters which have arisen during the past week. But I must have patience and perseverance until I mend!

The very sight of invaluable works serves, however, as a restorative to my mind. Excellence is the true universal panacea. I shall unceasingly seek to console myself therewith during these weary hours, until we are able by mutual intercourse to strengthen and re-invigorate each other.

Ottilie, with her friendly voice, has made me enjoy the music sent me. I cannot too strongly recommend to you this faithful artiste.

Let me hear from you as to your daily and hourly occupations, in which our industrious friend doubtless shows himself ever active.

I must now close with my most hopeful salutations.

G.

WEIMAR, *28th May, 1831.*

---

* Rochlitz was in Weimar, where he had become unwell; Goethe was also ill. (Correspondence with Zelter, VI., p. 196.) The following letter was also written under similar circumstances.

LX.

I can hardly express how very wearisome these last few days have been to me, on account of the mental obtusity and dislike of all bodily exercise by which I have been overcome. This would be difficult to bear in itself alone; but the knowledge, my dear Sir, that you, my worthy friend, although only separated from me by but a few hundred paces, are in like evil case, and whilst so near feel as far apart as though miles intervened between us, has caused a sadly hypochondriacal impression, just as an abortive attempt disappointing our hopes on the very threshold of success casts a dark shadow on our path. You doubtless suffer the same, and can realise my feelings perhaps even in a higher degree, as more aged than I; for when in years one is less inclined to renounce the enjoyment of the moment.

If at my age I am less greedy to possess than I may have been formerly—for why should one seek to obtain that which he must soon leave for ever—the old desire yet revives in certain cases; and particularly has this proved so at this time, as I am preparing to return you your magnificent portfolio, which my friends and I, always deploring your absence, have most carefully looked through.

Be this as it may, a certain feeling bids me distinguish the wish of a virtuoso from the words of a friend. In the shape of a *pro memoria*, I give you full license to reply, according to your own feelings and at your own convenience, to my perhaps indiscreet expressions.

Your again devoted and obliged

J. W. GOETHE.

WEIMAR, *4th June, 1831.*

TO YOUR KIND RECEPTION.

Amongst the excellent engravings submitted to us in the highly valuable portfolio is one, the possession of which is to me of the highest importance. The plate represents four fathers of the Church agreeing upon some vital point of Christian Doctrine, after Rubens, by Cornelius Galæ. I possess Rubens' original sketch of this deeply conceived and highly wrought composition, of exactly similar dimensions, and the engraving gives the clearest possible conception of the details of the work. I would have enclosed this sketch were it not that it would be buried in the already overstocked portfolio.

To an artistic friend and connoisseur I need not say how two such sheets, laid beside each other, enhance their respective value, since one bears witness to the other of what the painter intended and accomplished, and how the engraver, in transferring and interpreting the work, has shown himself worthy of so lofty a task; indeed it may be said that one only understands both beside each other, and with each other, and can only thus really possess them.

May this irrepressible wish be viewed in a friendly spirit, and be looked upon as any other passion which does not seek to excuse itself, because it cannot be helped. A lover surely pardons a lover's faults, a dilletante, the perhaps inconvenient demand of a dilletante, which he ventures to submit to a tried friend, without, however, daring in the smallest degree to restrict him in the exercise of his free discretion, according to his own feeling and desire.

Truly,

J. W. GOETHE.

WEIMAR, *4th June, 1831.*

LXI.

Permit me, my worthy friend, to make a hearty, laconic, reply.

As regards the first page of your letter : any communication will be welcome to me ; the reply must be left for the day and hour when it may be possible.

For the postscript on the second side :—

AD. 1.) We have learned with the greatest sympathy the disagreeable character of your journey home, and have endeavoured to lay the apparitions we had conjured up. A brief cessation of correspondence on the part of our friend Herr von Müller, so busily engaged and so much pressed, on and from all sides, you will pray excuse.

AD. 2.) I read beforehand the intended letter to Herr von Müller, and recommended him not to show it to any one, fearing certain disagreeable impressions. Whether he followed my advice or not I cannot say.

AD. 3.) May the common evil (however it may be named) which oppresses us all, take effect as lightly as possible on you.

AD. 4.) Pray make use of " The Malevolents," only not against me ; when young it caused a rupture between me and the sweetest of girls.

One particular source of pain to me was that, owing to the obstacles prevailing during your stay here, and your departure so unsatisfactory to us both, although you were actually seated alongside the excellent piano for which we are indebted to you, my grandchildren should not have played upon it even for a few minutes, in order to express to you practically how indispensable this instrument is to our domestic happiness.

For to-day adieu, promising myself an early reply,

Unchangeably,

J. W. GOETHE.

WEIMAR, *30th June, 1831.*

LXII.

To your by turns joyous, by turns sad letter, my worthy friend, as nothing can be decided, I would observe parenthetically :

Our worthy and active von Müller has gone to the Rhine, and if here, could not reply to your much esteemed offer. We receive our letters from Berlin, pierced through as usually only those from Constantinople are ; from the North-East an invisible tremendous spectre threatens us ; from the South-West a half visible, excited spirit of nationality, of which evil symptoms are traceable even in Leipzig. We have, therefore, only to follow your noble example to stand quiet and resolute at our post, and to let the unavoidable pass over, and, if fortune favours, beyond us.

No more for to-day ; and this little only, as a perhaps unnecessary token that we shall be found in true and respectful sympathy inflexibly at your side.

Ever yours,

Time and hour runns through the rougest day ! (*sic.*)

GOETHE.

WEIMAR, *11th Sept., 1831.*